C000184388

RODE

has published poetry in ai
gum in Philadelphia, stu
and worked for many yeai
students in scripting, recording and editing He lives in the
grounds of an old convent in Edinburgh.

He has a blog where he writes about life/his
autobiography and reading, including book reviews:

https://reinholdsite.wordpress.com/

Other Publications by Roderick Hart:

Time to Talk ~Set in Edinburgh. First person narrative.
Centres on Max Frei, who sets up as a therapist though
lacking the qualification to practice. The law catches up
with him in due course.

A Serious Business ~ Set in Edinburgh. Third person
narrative. Deals with events in a large department
store and the chaotic home life of its least ambitious
employee.

The Ears of a Cat ~ Set in Germany, California, Dorset
and Hungary. Third person narrative. Deals with the
doomed attempts of a group of idealists determined to
counter the destruction of the planet by human activity.

Interleaved Lives ~ Set in Edinburgh. First person
narrative. Deals with the attempt by Douglas Hunter to
set up his own agency, while being falsely accused of the
murder of his wife. First title in the Douglas Hunter series.

A Habit of Mind

by

Roderick Hart

EVENTISPRESS

A CIP catalogue record for this title is available from the British Library.

ISBN 978-1-7393286-3-4

Paperback published by Eventispress in 2023

Printed & Bound by PODW

For my wife, Audrey

1

BOXES WERE EVERYWHERE, dumped at random by the removal men: some in the front room, some in the bedroom, more in the hall. My fault. They'd have followed a list of instructions if they had one.

I found the kettle quickly enough, and the microwave, for me the basic necessities of life, but the bed defeated me. Four legs, no surprise there, and they all screwed off. After an hour I'd tracked down three but the fourth was nowhere to be found. Call myself a detective! Wearied by this setback, I propped the base against the bedroom wall, laid the mattress on the floor, took off my shoes, hung my pants on the door handle and bunked down under the duvet still in my shirt. My pyjamas were in a hold-all in case of emergency admission to hospital, always possible in my line of work, but the whereabouts of the hold-all was anyone's guess. I knew I would wake to the smell of stale sweat but that was too bad and it was only for one night.

If I'd thought that moving to a cul-de-sac would ensure a quiet night, I was wrong. In the small hours several drivers turned into the road and then, to make their morning departure easier, executed nine-point turns to face the main road. Thanks a lot, guys, very thoughtful. I knew the saying *try before you buy,* but it hadn't occurred to me to spend a night in the flat before signing on the dotted line. And even if it had, the letting agent would never have agreed. Rentals were hard to come by these days, they had the ball at their feet.

I rose earlier than usual and made my way from the toilet to the kitchen, still thinking about its Victorian wall-mounted cistern, the chain with ceramic handle decorated with cornflowers, blue against a white background. A work of art in its own right, but so far the only one in the house. What would prospective clients make of that?

The box of supplies was on the counter where I'd left it, water came out of the tap, so brewing up was possible. I was considering whether to go for up-market freeze-dried coffee granules or a simple tea bag when the entry phone rang. I wasn't expecting anyone, but maybe someone had found the missing leg. No harm hoping.

'Hello.'

'Delivery for Hunter.'

A woman's voice. I buzzed her up and she duly appeared.

'Morning Douglas.' She held out a bag. 'Croissants.'

I couldn't believe it. My old adversary, Maureen MacNeil, standing on the landing large as life and twice as unwelcome.

'We need to talk.'

'No we don't.'

But she walked past me anyway and showed herself round uninvited.

'Come in, why don't you?'

A waste of breath, sarcasm was lost on her.

'Not much in the way of amenity.'

'Just moved in.'

'So I heard.'

Right, but who had told her; she was the last person I'd want to know my new address.

'Bit of a come-down from your previous place, if you don't mind me saying.'

She didn't care whether I minded or not, came to rest in the kitchen, found a couple of plates and opened the fridge door.

'You realise the light doesn't come on.' Then after the briefest of pauses, 'Where's the butter?'

'Haven't bought any yet. Haven't had time.'

'Too bad.'

She noticed jam in my box of tricks and started spreading it on the croissants. The force being with her for the time being, I let her get on with it, boiled some water and dunked a tea bag from one mug to another. One would do us both.

Seated at the kitchen table, she made short work of her croissant and reached into the bag for another.

'So, Maureen,' I asked, 'what's the story?'

She paused before answering this question, partly because her mouth was full but mostly because it would involve an admission of inadequacy from a woman who was never inadequate.

'I need money. Like yesterday.'

This came as no surprise. She'd left the police service under a cloud and was lucky not to have lost her pension as well. But she was twenty years from pensionable age, so until that happy day dawned money was tight, her mortgage arrears increasing. She was on her second warning letter, did I realise that? Unless she started earning, she was out on her ear.

'It's fine for you with that house you had to sell.'

There was nothing fine about it. Half the proceeds had gone to my ex-wife, what remained reduced by legal bills. And anyway, the nerve of the woman.

'Come off it, Maureen, you're still a homeowner, I'm renting. Spot the difference. If it comes to the bit, you could sell too.'

Not to hear her tell it. By the time she'd paid off the mortgage she'd have very little left, so she might as well try to hang on.

Checking out this woman who, just a few short months ago had accused me of murdering my wife, I found it hard

9

to credit. Was I supposed to believe she'd turned a new leaf, become an upstanding member of the community, taken up crochet?

'I've changed.'

'You have?'

'I'm clean. Have been for four months.'

'Right.'

'I'm serious. Look at me!'

She hadn't changed so much she'd stopped barking out orders.

'Douglas, come on. Give me a break here.'

So I looked. She was wearing her hair longer than she did in her detective sergeant days and it didn't look so greasy as it had. Plainly she'd picked up an appropriate product. But there was no doubt about her complexion, it was definitely clearer, much improved. She'd never been one for makeup and that helped too. If she continued down this route, she'd end up looking good by mistake.

'Let's say we take your word for that, you're clean, but you didn't come here at this time of the morning to tell me that.'

'You know Grace Pettigrew?'

Under the catchy name Pettigroom, Grace had branched out from valeting pooches to walking them as well, and soon found she needed a bigger van. MacNeil bought her ten-year-old diesel at a knockdown price and started delivering for Just Eat. But it hadn't worked out.

'They'd call me all sorts when the order was wrong, but excuse me, people, I don't pack the orders, just deliver them, so I told them where to get off.'

'Sounds like you alright.'

She'd parted company with Just Eat after two weeks and was now to be found on sites such as Gumtree advertising her services as a delivery driver. Man with a Van, except she was a woman. And she was getting jobs, just not enough of them.

'Last week an idiot in a fourth floor flat asked me to take a piano to his daughter in Dundee!'

'You couldn't get it down the stairs.'

'Didn't try. Anyway, I was looking at your website.'

'Hunter Associates.'

'Private Investigators. Right. And your line-up hasn't changed. Still lists that IT nutcase David Wyness.'

'Our cybercrime expert, yes.'

'And that tame accountant of yours, Alison Eadie.'

'Our fraud investigator, her too. Oh, and me.'

'Of course. Anyway, I couldn't help thinking...'

Well, none of us could help that, but where did it get us? Where was she going with this?

'I could work for you.'

My face must have reacted before my mouth. She registered my astonishment at once.

'I don't mean officially, of course, nothing like that. Just when I might be able to help. On a case-by-case basis. You wouldn't be committed to anything.'

'Like a mental hospital for even considering it.'

'I mean,' she continued gamely, 'I know Wyness is hot on hacking and all that...'

'Which you are not.'

'And Alison has degrees and diplomas and knows when someone's cooking the books.'

'Beyond you too, I would have thought.'

'I'm not denying any of that, but Douglas, when it gets down and dirty...'

'At street fighting level...'

'Exactly. That I can handle, and they can't.'

There was something in what she was saying. Wyness led a sedentary life in front of his three screens. He had his work cut out climbing the stairs to his flat. He was so out of condition he couldn't fight his way out of a wet paper bag. Alison had a steely resolve and could mix in social circles where I would stick out like a sore thumb and MacNeil like a sore hand, wrist, and arm. She could also handle discreet surveillance; she'd proved that in the past. But if things got physical, that would be beyond her. She couldn't cope.

'I'm not talking about being on the payroll, Douglas, I wouldn't expect a mention on the website.'

Modest of her though this seemed, there was another explanation.

'You don't want to be on the payroll because you want your money up front. Untaxed. No National Insurance. You,' I said, pointing a weary index finger at her, 'are talking brown paper envelopes here.'

She nodded. 'I'm desperate.'

'Or you wouldn't have come here.'

She didn't reply to that since it was obviously true.

'Well,' I said, 'I don't have anything street level right now.'

I had to meet a prospective client later that morning, but my uninvited guest didn't need to know that.

She handed me her delivery driver's card with mobile number and email address.

'But you'll think about it.'

I told her I would, but I didn't really mean it.

2

THE MAIN DOOR was painted a solid blue. I pressed number four on the entry phone and heard an immediate buzz followed by the click of the door being opened remotely. The landlord was expecting me. I climbed the stairs to the first floor, noting a broken stair-light on the way, and arrived on the landing as he opened the door.

'Ah, Mr. Hunter, come in.'

Mr. Chen had no idea what I looked like and simply assumed that the stranger arriving at his door was the person he was expecting. Perhaps he was trusting by nature. Ushered first into the bedroom, I saw at once the scale of the problem. Not only was the furniture trashed, the walls had been spray-painted in a random mixture of red and black. The fact that *UP YOURS BITCH!* didn't refer to him was no consolation at all. I followed him to the living room, which had been at the receiving end of similar treatment.

'Please sit down, Mr. Hunter. Sorry about the sofa, but if you pick your spot. . .'

Its cover, worn though serviceable, had been slashed several times with a craft knife; at one end a spring showed through. I sat down carefully.

'If you could furnish me with details.'

The flat had been occupied by a Charles Plumstead Vellacott and his girlfriend, but the pair had fallen out. He had no idea why. After trashing the flat and selling certain items which didn't belong to him, Vellacott vanished from the scene.

'Certain items?'

'A fifty-two-inch flat-screen TV, a microwave and, believe it or not, a wing-backed chair which once belonged to my mother.'

'eBay?'

'Marketplace. Oh, and I should add that he was two months in arrears. So as we can see, theft can take several forms.'

'I assume you took pictures of these items for your inventory?'

He had, but it was not the first time he'd been faced with a problem of this sort and didn't expect them to help.

At a rough estimate, Mr. Chen was in his middle forties, in the region of five foot two, with early signs of male-pattern baldness beginning to thin his hair. It was only a guess, but the silver C-Class Mercedes parked outside probably belonged to him.

'I take it you required a deposit prior to letting.'

'Ah.'

Another problem. Though Vellacott had signed the tenancy agreement, he didn't have sufficient cash to hand, or so he said; he'd borrowed the deposit from his girlfriend, money which she now stood to lose.

'How much are we talking here?'

'Four hundred pounds.'

I took my notebook from my jacket pocket. Looking to lay it down, I glanced at the glass-topped coffee table, saw the initials CV etched large into it with a chisel or some such, and thought better of it. The top was still littered with shards of glass.

'I don't suppose you know her name?'

'I do. I also know where she works.'

He'd met Linda Hennessy only once, but during a short chat on the stair had learned that she worked at Body Art Studio on the High Street.

14

'She seemed a nice enough girl.'

'Ok Mr. Chen, so what do you want me to do?'

The question surprised him, surely the answer was obvious?

'Track him down, let me know where the miscreant may be found.'

A seemingly harmless request, I had to think about it for a moment. If I discovered that Vellacott was sofa-surfing in a flat in the Old Town for example, Chen might knock on the door, politely demanding back rent plus payment for stolen goods. And nothing wrong with that. But if he was a landlord on a large scale, he might have contacts with muscles whose first instinct would not be to demand money with menaces but to start with the menaces and leave the money till they'd beaten Vellacott to a pulp. I needed to know more about my client.

I checked my watch. My associate Wyness was late, which probably meant that he was still in bed and wouldn't arrive at all.

'I'll need a description, Mr. Chen, I wouldn't want to button-hole the wrong man. A photograph would be even better.'

'No photograph, I'm afraid.'

But he could provide a description. Vellacott was superficially pleasant, though I shouldn't be fooled: it was a front, nothing more, concealing a nasty streak when he didn't get what he wanted.

Interesting as this was, it wouldn't help much when it came to identification.

'Ah, of course. Good point. Please allow me to elaborate.'

In the light of past experience, I didn't expect much detail and was taken aback by Chen's thumbnail sketch. Vellacott was good-looking in an anaemic, Western sort of way, with a thick head of hair, brown, which often fell over his eyes, causing him to brush it aside. So ingrained had this habit become that he often brushed away hair which had yet to fall. He dressed reasonably well, though in tired clothes probably picked up in charity shops or stolen from clothes lines. When he'd seen him last, he was wearing burgundy corduroy pants, bagging at the knees, and a Harris tweed jacket with leather elbow pads.

'That's very helpful, Mr. Chen, very helpful indeed.'

Unfortunately, praise encouraged him to continue, an effect not confined to the young.

'It might also help you to know that when I interviewed him prior to entry he claimed to have attended a well-known school in England. I'd never heard of it, so I looked it up. Wellington College.'

I hadn't heard of it either.

His recollections were cut short by the entry phone, which I foolishly assumed was Wyness arriving late. But it proved to be the postman with a letter requiring a signature. Chen came back into the living room, turning it over in his hands, examining both sides for clues.

'It's for Vellacott.'

'Great. It might give us useful information.'

Mr. Chen looked doubtful. 'I understood it was illegal to open other people's mail.'

I had heard that too, had no idea if it was true and didn't really care. Despite a lack of acting skills, I did my best to sound outraged and turned up the volume a notch.

'What's illegal, Mr. Chen, is trashing someone's flat, selling items from it which belong to the landlord, then vanishing without trace owing two months' rent!'

3

Alison arrived just after six.

'Guess what, it's me.'

She was bearing gifts. Knowing my lack of interest in alcohol, she'd brought a bottle of elderflower wine. I was surprised the label didn't mention dandelion or burdock as well. And flowers. A bouquet which, to my eye, had an upmarket air about it, something to do with the ornate bow. None of your forecourt flowers for Alison Eadie.

'They'll need a vase.'

No doubt they would and there was one somewhere.

'I'll just pop them in the bathroom sink for now.'

This was an interesting development. In our culture, for lack of a better word, it was the custom for men to give women flowers, either to soften them up or to apologise for some misdemeanour, real or imagined. It was not the custom for a woman to give flowers to a man. And Alison, always attuned to the social norms, was well aware of this.

'Not for you, of course. For the flat.'

She had a quick look round, shook her head despairingly more than once, then opened the fridge to see if there was anything there she could make for tea.

'You realise the light doesn't work.'

Having two women point this out in the course of one day was a bit much. She produced her mobile phone and ordered food from a local takeaway.

'I ordered beef and black bean sauce for you, hope you don't mind. I know you like it.'

When our food arrived and in the temporary absence of plates, she spread it out on the kitchen table still in its foil containers.

'You haven't unpacked the cutlery yet, I take it.'

No, but I knew where it was, which was just as well. Neither of us liked eating with our fingers.

'So,' she said, ignoring the chaos around us, 'where are at we at now would you say, you and I? What's the position?'

She was referring to the heavy talk we'd had before I left Lauriston. And yes, moving in with her would have been easier than renting a new flat, the line of least resistance, but a house with chandeliers was too grand for a man like me. Then there was what it implied, that we were becoming a long-term item. I admired her, trusted her, liked her even, but that was not enough. And the fact that she felt much the same hadn't stopped her suggesting it. Perhaps she thought that having someone, anyone, was better than having no one at all.

'It was a generous offer, I realise that.'

'But?'

I fell back on the explanation I'd given her at the time.

'I have to stand on my own feet sometime. No point putting it off.'

'It's not as if I was trying to own you, Douglas. You'd rent a room and have your own key. Free to come and go as you please.'

But what I needed was not the appearance of freedom but freedom itself, not just from my ex-wife but from any other commitment as well. Commitment meant entanglement, the last thing I could cope with right now.

We talked things through for a while because Alison, though she'd given up trying to recruit me as a live-in lover, was less happy with my new flat than I was. When I'd borrowed keys to show her round, she thought the washing machine was on the small side, and her keen nose, close though it was to the scent of Lovestruck behind her ear, had detected a dank, mouldy smell from the kitchen sink. Dr Drain might fix it, but Dr Drain might not.

'Whatever you use should be bio-degradable, Douglas, nothing too corrosive.'

She'd been far ahead of my few modest thoughts on the subject: there was time enough for kitchen sinks when I moved in.

As the talk dried up and knowing The Eye was on me, I abandoned my normal practice and washed out the foil containers before dumping them in the bin. Alison put the bottle aside for recycling and washed the knives and forks. *We make a good team*, our actions seemed to say, as if synchronising tasks was all it took.

'What now? Help you unpack?'

'Where things have to go... I have it all in my head. But thanks.'

Alison's husband had been a serial cheat. It must have occurred to her that in his progress from one woman to the next he'd honed his skills. Sex and self-advancement, the two things he was good at. There was no danger of either with me. In a moment of weakness, I'd already told her that my ex-wife, Susan, had found my performance far from satisfactory between the sheets. And on our few occasions, so had she. I remembered the last time only too well.

'We could think of this as a fond farewell to the old place before you leave.'

She was stretched out on her back with her hands behind her head when she said this, looking up at the ceiling and noticing, not for the first time, cobwebs in the cornice and a spider which never seemed to move still resident in the corner. As usual her dark hair, disciplined by spray, showed no sign that she'd just engaged in anything energetic, not a single strand out of place. Who could live with such control? Certainly not me.

19

My recollection was interrupted by a phone call, a potential new client. He needed to talk but not so badly he was willing to come up with specifics. Not over the phone, he was sure I understood. So I arranged to meet him next day at his house. He worked from home. Alison, who'd only heard my half of the conversation, wanted to know more.

'Someone called Dan Drysdale. Sounded quite young, I've agreed to meet him tomorrow.'

'Where?'

'His house. Moat Terrace.'

'I don't know where that is.'

'Out Gorgie Road direction, I believe.'

She decided to make tea, and when she sat down again I knew I had to tell her.

'I had a visitor this morning.'

'Who?'

'You're not going to believe this.'

'Maureen MacNeil.'

I was amazed. How could she have known that? Had she been keeping a watch on the main door from her car on the street outside? It didn't seem likely.

'Well, Douglas, come on. When I went to make tea for us just now, I found two mugs on the draining board. So you'd had a visitor, but one you hadn't mentioned, one you were reluctant to tell me about. As far as I know, only that woman MacNeil fits the bill.'

Apart from her considerable skills in accounting, there was no getting away from the fact that Alison was an asset to a private investigation business. She was even more suspicious than I was and adept at figuring things out. She hadn't always been like that, but piecing together the moves of her cheating husband after his death had channelled her thoughts in this direction only too well. A pity, really. Innocence lost can never be recovered.

As I told her what MacNeil had said, including working

20

for me when the chance arose, I could tell Alison was unhappy.

'The cheek of the woman, the sheer brass neck!'

I could understand her reaction. Maureen MacNeil, then a detective sergeant, had not only accused me of murdering my wife, still very much alive, she'd gone on to suggest that Alison and I were somehow involved in the death of her husband. And our motive? She had that covered as well. Once relieved of our respective partners we'd be free to get up close and personal twenty-four hours a day, in my case, with the added advantage of access to money. Because, let's face it, the fair Alison wasn't short of a penny.

'I suppose we have to remember that she was suffering from paranoia at the time.'

But Alison wasn't having it.

'Cocaine-induced, if you remember. This beggars belief! I hope you told her where to get off.'

4

Moat Terrace wasn't hard to find, and since there was little in the way of housing on one side of the street, parking was easier than I'd expected. I was surprised to see that the main door to number eight was blue, just as Mr Chen's had been, but this blue was tired, crying out for some tender loving care though, from the state of it, less likely to get it. Drysdale's flat was on the first floor, and I found myself on a landing with a door at each end. There was no name on either but one sported DD in black marker, which I took to be Dan Drysdale. And so it turned out.

'Come in, Mr Hunter, this way.'

He ushered me into a room, probably intended as a bedroom but now his office.

'Good of you to come. The thing is, I mostly work from home and this is a working day for me.'

He indicated a chair and sat down at his workstation, rotating the seat to face me rather than the screen. As well he might, I'd come several miles, and though this didn't figure in his thinking, it was also a working day for me.

'So, Mr Drysdale, what can I do for you?'

'Dan, please.'

According to Dan, it was a delicate business, though the more he told me the less delicate it seemed. A few months before, Manor Place (I knew where that was, he assured me) had been closed for three days to allow filming a motion picture. I probably remembered the anger of residents at the time, it made the six o'clock news. No doubt it had, but I never watched the news; life was depressing enough.

'Well, I had occasion to be there then.'

'In connection with your work.'

'I was documenting a property about to go on the market.'

'Taking measurements, that sort of thing.'

'And photographs. We have a professional photographer, of course, but I find pictures useful as an aid to memory.'

'So when you've taken the measurements and the pictures?'

'I collate the information on any given property for our website. I get the text from the office, pictures and videos from the photographer. It's not so easy as it sounds. It has to look good on everything from tablets and laptops to mobile phones. It has to flow. And entries have to be constantly updated.'

'And you can do all this from home.'

'No distractions here. The office is too open plan. You wouldn't believe it. People keep talking, making remarks.'

Well, we couldn't have that, it wouldn't do at all.

'Okay, so we left you walking down Manor Place when they were filming.'

'And I'd every right to be there.'

'Of course.'

'So just have a look at this.'

While he engaged in some neat mousework, I moved my chair closer to the screen, soon to be rewarded with some two minutes of footage from Born Again 3, a film sufficiently downmarket to be streaming immediately after release, if not before.

'See what I mean!' He said this with an air of triumph I failed to fathom.

Realising that I hadn't seen it at all, he rose from his chair, went to the window and closed his floral curtains.

'It'll be more obvious with less light reflecting from the screen, and this time concentrate on the background.'

Then all would become clear. And maybe it did, because I detected a figure walking down the street who looked suspiciously like the lad himself, Dan Drysdale.

'That wouldn't be you, would it?'

'It would indeed.'

'Fame at last,' I told him, 'immortalised on celluloid.'

This statement didn't go down well. Firstly, as every schoolboy knew, many films, this one included, were entirely digital these days, no celluloid involved. Secondly, and here we came to the nub of the matter, at no point had he, Daniel Scott Drysdale, been asked if he minded being in this film, let alone been asked for his permission. His image rights were clearly infringed. And by the way, he'd timed it several times. He'd been on screen for a grand total of eighty-seven seconds, long enough to make tea.

'Well, Dan, I can see that, but it's done now, it's out there. It's not clear to me what you expect me to do about it.'

But Dan was a patient man for one so young, only twenty-three with all his hair and most of his teeth. And he was implacable with it. He'd studied the credits several times and found nineteen names listed either as producer, co-producer, associate producer, or executive producer. Nineteen! He'd since learned that one of them, Chester H Burt, had an apartment in Edinburgh. Having places in Cannes and Toronto as well, he didn't use it all year round, but there was reason to believe he'd be in residence during the Festival.

'And you want me to locate this apartment.'

'Exactly.'

He intended to sue Mr Burt for infringement of his image and have himself filmed knocking on the great man's door to serve the papers. At which point the clip would go viral.

'Poetic justice, I would say, nothing more, nothing less.'

Nothing more, that I could go along with, but there was a fair chance it was a great deal less.

'But suppose this Burt person can't be held legally responsible, what then?'

'Ah, perhaps I should have mentioned this. There are nineteen producers, like I said, but only three are listed as executive producers.'

'And Burt's one of them.'

'He is. And what does executive mean? It means he is responsible for making decisions.'

He said this with an air of finality, but it wasn't clear to me that he'd made his case, especially coming from someone who routinely claimed that houses he was marketing were "executive" apartments.

'Two questions.'

'Certainly. Fire away, Mr Hunter, shoot!'

'What about the other executive producers, why pick on the only one who happens to live here part of the year.'

'The way I see it, it would be an example, a test case. Get him and pursuing the others would be plain sailing.'

'In this jurisdiction, perhaps, but they're probably foreign nationals living abroad.'

'That may be, Mr Hunter, but we can only cross a bridge when we come to it.'

And sometimes not even then, though I didn't point this out.

'Your other question?'

'Yes, so who do you work for, Dan?'

'Linton Legal, solicitors and estate agents.'

I couldn't help but notice the word "legal" in there.

'Right, so they know about the law.'

'Ah, I see where you're coming from. Yes, well they know about the law as it applies to conveyancing, inheritance tax and so on. Yes, that's true.'

He paused briefly, the better to emphasise his next

point, though his disdainful tone would have done the job all on its own.

'But they don't have a clue about media law. Not a clue. Believe me, I've asked.'

I believed him. I was sure he had.

5

I'D JUST LEFT Drysdale's flat when my phone rang. Alison. Could I drop by that morning, something had come up? I expressed the hope that it wasn't something she ate, but either she didn't get it or, more likely, felt it was beneath her to reply.

Thanks to a combination of traffic and roadworks, it took me a good twenty-five minutes to reach Royal Terrace, there to be admitted to The Presence, still in her dressing gown, albeit an expensive little number with a silken sheen.

'Good morning, Douglas, do take a seat.'

Her lounge, or main public room, as Drysdale would doubtless have had it, was exactly the same as it had been when we first met: the same high ceiling, the same chandeliers, the same cold feel, regardless of the weather. There was only one exception. The picture which had hung over the mantelpiece had gone and in its place nothing, though it was just possible to make out the rectangle where it used to be, slightly lighter in colour than the surrounding wall. It had been a family portrait in oils showing Alison looking attractive, if austere, and her late husband, Alan Ogilvie, in landed gentry pose with two adoring dogs, neither of which had ever existed. Alison didn't like dogs.

'Thanks for coming so quickly. As I said, there's been a development.'

Her role with Hunter Associates was limited. She was a partner, took care of the accounts to a textbook standard and undertook the occasional surveillance job when no physical danger was involved. But her main source of income lay in her accounting skills, for which she was retained by several companies, large and small, most of them in the west.

'You may have heard of Ergonomica.' I hadn't, which drew the expected reply. 'Really, Douglas, you must pay more attention to the business pages.'

According to Alison, it was in the business pages that we could take the pulse of the nation. After all, economics *was* politics. And I suppose there was something in this since economists, like politicians, majored in drawing opposite conclusions from the same set of figures.

'Can I offer you anything. Tea? Coffee?'

'Later maybe. Go on.'

Ergonomica were big in furniture supplies and had recently acquired two smaller companies in the same field. She was sure I'd come across this before, but take-over documents always promised economies of scale and, as an added incentive, building on the synergies that already existed between the businesses. However, it seemed that in this case, as in so many before, these benefits were failing to materialize, and the problem lay in what she referred to as the back office. The plan had been to merge the functions of the three back offices and the stumbling block, as always, was software. Based on the software people I'd come across, notably our very own David Wyness, this did not come as a surprise.

'They're using completely different accounting packages, Douglas, and their attempts to harmonise them have been disastrous. It's absolute chaos through there.'

'Through where?'

'Oh sorry, didn't I say? Glasgow.'

'So how do you come in?'

'They've offered me a short-term contract, three months in the first instance.'

'To bring order out of chaos.'

'Well, I wouldn't go that far but, I suppose, yes.'

'And you're tempted to take it.'

'Let's just say it would pay my bills for the rest of this year and most of next.'

This was no small thing. Her house was large, the ceilings high, the heating expensive. On top of that she bought clothes, designer labels all, and patronised an upmarket hairdresser, Bernard (stress on the second syllable, please), whom she referred to as her stylist. Not that her hairstyle ever changed much, but he kept her black locks very neat and orderly. Very orderly indeed.

'So I've booked into the Sherbrooke Castle next week. I'll have to be on the spot a great deal, initially at least. I hope that won't be a problem.'

'Five star?' Alison liked the best.

'Four, but it's very good.'

I was sure it was.

'I'm glad that's settled, leaving you high and dry was worrying me a bit. But remember, Douglas, I'll just be a phone call away.'

Though true, this was a troubling statement. On the one hand, she meant that if I needed help with anything she would be happy to provide it. But it also meant that she could keep an eye on me remotely, at any time, just by phoning. I also had the feeling that while the events of the previous year had brought us together in more ways than one, the events unfolding now might cause us to drift apart to what might, after all, be a more manageable distance.

While she had me pinned to the sofa, she asked for an update on our current cases. Her starting point was, of course, financial. Had I informed Mr Chen and Mr Drysdale of our hourly rates, our position regarding expenses, and that all invoices should be settled within thirty days and preferably within seven? Had I been clear on these things?

Cash flow mattered, the last thing the business needed right now was having to borrow to keep afloat.

'I'm talking liquidity here, Douglas. These last few months have been tight.'

I was able to reassure her on these points, she had me well trained.

'So how did it go with Mr Chen?'

She was duly appalled by the devastation visited on his flat by the departing Charles Plumstead Vellacott, particularly by the spray paint on the walls, only too visible in the pictures I'd taken during my visit.

'And you tell me this Vellacott person went to a good school!'

'Wellington, I believe.'

Alison, a well-behaved lady who didn't have a malicious bone in her body, had trouble accepting the fact that some people who graduated from such superior establishments as good schools went on to a life of crime. She'd gone to a good school herself.

'About this Mr Chen, you think he might have muscle at his disposal.'

I liked her turn of phrase, here was a woman adapting herself to her role. In fact, Mr Chen seemed a solid citizen to me, though I intended to ask David Wyness to a bit of digging just in case.

'So your first port of call will be the tattoo parlour.'

'It's the only lead I have.'

'Rather you than me. As far as I can see, these places are always suspiciously dark and frequented by night-club bouncers.'

This was a pleasing flight of fancy, bouncers representing lowlifes and others Alison considered socially undesirable. I was willing to bet she'd never met one in her life.

'This afternoon might be a good time. Saturday. It's bound to be open for business.'

While this was true, it would also be at its most busy, the staff having little time to deal with a non-paying visitor like me. My plan was to spend the rest of the day, and most of Sunday, unpacking boxes and stowing things away where I could hope to find them later. A place for everything, everything in its place.

Having satisfied herself on the Chen case, she moved smartly on to Daniel Drysdale. When I filled in the background, she denied all knowledge of Born Again 3 which, in my book, was to her credit.

'Has it something to do with Hinduism? Reincarnation and all that?'

Coming somewhat out of left field the question took me aback for a moment, but I couldn't dismiss it out of hand since I hadn't seen the film myself.

'It's always possible, I suppose.'

I later learned that the film stretched credulity to breaking point, the villain, dispatched by the forces of good, returning to this life even more evil than before. Twice. According to Wyness, who checked it out one of his three screens, the film was so bad it was already bordering on cult status. But Alison wasn't interested in any of that.

'This Drysdale person, he's quite young by the sound of it.'

'About twenty-three or so.'

'Would you say he was over-impressed with his own appearance, a narcissistic young man?'

I'd detected a faint whiff of after-shave when we met, and he was neatly attired considering he was working from home at the time with no one there to see him.

'No one. I see, so he lives alone?'

I couldn't swear to it, I hadn't searched the flat, but that was the impression I had.

To forestall further questions I hadn't adequate answers to, I put one to Alison.

'So, Alison, suppose you found yourself in a film like that, what would your attitude be?'

She mulled this over for a moment before coming to the expected conclusion.

'As long as I was presentable, I wouldn't mind at all.'

This was Alison in a nutshell and nothing wrong with that. But it was an area outwith my experience, so she had some advice.

'You should talk this through with Louise.'

In principle, this was a good idea. Louise was the razor-sharp lawyer who'd defended her against the wild accusations of DS Maureen MacNeil and, later, the equally wild accusations against me. The same Louise who'd noticed before any of us that MacNeil was a user.

'Alison, let's get real here, she charges over four hundred pounds an hour. Her meter starts running the minute she opens her mouth.'

But as a friend from their university days, Alison was confident she could get me a free half hour with Ms Galbraith provided I paid for lunch.

'I'll phone her later today. I'm confident she'll be happy to help.'

Maybe. I wasn't so sure.

'This is the woman who thought I was after you for your money.'

'At first, yes, but not when she got to know you. I think I would characterise her attitude to you now as one of grudging respect.

6

ON MONDAY MORNING, after a Sunday of toil in the flat, I strolled from my new residence to the High Street, admiring the illustrations in the window of Body Art Studio when I got there. In my mid-thirties and without a vestige of style even about my hair, I stood out at once.

A young man with heavily tattooed arms and metal rings through his ears, nose and possibly other places as well, looked up from a desk.

'The barber's next door.'

'Good afternoon to you too.' I pointed to the metal. 'I hope that's galvanized.'

'Not your problem, mate, and just so you know, rust isn't poisonous.'

On the back foot already, I came to the point.

'I'm looking for someone.'

'Aren't we all.'

'Linda Hennessey.'

'Okay, you got me there, we're not all looking for Linda. You'd have to be desperate.'

'I am'

The man laid his magazine on the desk and looked me up and down.

'Alright, we can agree on that. The name's Brian, by the way. So what's this about?'

'I'm trying to save her money. Four hundred pounds to be exact.'

Brian was astonished. 'Pull the other one, pal, she never

has more than a tenner to her name.' Suddenly remembering he was running a business, he waved an arm round the walls, indicating blow-ups of the tattoo artist's skill. 'Any of these take your fancy? A butterfly, maybe, interlocking Celtic symbols?' Though I didn't respond he didn't give up. 'If you're not into art we can offer something useful: your blood group, for example or maybe, if you've had it with this miserable life, *Do Not Resuscitate*. In a tastefully chosen location, of course.' He paused for breath before one last throw of the dice. 'I could do you an introductory offer.'

Learning that I wasn't into adornment of any sort, he gave up and pointed to a door in the back wall. 'You'll find her in there. If she's sleeping, give her a prod. Everyone else does.'

I entered the back room and closed the door behind me. The suspended ceiling, painted black, was heavy with small, flush-mounted lights randomly spaced to suggest the sky at night. As Brian had suggested, Hennessey was out for the count, her head resting on a desk with some of the tools of her trade: cartons of ink, packs of needles, guns.

'Miss Hennessey.'

She stirred and opened an eye. 'And you are?'

'Douglas Hunter.'

'And that's supposed to mean something, is it?'

'You look knackered.'

'So would you if you'd spent the last three weeks dossing on an air bed in this shithole.'

'Since your boyfriend ripped you off.'

'You know about that?'

'It's why I'm here.'

Sighing, she sat up, lifted an atomizer from the desk, pointed the business end toward her face, shut her eyes and gave herself a generous blast.

'Revitalizing spray,' she explained, 'very refreshing. Does the trick for me.'

'Doesn't get your deposit back, though, does it.'

After a brief pause, she began to undo the good work of her spray by picking up a mirror and attacking her eyebrows with a black pencil and her lashes with Urban Rebel (102, Liquid Goth). I made a bet with myself that she'd go on to apply black lipstick as well, which she did, one of the few wagers I'd ever won.

'You can't leave it all to Nature.'

As Hennessey prepared her face for the afternoon, I looked round the room. The metal shelving along the rear wall supported yellow sharps boxes, a printer and a range of disinfectants. Below the bottom shelf, an autoclave with a short flex sat on the floor connected to a socket above the skirting board. But what really stood out was a large chair with many movable parts. Apart from outbreaks of chrome, its faux leather was as black as her hair. Or her pants. Or her jacket. And doubtless her underwear as well.

'Right, Mr. Hunter, if that's your real name...'

'It is.' I gave her my card as evidence.

'Chen's hired you to screw me for the damage to his flat.'

'Not quite.'

'What then?'

'He wants me to track down Vellacott and screw him instead.'

Suddenly wide awake, she sat up and looked me straight in the eye.

'You're not a debt-collector?'

'Do I look like a debt collector?'

'You don't look like anything much.'

She rolled herself towards me on her castor-mounted tattoo artist's chair.

'How can I help?'

'For a start you could give me pictures of the guy, Chen didn't have any.'

She produced a cell phone from her coffin bag and scrolled through the gallery.

35

'I have several.' She looked up from her screen and smiled. 'Close-ups of his privates any good?'

I didn't see how they could be, but she did.

'Post them on social media, embarrass the bastard into paying up.'

'That would be illegal, Miss Hennessy, and even if it wasn't, I don't see how it would work.'

'There's something you don't know.'

'And you're going to tell me.'

She rewarded me with a sly grin.

'For a big man he's not so well endowed.'

She had just started to show me when alarming sounds of violence came from the office outside. Brian's reception area was being demolished by a man with a cricket bat demanding to know where Linda Hennessy was. Despite his hard-man image, Brian was felled by a blow to the head and the attacker stormed in. He was plainly aggrieved.

'You bitch, you slag!'

Then he noticed me.

'Who's this tossser, your latest squeeze?'

He took a swing at me and missed. But the weight of the bat at the end of his arm, its sheer mass in motion, caused him to lose his balance and fall, Hennessey saw her chance and ran for it. A smart decision. Vellacott had heard she was spreading rumours about him: he was a thieving bastard who couldn't get it up. He was fine with first of these accusations, to him almost a badge of honour, but outraged by the second. Even without those little blue pills his prowess was second to none.

I helped Brian to his feet and out into the street, where I was amazed to see the police already in attendance. An officer I knew, Hector Robertson, combined looking after him till the ambulance arrived with asking him questions. A second officer I'd never met before, appeared in the studio door and beckoned me inside. I told her what little I knew.

'So let me get this straight, you were attacked with a cricket bat here in the Body Art Tattoo Studio by a tall man in burgundy cords.'

'That's correct.'

'A cricket bat? Really? Hardly a weapon of choice in these parts.'

'He was English.'

'I see.' She scribbled something in her notebook before returning to the attack. 'Subscribe to cultural stereotypes do you, Mr. Hunter?'

'Don't you?'

'No.'

I was being questioned in what was left of the Body Art office by DS Anastasija Cook, an officer I had heard of but had yet to meet. The glass frames of the tattoo blow-ups lately adorning the walls were in smithereens on the floor, so we had to watch where we put our feet. The pictures themselves were ripped and torn.

'You claim that the assailant was a Charles Plumstead Vellacott.'

'That's correct. Where is he, by the way?'

'Left through a window into the gardens at the back.'

She glanced at her notes.

'You say that you had never previously set eyes on Mr. Vellacott, so I have to wonder how you knew who he was.'

Though I had recently set eyes on graphic shots of his private parts, she had a point.

'He made it clear he was Linda Hennessey's ex. It had to be him.'

DS Cook, shorter than I was, looked up at me enquiringly.

'I'm sure she wouldn't mind me pointing this out, but Miss Hennessy is no longer in the first flush of youth.'

While this was true, I wasn't sure why was she saying it, something she quickly put right.

'You appear to assume that at the age of thirty-four she

37

had only clocked up one ex. Does that seem likely to you?'

Cook suspected that I had history with Vellacott and was trying to flush me out. I pointed to the street outside; Robertson, was still interrogating the remains of the manager, now in the care of two paramedics.

'Ask Brian if you don't believe me, he'll have no trouble identifying Vellacott.'

DC Robertson was strong on notetaking too but played his cards so close to his chest I sometimes wondered if he had any. DS Cook subjected me to a brief visual inspection and came to the obvious conclusion.

'You're not into tattoos yourself, I see, so an obvious question arises: what were you doing here in the first place?'

I assumed she would know my back story so I made no attempt to disguise it.

'Acting on behalf of a client.'

'In your capacity as a private investigator?'

'Yes.'

She sighed, surveyed the devastation again and summoned up a world-weary tone.

'But on grounds of confidentiality, you can't tell me who that client is?'

'No, but I'll ask him to contact you. I'm sure he'll be happy to oblige.'

'Excuse me one moment. Don't go away.'

She left the studio to have a word with Robertson on the street outside. A small crowd had gathered, some just curious, others recording what action they could on their mobile phones. For a second, I thought I saw DS Cook's predecessor, Maureen MacNeil among them, but before I could verify that, Cook joined me back in the shop.

'This Vellacott, know anything about him?'

'He's violent.'

'By *anything,* I mean anything which isn't blindingly obvious.'

'He has it in for Linda Hennessy, an employee of the studio here.'

'A tattoo artist.'

'Correct.'

'So where is she now, the elusive Miss Hennessey?'

I had no idea. She'd made a sharp exit at the first sign of trouble and quite right too.

'According to my colleague, several witnesses saw a woman matching her description run from the premises and disappear down the road towards The Pleasance. I don't suppose you know where she lives?'

'To the best of my knowledge she's been sleeping in the studio lately, on an air bed I believe.'

'And Vellacott? Any idea where he lives?'

'That's what I'm trying to find out.'

'For your client.'

'Yes.'

Further questioning was cut short by the blare of car horns. Several drivers were taking exception to the double-parked ambulance blocking the street.

7

SOMEONE DEALING WITH crime and criminals should be able to handle violence better than I do. MacNeil certainly could, I'd seen her in action. As the saying goes, you wouldn't want to meet her on a dark night. But in this respect, and maybe some others, I wasn't in her league. Violence always left me feeling fragile, tremulous even, as if my heart was about to pack in. Even in films, when the going got nasty I turned the volume down. Pathetic, I know, but we all have our weak points.

Picking up a sandwich on the way, I walked back to the flat, washed it down with a mug of builder's brew and lay on my mattress for a while, thinking. I had the feeling that events were leaving me less room for manoeuvre; I needed more mental space to cover the angles. And I still hadn't found that elusive fourth leg. Eventually, without feeling a bit like it, I took one of the three remaining legs and drove to the nearest bed shop in the hope of finding a match.

'Ah yes,' the salesman said, 'a standard thread, alright, but I don't know about the length. We may not be able to match that. Just give me a moment.'

He disappeared into the back shop and I waited in the showroom, clocking how cavernous it was and how few customers there were. I saw a family in the distance, their small boy mistaking a bed for a trampoline. Apart from that, nothing. Maybe people didn't shop for beds on a Monday afternoon, or maybe it was usually like this.

The salesman returned, all smiles.

'Yes, we can do you a set of these, sir.'

'I only need one.'

He realised that, but he couldn't break up a set, it wouldn't make business sense. What could they possibly do with the remaining three legs if he gave one to me?

So what was I to do? Embark on a grand tour of other bed shops or go for his solution. I opted for a new set of four, wasteful, but it would work. I needed less weight on the brain, I needed solutions.

'Fine, I'll go with the set of four.'

'They'll be in within five to seven working days, guaranteed.'

I couldn't believe it. 'You don't have them in stock?'

No, but his computer had shown seven sets available in their warehouse.

'I could have them delivered. Save you coming back out here.'

He seemed quite pleased, perhaps even relieved. Small though it was, mine may have been the first sale he'd made that day.

I left Benjamin's Beds with the feeling that at least I'd struck one task from the list and called my friend John Banks before leaving the car park. He didn't need to talk to me, but I needed to talk to him. We usually met at the Royal Oak, but when he heard that David Wyness wasn't coming, he suggested a café, which suited me fine. Not that I was signed up to the Temperance League, just that for me alcohol seldom hit the spot.

But here we met a snag. In our fair city, hospitality worked in shifts. Coffee shops opened their doors much earlier than public houses, taverns and the like, but they also closed them earlier too. Try getting a coffee at seven in the evening and you'd be stuck with filter coffee in a pub or, failing that, if you were dead set on a latte or a cappuccino, you could get one in a restaurant provided you had a meal as well. Which increased the price of your favourite brew just a bit. But on this occasion, though I'd done a deal of tidying up, I'd yet to shop for groceries, so eating out made sense. I talked John into joining me for a fish supper in the Reverie. The description in the menu was longer, more impressive, but that's what it was. The whole thing being my idea, he accepted my offer to pay.

'From your ill-gotten gains selling the house.'

And for the inside information I hoped he might provide. Though not a police officer himself, John was a civilian employee of the force and knew what was going on.

'Just as well Wyness couldn't come. He'd have wanted three beers at least.'

Wyness might have come if I'd asked him, but I'd a lot to talk through with him, better accomplished one to one, and in any case, he was increasingly reluctant to leave his flat.

'And we both know why that is.'

Climbing the four flights of stairs to his front door was more of a challenge than before, and much more than it should have been for a man still only forty. He inhabited a smoke-filled room, curtains drawn, interrogating his three screens as if his life depended on it. Which, in a way, it did since he made most of his money trading currency. And the result of this sedentary, nicotine-stained lifestyle? He was three stones heavier than he should have been and his lungs were labouring at the slightest effort.

'He explained to me how it worked one time, something to do with real time indicators, red and green candles. And wicks. Rice came into it somewhere too, the Lord alone knows how. Alison was there as well.'

'I bet they didn't hit it off.' John was spot on. 'Chalk and cheese.'

He'd tried to impress her with his handle on the markets, his top-end gear, and catchy phrases like tomorrow's technology today. But she hadn't been impressed. As she saw it, Wyness contributed nothing to society. He was a leech, a parasite. Not that she said this to his face, she was too polite.

As we attacked our battered haddock, John, who knew why I'd invited him, got to the point.

'So, Douglas, what do you want to know?'

I told him about the morning's events at the Body Art Studio, only to find he knew about the incident already.

'Sounded quite bad.'

It was. And I'd been questioned by a detective sergeant I'd never met before. Anastasija Cook.

'Ah yes, MacNeil's replacement. How did that go?'

I wasn't sure, I'd found her hard to read. John wasn't surprised to hear that she'd got me on cultural stereotypes.

'She would. She's from Latvia.'

With a surname like Cook this wasn't immediately obvious, though I thought I'd detected a faint East European twang when she spoke. Very slight, but it was there.

'She's married to Jim Cook, the bloke who runs Ruby's bookshop.'

I was amazed. Jim, popularly known as Cook the Books, was ten years older than she was.

'True, but you need to engage in more flexible thinking, Douglas. Susan and you were the same age and that didn't exactly work out. Where is she now? Lake Tahoe, I believe you said?'

He had a point. 'Right. Fine.'

'Is this Cook woman any good?'

'I think so. Robertson rates her.'

I was surprised to hear this because Robertson's custom, if he had any opinions, was to keep them to himself.

'How do you know?'

John tapped the side of his nose with his index finger, a gesture which seemed to suggest privileged knowledge.

'You can always tell. It's in the air.'

As I ate my last chip, I looked round the restaurant and liked what I saw. I was particularly impressed by the low-hanging lights suspended on long leads above each table. You had the feeling that you were but one island in a little archipelago, each one tastefully lit.

'Right, so John, here's the thing.'

There had been an assault at commercial premises and the police appeared in seconds. This was astonishing in itself, but why detectives, why not uniformed officers? And how had they got there so quickly? It only made sense if they'd been close by already. And they were. An informant had claimed that Class A drugs were being dealt from the studio, not by Linda Hennessey but by the manager, Brian Doyle. Since Doyle erred on the rude side, I was ready to believe it, but DS Cook needed better evidence than that and had the studio under observation from a second-floor flat in the tenement opposite.

'Airbnb,' John said, by way of explanation.

'Does the budget stretch to that!'

'Just for three days. According to Cook we had to cover the bases.'

Which explained how they were on the scene so quickly. And John wasn't finished yet.

'Something else you should know.'

'Which is?'

'She's not a natural blonde.'

8

THE FOLLOWING MORNING, I woke up early again, conscious of a draught coming in under the bedroom door, noticeable to a man still marooned on a mattress at floor level. But I had bran flakes in a kitchen cupboard, milk in the fridge, and I'd pushed the boat out the day before and bought a tin of prunes. Susan, my ex-wife, winter sports instructor to the families of the privileged few, had advised that prunes would keep me regular. And she should know, she had qualifications.

I was just beginning to relax into the day when my phone rang. Louise Galbraith.

'Alison contacted me. I can give you half an hour, today, twelve thirty. That's it. Take it or leave it.'

She had such a warm way with her, the woman oozed charm from every pore. But having no other source of advice on Drysdale's particular point of law, I accepted her invitation. It was tempting to drop in on Wyness before my designated time, but he seldom got up before noon and sometimes not even then, so I rested my soul in patience and prepared to meet my doom in Galbraith's legal offices high up in a concrete and glass structure off Conference Square. No harm looking neat and tidy for the occasion. Who knew who I might meet.

The half-hour window being tight, I arrived ten minutes early and was ushered into a waiting area by one of the secretaries. The chairs were so plush I wondered how some of their older clients managed to rise from them, the ones wanting trust funds for their grandchildren or shelters for their savings against tax. They called to mind those armchairs in eventide homes where the residents are parked in the day room, never to escape till a member of staff helps them up. Simple, really. No drugs, required, no restraints. And there they stay, like it or not, watching re-runs of the Black and White Minstrel show or The Good Old Days. Anything thought likely to appeal to their long-lost youth before the advent of flat screen TVs and mobile phones.

A self-service counter was on hand for those wanting tea, coffee and rich tea biscuits. I was tempted but resisted. The last thing I needed was having to excuse myself halfway through my allotted half hour. And right on the stroke of half past twelve, Ms Galbraith came to lead me down a corridor to her office. The first time I'd met her she was wearing a sweatshirt bearing the words SEE YOU IN COURT in letters as red as her hair, but today she was sporting a business suit tending to the charcoal or black. Power dressing, no doubt. She pointed to a chair and I sat on it.

'Alison told me about your meter wisecrack, Douglas, so I shall tell you right now that it will start counting the minutes at one o'clock exactly. At which point,' she added, 'you will also hear me address you as Mr Hunter.'

It seemed she was troubled by a sore throat, it certainly sounded like it, but I politely declined her offer of a Fisherman's Friend.

'So tell me, concisely if you can, what this is about.'

As I outlined Drysdale's case against the makers of Born Again 3, she listened impassively, quite an achievement really. But her first question threw me.

'Is he a footballer?'

'Not as far as I knew.

'A pop star? A celebrity of some kind, however minor?'

I didn't think so. I had no reason to believe that.

'In which case the young man's image rights, if he has any, are of no value whatsoever. I mean, who watching this film would notice him?'

'Apart from himself and his mother?'

'Exactly. I really don't see the point. His complaint is frivolous.'

She said this in such a way as to suggest that my presence in the inner sanctum must also be frivolous by extension and rammed this home by turning her attention to papers on her desk.

'Mr Drysdale regards it as a matter of principle.'

'Which you can articulate on his behalf?' She said this in a tone of mild incredulity.

But I believed I could, my starting point being a principle we'd been taught at the police college, namely, that everyone is equal in the eyes of the law.

'For example,' I said, 'if a hairdresser and a belted earl were each caught shoplifting in a department store both should be charged.'

She replied very quickly. 'Or neither.'

'Ok,' I continued, suddenly feeling on less solid ground, 'but if a highly paid footballer can sue over image rights, why can't the humble employee of an estate agent?'

She looked at me for a moment, as if trying to assess if I still had what it took between the ears.

'Douglas,' she said with a throaty sigh, 'it isn't a question of how much they are paid, what matters in a case like this is whether they have any public profile to speak of in the first place. This Mr Drysdale of yours; if a hundred people passed him in the street, not one of them would know who he was.'

This was highly likely, the more so since he worked so much from home.

'There you are then. He doesn't have a leg to stand on.'

Maybe not, but he was determined to stand on it anyway, bring a test case, if necessary.

'Have you any idea what that would cost?'

'No.'

'Has he?'

Probably not, but he was crowdfunding against the day.

'God give me strength!'

'Come over here a moment,' she said, going to the window. 'Look over there.'

I did, and saw a roof-top swimming pool I hadn't known existed.

'You know who uses that pool? Guests at the Sheraton, some of them very high profile indeed. I know because I've seen them. These are just the sort of people who might claim image rights. And I say "might" because even there, most of them aren't in that league.'

'Who are you thinking of, Gillian?'

She thought for a moment, probably selecting a name from a long list of celebrities she'd eye-balled through opera glasses from her vantage point on the sixth floor.

'Addison O'Dowd used that pool as recently as last week.'

The name had a faint ring to it, but I couldn't place it.

'You've never heard of her, have you?'

'No.'

'Supermodel. Poses on catwalks in handkerchiefs and high heels.'

'You're making this up.'

'If only.'

She rose, a prelude to ushering me out.

'Now there's a woman with a legitimate interest in image rights.'

I didn't doubt it for a moment.

9

WHEN I GOT back to the flat, there were several letters behind the door, including the first of many from TV Licensing. Walking over it felt good. I made for the kitchen and spread some farmhouse pâté on a slice of wholemeal bread. In line with my latest attempt at healthy living, my intention was to wash it down with cool, clear water, which I was about to do when my mobile rang.

'Mr Hunter? Of Hunter Associates?'

'Yes.'

'My name is Anna van Leeuwen. I have a problem.'

Don't we all, I thought, but forbore to say it.

'What can I do for you, Miss van Leeuwen?'

She hoped to drop by my place in Royal Terrace to discuss it. She'd evidently checked out Hunter Associates and found that Alison's house was our registered office. As a choice it made sense; a select location suggesting a level of reliability, and also, unlike my address at the time, reasonably permanent and unlikely to change. When I set her straight, she revised her offer.

'OK, I can come to Gifford Place, it's not so far from my work.'

When the bell rang, I was stowing away bubble wrap recently used to pack the plates.

'Mr. Hunter?' She held out her hand and introduced herself. 'Anna van Leeuwen.'

And there she was, another woman on my doorstep, the third in as many days. By comparison with me, women

49

tended to be well turned out and strong on detail. They would be my downfall, no doubt about it.

Her grip was weak, fingers only, not extending to the palm of the hand, though if that signified anything I didn't know what. I led her to the living room and indicated a chair with nothing piled on top of it.

'Sorry about this, I'm in the process of flitting.'

She raised an artfully defined eyebrow. 'Flitting?'

Registering a mild transatlantic accent, I helped her out. 'Moving house.'

'Ah.'

I could almost hear the cogs whir as she considered what this might imply.

'So you may have too much on your hands right now to take on more.'

The only clients currently on my books were a landlord with a problem and a young man keen to protect his image so, flitting notwithstanding, I probably had enough slack to consider her. But until I knew what her problem was it seemed wiser not to admit it. At five foot four or thereabouts she was small, an impression increased by her hair: also short, light brown, but with a faint shine to it.

'I'm being followed at work. Maybe at home too, not so sure there, though.'

'You're being stalked.'

'I believe so.'

'By a man?'

'Yes.'

I moved some papers from a chair and sat down facing her, hoping to build up a picture.

'In cases like this an ex-partner is often involved.'

'Max is in New York right now, so he'd be going some. Anyway, he's not one to hold a grudge.'

'Ok, so where do you work, Miss van Leeuwen?'

'Capital House, Bank of New York Mellon. I'm a risk and

compliance manager.'

Her clients, none of them short of a penny, wanted to be confident that their assets were safe in the event of market turmoil; all the more likely, she told me in too much detail, what with uncertainty regarding Brexit, tariff barriers and the projected slow-down in global growth.

'I advise them how best to hedge their bets against disaster. Absolute return funds and so on.'

'I see.'

'I'm not sure you do but it doesn't much matter.'

If she was right, if there really was a stalker, his interest in her could be personal but it might also centre on her role at the bank.

'Do you have access to codes, combinations of any sort, for example, to the vault?'

'You think he wants to kidnap me for a code?'

'It's a possibility we should consider. As I'm sure you know, it's happened before.'

'New York Mellon isn't a retail bank, Mr. Hunter, I thought I'd made that clear. We have a safe for confidential documents, of course, but no cash, no diamonds, no gold ingots. In short,' she added a little sharply, 'we have no need of a vault.'

I should have picked up on this but found an easy way out.

'All well and good, Miss van Leeuwen, but your stalker may not know that.'

Perched on my armchair she looked, as my grandmother used to say, quite the thing, an effect increased by her tailored suit, cream background with discreet grey and black lines. She glanced at me enquiringly.

'Shouldn't you be taking notes?'

I should have been but couldn't remember where my notebook was, so I pointed to my head.

'I am.'

Her sceptical tone was unmistakable. 'You'll remember all this?'

I nodded, noticing the glint of small stud earrings when she moved her head, probably there to keep her pierced lobes open.

'So, Mr. Hunter, about your associates.'

She was looking for reassurance; I would have done the same.

'My business partner, Alison Eadie, is a forensic accountant,' I said, giving a modest boost to her area of expertise, 'the other is our resident IT expert, David Wyness. Both are available for surveillance as required.'

They weren't, of course, but I was learning to live with the imperatives of marketing.

'Well, what I need to know is whether you and your team can check this out for me, or are your hands full at the moment,' her eyes straying to the corner of the room, 'like these boxes of yours still to be unpacked.'

It seemed to me that this woman was sharp as a boning knife and would expect her case to be handled quickly and efficiently.

'If you give me a contact number, I'll run it past my colleagues and get back to you with a response by close of play today.' She didn't reply at once. 'Provided that is satisfactory to you.'

She shifted in her seat and looked out the window, she wanted to make a point.

'There is a logic to all this, Mr. Hunter, but also what we might call a psycho-logic. As I'm sure you will understand, being followed is unsettling to say the least. Yes, you might be imagining it, but either way you're constantly on edge. What's the motive, what might happen next? Put yourself in my shoes.'

When I looked at them, I noticed for the first time that they were not the high heels I had expected of a female executive, but sensible flat-heeled numbers. Anna van Leeuwen rose in my estimation at once.

'You want a solution as quickly as possible.'

'Wouldn't you?'

When she left, my head was awash with the factors I had to balance, Chen, Drysdale, and now Anna van Leeuwen. There was no way I could handle all this on my own, but the liquidity problem much mentioned by Alison meant that turning work away wasn't an option either. I had to visit David Wyness that evening anyway, by which time he'd be fully awake. But by the look of it, and for lack of an alternative, I would also have to pull in someone capable of leaving the room and walking several yards without stopping for breath. Which ruled him out and, anyway, his talents lay elsewhere. Alison had counted herself out by going to Glasgow. Which only left one candidate, however unlikely. Maureen MacNeil. I was loath to do it, and Alison wouldn't approve, but she didn't need to know. In fact, if she hadn't gone west, she would have been available herself. So really, looked at clearly, it was down to her I was having to think the unthinkable. And so, in order to keep functioning, we rationalise decisions we wouldn't otherwise have made.

10

HIS FLAT WAS as toxic as ever, the curtains stiff with stale cigarette smoke. What was left of them. Wyness blamed the holes on moths, but any there had ever been had died long since of nicotine poisoning. I began with Drysdale.

'Right, so you want me to find out where this film producer lives.'

'Chester H Burt.'

'If he's a bird of passage that could be difficult, you realise that.'

I did, but there was always a way in, and moved swiftly on to Chen.

'So let me get this straight, you want to know if he's the Mr Big of a property empire, a man with hired hands, black belts in karate or taekwondo?'

'Exactly.'

'Seems a bit far-fetched to me, Douglas.'

It probably was, but I had to be sure, so I left him with that one too and moved on to van Leeuwen.

'Stalking? That's not funny, but if she's imagining this we could waste hours, days. I take it you realize that?'

'She didn't seem the paranoid type to me.'

'That doesn't mean she's right.'

'True.'

Since it was usually possible to talk him round with money, I reminded him that we charged the same for a wasted hour as a productive one. Though this was self-evident, Wyness was strangely reluctant to concede it. He wanted to know more.

'This bank of New York Lemon . . .'

'Mellon.'

'It has no vault?'

'That's what she said. Not a retail bank.'

Suddenly struck by a thought, he looked up from his live-stream currency feeds and laid down his cigarette to smoke itself out in the cracked saucer he used as an ashtray.

'We're forgetting something here.'

Anna van Leeuwen managed funds and therefore accessed dealing platforms requiring IDs and passwords. Someone gaining access to these data – I could tell he liked this expression, it had a pleasingly pedantic ring to it – could syphon off large sums of money in seconds before their activity was detected.

'Assuming they know how to do it.'

He was referring to an expert like himself.

'Of course.'

Van Leeuwen lived in a basement flat at St. Patrick's Square. If she agreed, we would meet her there tomorrow in her lunch hour. Wyness would install a camera giving a view of the street outside. I would tail her when she went back to work and keep an eye on her for the rest of the day. And several days thereafter if need be.

'Unobtrusively, of course.'

'Sounds boring as hell to me.'

Maybe, but at least I'd be outside, not trapped in an airless, smoke-filled room watching red and green rectangles rising and falling for no obvious reason.

'This Dutch girl. . .'

'She's American.'

'As I say, this Dutch girl – what would *she* make of her?'

'Who?'

'Your bosom buddy, Alison.'

'Ask her yourself.'

'No way, Jose. She's made it very clear I'm totally unproductive, a gambler pure and simple. According to Alison Eadie,' he said with increased edge, 'I contribute absolutely nothing to society, nothing at all.'

'I wouldn't go that far, David.'

'Maybe not, but she would. You told me so yourself. When you come right down to it, though, the funds this van Leeuwen dame invests for her clients, and let's not beat about the bush here, for the filthy rich of this world, she has to buy and sell like anyone else. Stocks and shares, government bonds, tracker funds, managed funds. She gets her hands dirty too.'

'I suppose.'

'There you go then, she's gambling as well, except she's doing it with other people's money. I, on the other hand,' he said, looking pleased with himself, 'only risk my own.'

I didn't much care whose money he risked as long as it wasn't mine.

'Anyway, David, I'll get back to van Leeuwen tonight.'

'You do that, Douglas,' he said, giving me the nod, but looking anxiously at his screens as he spoke.

Despite the impression he gave of coining it in hand over fist, he clearly wasn't doing so well. To the outward eye his set-up looked slick, and it was, yet having the latest gear was no guarantee of success. Betting on currency fluctuations was easy, winning those bets was not. He'd gone big on technical analysis, assuring me often over the years that the trend was his friend. Well maybe it was, but he'd been finding of late that friends can let you down, a problem he would have to deal with alone since the one person who might have helped him, the same Alison Eadie, disapproved of gambling, no matter how artfully dressed up. Worse, she disapproved of him full stop and he never dressed up at all.

'Beer?' he asked, but only because he wanted one himself.

Sitting in front of his screens with a can and a packet of crisps, both of which I declined on health grounds, he gave me the low-down on the losers of this world.

'Alison spends hours chasing down other people's paperwork. I know she's good at it, but that's no way to live. As for this van Leeuwen girl, she'll be making serious money alright, no doubt about that – for everyone except herself. The best she can hope for? A decent annual bonus.'

This was company he intended to leave and suddenly, unusually animated, he chose to hint at his latest money-making scheme which was, let there be no doubt about it, a sure-fire winner.

'Some people just can't cut it,' he said, 'inadequates all.' He fixed me through the smoke with a febrile eye. 'Heard of a guy called Naismith?' I hadn't. 'Topped himself last week. No great loss, but there you are.'

He'd strung himself up in his garage after his wife of fifteen years found pictures of his bigamous wedding in Mexico to a woman twenty years younger than she was, when, according to him, he'd been on a business trip to Antwerp at the time. He was forty-two. In exchange for an undisclosed sum, the grief-stricken widow had granted an exclusive interview to a national newspaper. 'Take my word for it,' she said, 'keeping secrets never pays.'

But Wyness never took anyone's word for anything and emerging details of the story confirmed him in his view. Naismith's new woman had posted pictures of her wedding on social media sites, which she might not have done had she known the groom was married already. But what really enraged his wife was the fact that he had chosen to return to their honeymoon destination to tie the knot. No doubt Playa del Carmen had its attractions, but in choosing this location he was asking for trouble and she made sure he got it. *Wave goodbye to the house, Andrew, and the kids and oh*, she'd added as a killing afterthought, *did I mention*

Dexter? That had been the last straw. Unlike him the dog was faithful, a friend he couldn't bear to be without.

'She actually said,' Wyness added, still in a state of disbelief, 'that the truth will always come out!'

Well he, David Wyness, begged to differ. If Naismith had been better at keeping secrets, he'd still be alive today. All he had needed was help, help that a true professional was equipped to provide, an expert like him. And though he didn't put it this way, it had been a lightbulb moment which, after much research and several drafts taking him well into the small hours, had led him to place a carefully crafted ad on several marketing platforms. But when I asked what the ad contained, he was suddenly tight as a clam.

'It's a side-hustle, Douglas, nothing to do with the business. Better you don't know.'

11

THE FOLLOWING MORNING, I met MacNeil at her favoured watering hole in the Grassmarket.

'I had to postpone a delivery for this.'

Which meant that in order to meet me she'd lost money, so I should compensate with an offer of work. Though it was still early April and not especially warm, she wanted to sit at an outside table. The reason soon became clear.

'I'm keeping the pangs at bay with nicotine.'

She took a small green pouch from her pocket and rolled her own.

'I know what you're going to say, replacing one drug with another, but coke's no joke.'

She was right there; thanks to cocaine she'd lost her job.

'You don't, of course. Don't drink, don't smoke. What do you do?'

'Listen to music, walk.'

This was rewarded with a dismissive look.

'Hark at Saint Douglas! How virtuous can you get?'

It was true I'd never smoked and hardly ever drank, but it wasn't down to resisting temptation. I wasn't tempted in the first place. Virtuous I was not.

'So, let's have it, Hunter.'

'I ran into trouble on the High Street, don't know if you heard.'

'Saw that, I was passing at the time. You were collared by DS Cook.'

'Your successor. What do you make of her?'

'Haven't met her, but I hear she reads books.'

'We can't have that.'

MacNeil agreed. 'No we bloody can't!'

According to her, that way softness lay, and soft people were weak. Couldn't look after themselves, never mind other people.

'She probably likes jazz.'

'I wouldn't know, Maureen, and neither would you.'

As I filled in the background, she took the occasional puff, arching her head back when she exhaled, adding her toxic fumes to those of passing cars and vans. A modest contribution, but we all have to make one.

'To hear you tell it, this Hennessy girl's done nothing wrong but she skipped anyway.'

Who could blame her? Vellacott had been out to fell her with a cricket bat.

The more I told her the angrier she became. 'What a bastard.'

'Exactly. So what we need to know is where he's shacking up right now.'

But hearing what I wanted she suddenly took a stand.

'You think,' she said, pointing her cigarette too near my face, 'that just because I'm down on my luck I'm operating at street level.'

That was exactly what I thought.

'And some of the junkies and lowlifes I rub shoulders with will point us in the right direction.'

'No harm hoping, worth a try.'

At that point, amazingly on cue, an old man in tired clothes walked unsteadily by. He was either leaving or returning to a nearby hostel for the homeless, he'd find out which in due course.

'If it isn't my old friend, Mo.'

'Bugger off, Greg. Busy right now. Catch you later.'

Gregory swayed in the breeze for a moment before doing

as he'd been told. He knew MacNeil and probably wanted to live longer, though why was another matter.

'He's harmless,' Maureen assured me.

No doubt he was, though whether being harmless is enough to justify existence is surely an open question. Don't we have to do some good in the world as well?

'Right,' Maureen said, returning to the topic uppermost in her mind, 'so payment by the hour then?'

I had to disappoint her.

'Information leading to an arrest, fifty pounds.'

Strapped for cash she wanted more, but that was too bad.

'Suck it and see, Maureen. For now.'

A waitress came out expecting an order for the use of her table. When she saw her, MacNeil rose to leave. That was how short of money she was.

'It's on me, Maureen. Don't worry.'

On her feet anyway, she gave me a twirl before sitting down.

'Like the jacket? Zara. Chest Heart and Stroke.'

'Suits you.'

It actually did, and she was telling me she'd bought it in a charity shop to let me know that when it came to change, she wasn't just saying it, she was doing it.

When her coffee arrived, she relaxed a little. Not all the world was against her. But as I told her about Anna van Leeuwen she began to get angry again, the old Maureen MacNeil putting in an appearance. Crimes against women enraged her, as well they might.

'You want me to follow her.'

'It might come to that, yes. From a discreet distance, to see if she *is* being stalked.'

'That could take hours, you know that.'

She was right, of course, so I proposed forty pounds an hour by way of a trial run, the rate I'd charged myself as recently as the previous year.

We sat in silence as she smoked. I don't know what she was thinking, but I was taking stock of my position. Alison wouldn't like this development, she'd be incensed. Here I was employing this woman, abrasive, and sometimes aggressive with it, who'd given us so much grief the year before. Come to think of it, though, she'd only be furious if she knew, and she didn't have to know. But as I finished my coffee, I noticed a flaw in my reasoning. Alison did our books, recorded every payment, large or small. Sooner or later she would know, of course she would. It was a dilemma alright, and a tricky one till Maureen stated her terms.

'OK, I'll do it, but only cash in hand. At these miserly rates I can't afford tax.'

And that was it, she'd solved it for me. I could slip her the money from my savings from the sale of the house and no one would be the wiser.

'Does she know about this, that stuck-up lady-friend of yours?'

I could hardly tell her the truth. If MacNeil suspected I was going behind Alison's back, she'd have something over me and I couldn't have that.

'Of course.'

'Changed her tune a bit, hasn't she?'

Unlikely, but not impossible.

'She has, and so should you.'

12

I WAITED AT the top of the stairs to van Leeuwen's basement flat and looked round for Wyness, still nowhere to be seen. This was a job we would lose if he didn't show with his security camera and set it up as promised. But he appeared a minute later, minus his trademark overcoat though still sporting his leather bush hat, something he refused to abandon regardless of the weather. I sometimes wondered if he slept in it.

As always when he rose at the crack of noon, Wyness looked half asleep and bleary round the eyes, but I noted with relief that he was carrying a gadget-bag containing the camera and the tools necessary to install it.

'I thought you weren't going to make it.'

'Ah, yes, sorry about that, but if I hadn't stayed online I stood to lose a four-figure sum.'

'So you saved it.'

Wyness looked abashed. 'Actually, no, but you can't win them all.'

At that point Anna van Leeuwen arrived and saved him further embarrassment.

'Good afternoon, gentlemen, follow me.'

She led us down the steps and opened the door using a key connecting with a surface-mounted lock on the inside. Her setup was far from secure.

'There's no way he can see into the back of the house, so really my problem is the living room. I could always draw the curtains, but it's dark enough down here at the best of times.'

'Which these are not,' Wyness said, eying the curtain rail running the length of the windows. 'Did you see him again this morning?'

'I think so, yes.'

If she was right, there was a danger that the stalker had seen us entering the house, a risk we would run only once.

Wyness unzipped his bag and removed a box containing the camera, several screwdrivers, assorted pliers and rolls of tape, laying them out on the window ledge in an ordered sequence understood only by himself, and maybe not even by him.

'Right, that should be me. If you two like to talk among yourselves for a while, I'll fix this beauty up.'

I was always uneasy when Wyness was at work, having no idea what he might do next and even less what he might say. So in joining van Leeuwen on the settee, my attention was split between our client and keeping an eye on my associate who, with one exception, had brought everything he might need.

'You don't have stepladders, I suppose?'

The landlord hadn't provided any. When she'd changed a lightbulb the week before she'd stood on a kitchen chair. She watched as he went for one and turned back to me. I couldn't help but be impressed by her trouser suit. The creases were sharp enough to cut cheese.

'So, Miss van Leeuwen, could you give me some idea of your movements since you came over from the US, any location where our stalker might have seen you?'

When she first arrived, she'd stayed at the Sheraton, all expenses paid, while looking for a place to rent. She'd been there three weeks in all and had naturally availed herself of the facilities, including the fitness centre.

'They have personal fitness trainers?'

'Of course.'

'Did any of them assist you in your training, work out a fitness plan, for example.'

'There was one. Farhad someone. Iranian. Short and stocky. Very strong.'

At this point Wyness, as if he didn't have enough to do, saw fit to ask a question.

'And this Farhad fellow, did he show undue interest? After all, you're an attractive woman.'

Van Leeuwen shot me a quizzical look then glanced up at Wyness, one foot on a chair, the other on the window ledge, attaching his camera to the curtain rail with gaffer tape. He looked unsteady to me.

'In my opinion, no. Such little interest as he showed did not seem unusual. Oh, and for future reference, I would hold that anyone, seen clearly, might be considered attractive.'

Wyness' head was near the ceiling and his spreading belly showed clear signs of a sedentary life, the more so seen from below, as van Leeuwen was seeing it now.

'So that makes me attractive,' he said, turning to look down at her.

'Indeed it does, Mr. Wyness,' she agreed, though with little conviction.

'Can you think of anyone else?'

'Not really.' Then she paused, taking the time to think back. 'Actually, I did notice one person who might have been keeping an eye on me, but we didn't exchange a word, ever, so it wouldn't be him.'

It had been some time since I'd read up on the psychology of the stalker, but this assumption, on the face of it perfectly logical, struck me as too easy.

'You didn't converse, but did he ever come close to you? Within two or three feet?'

'I can't say he did. Though when I was on a rowing machine on one occasion, I thought he might be checking me out from another machine. But there were two or three people between us.'

'Which might just mean he was taking care not to be too obvious. At the moment we have to check out every lead, however slender. The Iranian will be easy, we know his name. This other guy, though, what do you know about him?'

She hadn't paid him much heed: he was maybe twenty-four or five, with what might be thought of as a natural suntan.

'What you're really saying,' Wyness said from ceiling height, 'is that he was of mixed race.'

'Yes, Mr. Wyness, that's always possible, as most of us prove to be when we subject our ancestry to detailed scrutiny.'

When he had the camera securely in place Wyness returned to floor level, showing a degree of stiffness which might have worried a lesser man. But due to his dependence on the life online he was resigned to the gradual failure of his moving parts and had no interest whatever in following van Leeuwen into a health centre, places which, as he saw it, were packed with medieval instruments of torture.

'So, Miss van Leeuwen, what I have to check now is that the camera is providing an optimal view of the street outside – as far as that is possible from below pavement level.'

'What if the stalker sees it, Mr. Wyness?'

'A risk we have to take. To work at all, line of sight must be maintained. If the camera can see the stalker, then the stalker can see the camera. But relative to a man, it's small and inconspicuous. Easily missed.'

Then, to the surprise of van Leeuwen and myself, he squeezed between us on the settee, ignoring both the empty armchairs completing her three-piece suite. He woke his mobile phone, scrolled to the relevant icon and showed us what the camera was seeing, a mongrel relieving itself against the railing, pages of a newspaper blowing by on the breeze.

'Unedifying, Mr. Wyness, but remarkably clear.'

'It would be. I have set that little gem,' he said, pointing up at the curtain rail, 'to a resolution of 640x480 and thirty frames a second,' he said proudly, as if he'd engineered the device himself. 'You can monitor the output via the dedicated Private Eye app. Once you've downloaded it, of course.'

Van Leeuwen liked the sound of that, unlocked her phone and handed it to him. Shortly afterwards, she was getting the low-down on street life. Then, looking at her watch, she stood up.

'Sorry, gentlemen, time presses, I have to get back.'

'Right,' I said, 'I'll wait a minute and follow you from a safe distance. David here will tidy up his gear and pull the door shut behind him when he leaves. And on the subject of security. . .'

'Yes, I realise it isn't good, but the previous tenant left with the keys to the mortice. The agency say they have it in hand.' I must have looked sceptical. 'I know. How likely is that?'

13

I TAILED Ms van Leeuwen all the way back to her place of work. Though I wasn't sure, I thought it possible she was being stalked by a man on a bike and took photographs of him from a safe distance. If he kept appearing where and when she did, then we'd be on to something. Feeling a good start had been made, I was about to treat myself to a coffee and a cookie when my mobile rang, another possible client. She wanted to meet as soon as possible.

'I can tell from the traffic noise you're in town at the moment.'

She was right, I was in Lothian Road at the time. The traffic was heavy and loud with it.

'So am I, as it happens. I wonder if we could meet.'

There was no way I could cope with yet another woman casting a critical eye on my flat, so we agreed to meet at the Elephant House. It was handy for me. If it wasn't for her, too bad: she hadn't said what she wanted and as yet I owed her nothing.

When I entered the café, I couldn't see her at first; she'd found a seat round the L-bend to the rear and saved one for me, draping her jacket on the back of a chair. A light pastel violet, it was making no impact whatsoever. I hoped the same wouldn't be true of her. Seeing me looking round, she rose to greet me.

'Mr. Hunter?'

'Yes.'

'Of Hunter Associates?'

'The same.'

'Good of you to meet me at such short notice.' She held out her hand, which I took.

'Sylvia.'

She was drinking hot chocolate, asked me what I wanted, went to the counter and ordered me a coffee.

'It's a sensitive matter, I hope you don't mind.'

I told her I was all ears but really, at that point, my body notwithstanding, I wasn't entirely present.

'It's about your associate, Mr. Wyness.'

What had he done this time, hacked her email, syphoned money from her current account? Whatever it was she had my attention now.

'I trust this conversation will be entirely confidential. I have to be sure of that. Mr. Wyness must never know it took place.'

Seeing through the adipose tissue to what had been the girl below, Sylvia, if that was really her name, was still in good shape. I put her age at sixty or thereabouts. I assumed her grey hair had once been brown, and as befitted a woman of her years it was cut relatively short and neatly parted. Though she had requested the meeting, I sensed an understandable reluctance to discuss a sensitive matter with a stranger.

'So, Sylvia. . .'

'Alright, I have a problem you may be able to help me with. You will have heard of Parallel Lives.'

My expression clearly gave me away, a blank look, perhaps.

'Ah, I see you haven't.'

Parallel Lives was an organization which enabled a client to appear to be in one place while actually being in another.

'Nothing illegal, you understand, nothing fraudulent.'

Great, but I could think of no reason for such a proceeding unless fraud of some sort was involved. What would be the point? Her answer was clear enough. She was a married woman who didn't want to leave her husband. On the other hand, she wanted to branch out, an expression which required clarification.

'Branch out?'

'I'm sure you know what I mean, lead a life of my own he doesn't know about.'

'A parallel life.'

'Exactly.'

At first, she didn't say why she wished to do this, probably something to do with sex or money. Whatever the reason, she had reached a point in her life when she needed more than her marriage was providing.

'You want to squeeze more juice from the orange.'

She gave me a doubtful look, suddenly uncertain if she should be confiding in someone who expressed himself so crudely.

'I'm not sure I would put it quite like that.'

A noise from a neighbouring table distracted her enough to look round: four young people were playing cards and getting excited about it. To judge from their accents they were foreign, as were many of the other patrons.

'You have to understand that my husband has many good qualities.'

Since I had yet to meet anyone of whom such a claim could safely be made, I didn't believe her for a moment.

'But he's cheating with other women.'

Sylvia laughed. 'Heavens, no, he's much too indolent for that. As a matter of fact, I have the utmost difficulty getting him to cheat with me.'

I took this to mean that her husband had lost interest in her body and she was now seeking solace elsewhere, Parallel Lives to provide the necessary cover.

'So would I be right in thinking,' I enquired, 'that as a result you're losing interest in him?'

'Between the sheets, yes, though not in other respects. He remains strong on existential philosophy.'

Though she said this with a straight face, I knew she was having me on. People like that are tricky. They seldom say what they mean or mean what they say, and even when they do you can't be sure that they have. She opened the small plaid bag she had placed on the table. What was in it? Perhaps this woman was an investigative journalist, her bag concealing a digital recording device.

'Anyway, I need your advice.'

Hearing all this, I believed I could put the pieces together.

'You mentioned my associate, David Wyness.'

'Mr Parallel Lives himself, though you clearly didn't know that. Which concerns me more than a little.'

It concerned me too, more than a little. She removed a neatly folded A4 sheet from her bag and handed it to me. I was astonished. Wyness had prepared a flier listing his services, which he had classified in three levels for ease of over-charging. Pleased with his handiwork, he had given one to Sylvia, who had quickly passed over Service Level One which most people, with half a brain and minimal effort, could easily provide for themselves.

'Well,' I said, buying time to catch up with this new development.

But I now began to understand what he'd been hinting at when he told me about the man who'd hanged himself in his garage. If he'd been better at keeping secrets, he'd still be alive today. All he had needed was help. And here it was, Wyness' gift to the world, Parallel Lives.

'As you can imagine, only Level Three would fit the bill for me.'

'The most expensive.'

'True, but providing the best cover. As I explained to him in an email exchange, I would like to spend several days at a time away from home without attracting suspicion.'

71

'How often?'

'Three or four times a year.'

'If you don't mind me asking, what do you do for a living? You come across as a professional person.'

'I'm with a leading medical supplier, Anderson and Blumenstein. You may have heard of us.'

'Ah,' I said, making a complete fool of myself, 'scalpels, sterile dressings, that sort of thing?'

'I'm afraid we're higher up the food chain than that, Mr. Hunter. We're currently leading the field in multispectral analysis of tissue morphology.'

'Right.'

She probably saw my eyes glaze over but ploughed on anyway.

'We're getting a lot of interest right now in our transdermal biosensor, a neat little device which reads blood analytes without puncturing the skin. And that,' she added, 'is just the tip of the iceberg.'

'Then it would be safe to say you're well qualified.'

'If a doctorate in cell biology fits the bill. Anyway, to my concern. To utilise this service will require me to reveal considerable information of a personal nature to your associate Mr. Wyness. And it occurred to me to wonder whether that was a good idea. Apart from what he's told me himself, I know absolutely nothing about him. But I assume that you, as his business partner, will know whether or not I can safely proceed.'

I could see her point. Any information she gave to Wyness would have to be totally secure. What if Wyness leaked like a sieve and word got back to her husband? That wouldn't do at all. But her worry proved more radical than that.

'The thing is, Mr. Hunter, an unscrupulous person having this information might put it to use.'

And late in the day, the light dawned. She was afraid that

Wyness might blackmail her by threatening to reveal all to her husband. She was looking to me for reassurance. On subjects such as online security, there wasn't much Wyness didn't know, her data would be safe with him. But what concerned Sylvia was his character, not his IT credentials.

'You're a private investigator, Mr. Hunter. Surely you can see the danger to any prospective client exposing herself in this way. I can't believe you don't.'

Because I knew Wyness, this was something which had never occurred to me, but Sylvia didn't know him from Adam and she was right to be thinking about it.

'You're worried he might put the black on you.'

She gave me a direct look.

'There we are, got there at last. Convince me. Tell me I'm wrong.'

While no one would mistake Wyness for a lay preacher, it was my opinion that he wouldn't blackmail anyone either.

'And yet you look worried, Mr Hunter.'

I was. Wyness presumably thought that his Parallel Lives scheme was perfectly legal provided there was no fraudulent intent. If the scheme were used to provide an alibi for a heist, then that would not be legal. If, on the other hand, it was used by a husband or wife to conceal an affair, then the law would have no problem with it. And this was what I didn't get. In order to become a husband or wife you entered into a contract with another party. In engaging in an affair, you were clearly in breach of that contract. So surely, in such a case, Parallel Lives would be enabling fraud. Was I missing something here?

'The thing is, Sylvia, what you're proposing seems fraudulent to me. Duplicitous.'

'Then the same might be said of what your colleague is enabling.'

She toyed with her mug though there was no longer anything it.

'You're afflicted by moral qualms.'
'We all have our weaknesses.'
'True. You're married yourself?'
'My wife left me.'
'Ah. I see.'
If not for me, for her it had all become clear.

14

SOMETIMES WE FEEL that events have us by the throat, that life is in control of us while we, try as we may, are not in control of life. That's how I felt the following morning. I should have brushed my teeth the night before, but I'd forgotten, so when I got up I attacked them with fluoride toothpaste in my stylish Victorian bathroom. There was too much on my mind for comfort and forgetting anything else wasn't an option. Vellacott, Drysdale, Anna van Leeuwen and now the strange case of Sylvia Gathercole. Did I need to do anything there? After all, I wasn't supposed to know who she was. Yet some research was called for. The last thing I needed was guilt by association if Wyness' latest money-making scheme went wrong, and this was one subject I couldn't ask him about without giving the game away.

Though I was still sleeping on the floor, most of my clothes were now draped on hangers in the wardrobe, such plates and cutlery as I had stowed away in kitchen cupboards, and the fridge boasted milk, cheese, and a brand of yoghurt which made bold claims about aiding the digestion. I even had real coffee and teabags in stock, chamomile and builder's brew, granulated sugar for the occasional caller who didn't mind their teeth rotting prematurely, and a value pack of custard creams which might well have the same effect. All in all, I was slowly getting there, except for Alison's flowers, now in their autumn colours because I'd forgotten to put them in water. But, I reasoned, they'd already been cut, they were going to die anyway, they never had a chance.

After my customary bran flakes and prunes, I opened my laptop and had just entered the name Gathercole in my search engine, there wouldn't be many of them, when a text arrived from John Banks or, as I thought of him in lighter moments, my Deep Throat in the local police. A certain Mr Charles P Vellacott was currently being questioned in St Leonard's police station by none other than Detective Sergeant Anastasija Cook. All I had to do, he assured me, was lurk in the vicinity and follow him home when she released him. That way I'd find out where he was living, report back to Chen and, hey presto, another cheque to swell the business account!

I liked John, he was a nice man, but seriously, all I had to do? Cook could hold him for twelve hours, but when had the clock started, when would her twelve hours end? And the fact that she could lawfully detain this man for twelve hours didn't mean she had to. She might release him after six, or three. So the sooner I started lurking the better or I might miss him and the game would be up.

I dressed hastily, exited the building, and left for St Leonard's Street in my Saab 900. Clapped-out it may have been, but at least it had the virtue of not drawing attention to itself. And, I liked to think, only a fool would steal a car as old as that. I had the expected trouble parking and ended up in the grounds of a private housing development off St Leonard's Lane. The residents had stanchions to keep intruders like me from borrowing their bays, but several had driven off without putting them up, probably tired of yet another daily task. They might even have thought that being near a police station offered some protection.

My view of the entrance to the station would have been better if I'd got out of the car, wandered closer to it and leaned against a wall, but how many hours could anyone keep that up? So I sat in the car and observed. Which was when it occurred to me, something else I'd come close to forgetting;

I was supposed to be tracking Anna van Leeuwen that day. But out of the blue I was following Vellacott instead, so what was I to do? Wyness would have trouble tracking his own shadow and Alison, who could have done it, was in Glasgow reconciling back-office software. I did the only thing I could, phoned Maureen MacNeil.

'What do you want?'

I explained that Anna van Leeuwen, an investment banker, believed she was being stalked, told her where she lived and where she worked.

'Where will she be right now?'

I looked at my watch, approaching twenty to nine.

'Either at work or on her way there.'

'Forty pounds an hour plus lunch.'

She sensed my back was to the wall but her terms were reasonable. I could live with them.

'Ok.'

On that happy note she ended the call before I could change my mind. Prematurely, as it turned out. My phone rang five seconds later.

'This van Leeuwen, what does she look like?'

And that was the only significant event of my first two hours surveilling the police station. As can happen, my mind began to wander after a while. I read news stories on my phone and searched the car radio for anything worth listening to, switching it off when I heard a man ask a team of experts how to ensure his acorn would germinate. He hoped it would grow into a mighty oak, and good luck to him, but another thing I didn't have any more was a garden of my own.

All that ended when someone knocked on my window. Hector Robertson, detective constable. I opened the window halfway.

'Hi Hector, how are you?'

He ignored my question and came straight to the point.

'He'll be leaving in ten minutes.'

'Who?'

'Charles Plumstead Vellacott, the man you're waiting for.'

'Ah.'

'Ah, indeed,' he said, in his usual inscrutable tone, 'so you can either come in now or later.'

What was he talking about? I couldn't risk Vellacott clocking me, he had to know that.

'Why would I do that?'

When it came, the reason was painfully obvious; I was still to give a formal statement regarding Vellacott's attack on Body Art Studio and its occupants. Something else I seemed to have forgotten. I began to wonder why I'd bothered getting out of bed.

'But if you've pressing business just now, you could always come back this afternoon.'

It sounded good to me, but one thing puzzled me. How had the police caught Vellacott so quickly? According to Robertson, they hadn't. He'd caught himself.

'He ordered food and drink in a bar and tried to leave without paying. The staff didn't take kindly to that. When he tried to force his way out, they hit him over the head with a bar stool, locked him in a cupboard and called us.'

I liked the sound of this. It couldn't have happened to a nicer man.

'So, Hector, if you have him in for questioning, you should know where he's living.'

Unfortunately not. According to Robertson, he'd given as his address a certain flight of steps connecting High School Yards to the Cowgate. And while this was a popular spot with gentlemen of the street, the steps being covered against the elements, neither Cook nor Robertson believed him for a moment.

'For the time being we've listed him as no fixed abode, but we need to know where he's staying. You could help us with that and get in Cook's good books while you're at it.'

'Two for the price of one.'

'Exactly.'

When Vellacott left the station, I followed him to a Swedish bar on Holyrood Road. Through the plate glass windows at the front, I saw him buy a drink, search out a seat and collapse into it. I reckoned I had ten minutes at least, probably longer, so I parked in a nearby council estate and waited at a bus stop across the road from the pub for my mark to come out. I'd learned the hard way that following a suspect by car ranges from the tricky to the impossible when the suspect is on foot.

After two long hours, most of which he spent buried in his phone, he finally left the pub, cut through to the Canongate and slowly weaved his way through the crowds to the High Street and on to the Lawnmarket. Just as water flows downhill, so with the sightseers. Vellacott walked upstream very much against the current, and I had no choice but to follow him.

I just kept up with him enough to follow him to Lady Stair's Close. The area was swamped by several groups of tourists, each with its own guide giving them the historical low-down in Spanish, Mandarin and, for all I knew, Melanesian Pidgin English. There was never a good time of year to follow up a lead off the Lawnmarket, but what choice did I have? And there he was, leaning against the central lamppost as if he owned it, sharing a smoke and the time of day with an older woman and her Staffie, secure on its lead just in case. Pretending to an interest in the Writer's Museum, I kept him in sight till he said goodbye to his friend, clapped the dog and entered one of the tenements just as a man was coming out. Well, I'd tracked him down to a building. Though I didn't know which flat yet, I was well on my way. But I wasn't going to act on it till Wyness came up with the background on Mr Chen.

15

I'D EXPECTED SOMETHING as simple as giving a statement wouldn't require the presence of a detective sergeant, but I was wrong. She joined me in an interview room for what would normally have been a relatively short time.

'So, Mr Hunter.'

'DS Cook.'

'Tell me exactly what happened, I'll take it down, you check for accuracy; if you're happy with my account, append your signature.'

'Or I could write it myself and save you the trouble.'

'You could.' Then she had second thoughts. 'How's your handwriting?'

I had to admit it was bad, so bad I sometimes couldn't decipher notes I left for myself on the kitchen table. This was not a problem shared by Cook.

'My writing is excellent.'

I didn't doubt it for a moment; she was starting to come across as a one-woman centre of excellence. So I spoke and she wrote.

'You were talking to the Hennessy girl in the studio to the rear.'

'I was.'

'Interesting. You don't come over as the tattoo type.'

'I was there on another matter, as you know.'

'I think you can give me some indication as to what that other matter might be.'

If I didn't mention Mr Chen by name, then I probably

could.

'Linda Hennessy shared a furnished flat with Vellacott. They did a moonlight when they couldn't pay the rent. As far as I can see, Hennessy worked but he didn't.'

'And that was the problem.'

'I don't know this for sure, but they fell out, probably over money. Vellacott trashed the flat before they left.'

'Badly?'

I showed her the photographs I'd taken at the scene.

'My God!'

'Something else you should know. Vellacott removed several items from the flat and sold them.'

'Such as?'

'A fifty-five-inch TV and a wing-backed chair.'

Cook wrote rapidly and read back the gist of it to me.

'He owed rent, vandalised rented property and stole items from the landlord for resale.'

'Exactly. And,' I added, taking sides in the matter, 'he conned Hennessy out of four hundred pounds for the deposit. Probably cleaned her out.'

Cook looked up from her notes, clearly following her own line of thought.

'But Mr Hunter, the flat being trashed there was no way she could reclaim that deposit.'

'Not from the landlord, no.'

'You can't possibly mean she hoped to get four hundred pounds from Vellacott.'

Looking back at our conversation, I had to admit that thought hadn't entered her mind till I put it there.

'Vellacott's so strapped for cash he tries to leave pubs without paying. Where could a man like that lay his hands on four hundred pounds?'

'To be fair, that incident had yet to take place.'

'Okay, but to be even fairer, you already knew he couldn't pay the rent on his flat.'

That was me told. I took a second to check her dyed blonde hair before meeting her eyes. There were signs of her natural colour along the parting.

'You're right. I don't know what I was thinking about.'

In fact, I knew perfectly well. I'd been motivated by anger at Vellacott's treatment of Hennessy and was acting on the basis I might be able to help.

'Well, this is all very interesting, but we've yet to establish *why* you were visiting Linda Hennessy.'

'I hoped she might give me some idea as to Vellacott's whereabouts on behalf of my client.'

'Let's not be coy here, Mr Hunter. On behalf of the landlord.'

'Yes.'

'I take it you haven't discovered where he's living yet.' I nodded. 'Well in the unlikely event that you find out before we do, I shall expect you to inform us at once. This attack was serious.'

Having satisfied herself on that score, she moved on.

'Right, so you were talking with Ms Hennessey when the attack took place.'

I gave her a full description of everything I'd seen. None of it came as news.

'This confirms what other witnesses have told us, notably Brian Doyle, who has now been released from hospital.'

'I didn't take to him at all.'

'Neither did I,' Cook said, 'but that's no reason to hit him with a cricket bat.'

'What about Hennessy, have you found her yet?'

She didn't need to answer this question, but I was pleased when she did, regarding it as a sign of confidence in my integrity, however misplaced.

'She's working in another studio for the time being. Pins and Needles. West Nicolson Street. Owned by the same people. DC Robertson's on his way there as we speak.'

'She's had a hard time of it.'

Cook agreed. But now, unfortunately, she had a problem with Hennessy as well. The girl had decided to retaliate. Fair enough, who could blame her? But the detective sergeant had an answer to that one too.

'I could. She's posted what I shall call, for want of a better term, intimate pictures of Vellacott's tackle, accompanied by claims that he's far from well endowed.'

I thought she might do this. If only I'd had longer to talk with her I'd have advised against it, but Vellacott's violence deprived me of the chance. So really, he only had himself to blame.

Cook opened a folder on her side of the desk and read part of it out. Under the Abusive Behaviour and Sexual Harm Act (2016) Section 2, it was an offence to disclose or threaten to disclose an intimate photograph or film of a person without their consent.

'She's left us no choice. It's a clear-cut case of what's popularly known as revenge porn. We'll have to charge her. Too bad, really.'

At that point she offered me tea or coffee, from a machine, but refreshment nevertheless. And why was that? I'd told her everything she needed to know. Clutching our plastic cups, she ran an idea past me. The papers concerning Vellacott wouldn't be sent to the fiscal for some days pending, among other things, a statement from Linda Hennessy and a report from the insurance company's loss adjuster estimating the total cost of making good the damage to the studio.

'So,' Cook said, 'I could also charge him with criminal damage to your client's flat plus theft of the items you mentioned.'

Provided she knew where the flat was and who owned it.

'I'll be reporting back to my client tomorrow. I'll run this past him. I'm sure he'll be happy to come forward.'

'Good. Your cooperation in this matter is appreciated.'

She paused for a moment, looking down at her files, her mind elsewhere.

'I have your back story. Robertson told me.'

'But you had to ask him first.'

'He doesn't give much away.'

How right she was; Robertson gave clams a bad name.

'My name is Douglas.'

She came close to smiling.

'I know.'

16

By the time I'd collected my car and made it back home, I didn't feel like cooking. There was nothing new there; I never felt like cooking. I strolled to the nearest food store and came back with a meal for one, that old stand-by, ham and mushroom tagliatelle. And the microwave did it proud. After a mere four minutes thirty seconds there it was, steaming on the plate. I set it down beside my laptop, resolved to continue where I'd left off that morning, in search of the elusive Sylvia Gathercole. And sure enough, she was listed under the heading OUR TEAM on the website of Anderson and Blumenstein, Medical Suppliers. Since members of this exclusive group were dignified with mugshots, there could be no doubt about it. I had been privileged to meet the lady herself and what she had told me was true.

So far, so good. Wyness had provided her with an A5 flyer, which was fine as far as it went, but an IT person like him would surely have created a website where more could be done to reel in potential customers. Every second person I met was dissatisfied with life in one way or another. They were out there alright, what might be thought of as a large client base. So my next search was for Parallel Lives. Unfortunately, this was a title used by many to promote books ranging from the writings of Plutarch, long gone, through Victorian marriages, to a tome about Hitler and Stalin. There was also a film of that title. All of which meant, if my grasp of internet marketing had anything going for it, that Wyness' new service would be harder to track down than it should have been. Yet I had to admit it was a fitting name for this dubious enterprise of his and it did have a ring to it.

Skipping the first two levels, I went straight to Service Level Three, the most expensive but the one Mrs Gathercole was interested in. Wyness had thoughtfully provided three case studies, one of which was close to her situation. Parallel Lives had arranged four conferences in the course of a year for a certain Mr H, complete with back-up documentation. To satisfy his wife's natural interest, Mr H had shown these documents to her by way of explanation. And what might have happened had she taken the trouble to check out any of these events? Parallel Lives had provided the client with links to web pages purporting to document the events he was attending, complete with opening welcome and registration, addresses from the floor, workshop groups and plenary sessions. Mr H had duly furnished his wife with these links, and for added credibility his name appeared on the list of delegates.

So engrossing was all this, my tagliatelle lingered longer on the plate than it should have, the sauce starting to coagulate as it cooled. Something was troubling me. Wyness had dropped his hint two days before, but one thing he said had stuck in my mind; he'd got the idea from the sad case of Andrew Naismith, now deceased. According to Wyness, Naismith had topped himself the previous week. If that was his starting point the business, for want of a better word, was less than two weeks old. These case studies of his were as fictitious as the testimonials he quoted from satisfied clients.

I was considering the implications of this when my mobile rang.

'It's me. Open the door.'

MacNeil came in at speed with a sandwich she'd bought

en route and made straight for the kettle as if she owned the place. She'd never been one for petty distinctions.

'Want anything?' she asked, as she raided the teabags.

She joined me at the kitchen table, her tuna and sweetcorn sandwich on a plate, and put a mug of tea beside me.

'So,' I asked, 'how did it go?'

She thought van Leeuwen was right. In the course of the day, she'd spotted a man on a bicycle in her vicinity several times. When she entered her place of work, the Bank of New York Mellon, he disappeared into the fitness centre to the rear of the Sheraton but left in good time to catch her leaving again – when she went for lunch with a colleague and also at close of play when she left to go home.

'What did he look like, this guy?'

MacNeil had a problem there. He'd been clad in cycling gear, complete with helmet-mounted camera. His reflective goggles were large. Together with the helmet, not much of his face was visible. He was young, though. She could tell from his slim frame and general fitness level.

'Height?'

'About five eleven.'

'Taller than the fitness trainer she told us about.'

'Definitely. He hung around St Patrick's Square for a while then buggered off, probably going home. I followed him as far as Salisbury Road but it's one way. He's a cyclist and you know what they're like. Don't give a damn. He cycled up it anyway, on the pavement, but I couldn't follow him, not in the van.'

She had a plan, though. Tomorrow afternoon, she'd be waiting at the far end of Salisbury Road and pick him up from there.

'That's a major junction. Where would you park?'

'Salisbury Arms, it's right on the corner.' So it was, it couldn't be better. 'And in the meantime, you might check for images from that camera Wyness installed. 'Never know, we might be lucky.'

Noticing my laptop open, she got up and appeared at my shoulder. I'd never had a parrot and wasn't sure I wanted one now.

'What have we here?'

For a horrible moment I thought I'd landed Wyness in it, but he'd taken the wise precaution of ensuring he couldn't be identified from his website. Finding what she saw of interest, the case study of Mr H, she drew her chair up beside mine, her curiosity piqued.

'I was looking for the works of Plutarch when this came up.'

'Yeah, right!'

'Seriously. Same name. Parallel Lives.'

'I believe you, thousands wouldn't.'

And thousands would have been right, but wheeling out the venerable Plutarch saved me explaining why I'd really been looking for Parallel Lives.

We scrolled through the pages together, MacNeil not saying a word; a habit of hers when drumming up the thinking. But after five minutes or so, she was forming conclusions.

'Right, so if an emergency crops up at home and the husband or wife phones the hotel they're supposed to be staying in?'

'According to this, the call will be diverted to Parallel Lives. They take the call, contact the cheating partner, and have them call back home.'

'Might just work,' MacNeil conceded, 'but how about this. The cheating partner falls ill and has to be flown back from Madeira when he's supposed to be angling in Ardnamurchan.'

'Ah, yes, well that would be tricky.'

'To say the least. And what about these lists of delegates.

Are these people real?'

I had no idea, so we chose a name at random from the sample given.

'Right,' she said, 'so this Dr Archibald Patterson MBBCh, MRCS actually exists.'

'He does.'

'Well good for him, but that's a problem.'

If a listed delegate existed, then it would be possible to find out where he really was, as opposed to the event Parallel Lives claimed he was attending. Dr Patterson worked at Brigham Young. One call was all it would take.

'In any case,' she added, ramming home her point, 'these fake events have to be at genuine venues, right? Anyone in doubt could contact the venue and quickly establish that they weren't hosting the conference at all. This,' she said, pointing an accusing finger at my screen, 'is total crap. It's shot full of holes!'

And so it should be, I thought. And what was going on here anyway, why I was I sitting in my kitchen, side by side with Maureen MacNeil? Why was I letting this happen? The answer slowly dawned on me after she left.

In the short time my business had been running, I'd been accustomed to talking through cases with Alison. Since she had departed the scene, if only for a month or two, I was bouncing ideas off MacNeil instead and this was something she was good at. Hardly surprising in an ex-detective-sergeant. And that wasn't all. While we were there, I'd noticed that MacNeil Mark 2, the new going clean MacNeil, smelled better than she used to. Wholesome even. Was my sense of smell really that good? Was I a dog? Not the last time I looked.

17

THE FOLLOWING MORNING, Friday, marked the end of my first week in Gifford Park, so I should start as I intended to go on, celebrate the beginning of this new chapter in what passed for a life by improving my domestic arrangements. The only trouble with that was knowing where to begin.

Guided by my nose, I poured some bleach down the kitchen sink, hoping the bulk of it would settle in the S-bend and go about its work without any further help from me. Alison had been right, there was a mouldy smell from that direction best tackled at once.

Then there were the many objects I'd stowed away in cupboards and drawers. Very neat, no doubt, but all too often I opened the wrong cupboard, pulled out the wrong drawer in my search for scissors or socks. What I really needed was a logical disposition of items like these before the search for them wore me down, or worse, put me off my new flat altogether.

The chest in the bedroom had four drawers. In a blinding flash of inspiration, I decided to mirror my body, starting from the top and working down. So, gansies in the top drawer, shirts one drawer down, smalls one further down again, leaving the bottom drawer for socks. And with a bit of thought I could improve on that, light summer socks to the left, heavy winter socks to the right. I knew that anyone catching me at this would convict me of something unpleasant, like being anal retentive or worse, but having routines in place, routines you can rely on, saves on thinking time. And as Alison had told me more than once, time is money. In any case, who would know? I lived on my own now.

I was halfway through sorting my socks when I heard post pop through the door, a letter from the council telling me what I owed in tax for the current year. I'd known it was coming, of course, but as I checked it over I noticed a reduction, a discount for those of us unlucky enough to live alone. And this discount, small though it was in the great scheme of things, proved to be the first and only benefit I was ever to derive from the departure of my wife.

I was sitting at the nerve-centre of my operation, the kitchen table, wondering where to store this piece of paper, a document of world-historical importance, when my laptop and phone rang simultaneously.

I knew from experience it had to be Wyness, who'd taken to video calling big time. It saved him going out to meet people and, further to that, saved him having to climb back up four flights of stairs to his flat. I, on the other hand, didn't like it one bit.

'David.'

'Hi.'

'You're up early.'

By his standards, half past ten was equivalent to daybreak.

'Couldn't sleep, too much on my brain. Anyway, I have some news. You have a sharpened pencil ready?'

'No.'

'Good, then I'll begin. This Mr. Chen of yours, he owns five properties, all here in the city. He also owns the Heavenly Garden Market at Tollcross, Chinese and oriental produce, and lives in the flat above it. He never married, not here in the UK anyway, and as far as I can tell he isn't shacked up with anyone either.'

'He's lived here all his life?'

91

'Came over from Hong Kong when the lease ran out in ninety-seven.'

'What age was he at the time?'

'Twenty-three.'

So he might have been married back then, but it didn't seem likely.

'On the other question, I can find no evidence of involvement with heavies. Oh, and get this,' he added, with a wink whose significance escaped me, 'he lectures on Chinese art at the Confucius Institute.'

'A man of culture, then.'

'Chinese art! Culture! You must be joking.'

According to Wyness, an authority on this subject as on so many others, Chinese art consisted entirely of mountains, waterfalls, mists, and bearded men sitting under trees thinking sad thoughts.

'With a bit of calligraphy thrown in for good measure,' he added as an afterthought, 'not a bit of perspective to be seen. Anyway, that's all I can dig up on the man. Seems a solid citizen, though. You can safely tell him where to find Vellacott.'

'When I know myself.'

'Close?'

'Getting there. Chester H Burt, anything on him?'

The answer thus far was no. Our film producer friend was tricky to track down, though Wyness was logging references on social media sites which might get him there in the end. I had a suggestion.

'If he only lives here part of the year, he might rent out for the rest of it, Airbnb, Bookings.com.'

Wyness had this on his to-do list when he'd finished trawling the social media. I wasn't to worry, he was on to it. Which left Anna van Leeuwen and anything the Wyness camera might have picked up. And there he had useful information. A cyclist had wheeled his bike along the pavement three times, all after van Leeuwen had returned home after work. On one of these occasions, he'd propped his machine against the iron railings directly above her basement, supposedly adjusting his gear change. But in Wyness' opinion, which I readily believed, he'd been doing his best to check out her front room.

'Get his face at all?'

No, it had been obscured by his crash helmet and goggles. But his jacket stood out from the crowd, black with a yellow diagonal stripe, about six inches wide with a luminous look to it. As he was giving me his take on this, namely, that the function of the stripe was to stand out in poor light, protecting the wearer from careless drivers, I realised that he was looking not so much at me as what was visible behind me.

'Let's have it then.'

'What?'

'The guided tour.'

With great reluctance I switched my laptop to its back camera and started walking round the house.

'Kitchen seems a bit basic.'

True, but it was good enough for me and, anyway, he was a fine one to talk. The last time I'd seen it, his was a tip.

He was even less impressed by the bedroom, still with my mattress on the floor along with several boxes. Though some of them had been emptied, this wasn't obvious to the distant Wyness. Moving on, he felt that the chairs in the living room, foldable directors' numbers, were a bit basic.

'What happened to those chairs you had in Lauriston?'

Along with several other items in the same category, I'd sold them out of a feeling that I couldn't offer them a good home.

'Too bad, they seemed alright to me.'

And with those well-chosen words of encouragement, he signed off.

Back in the kitchen with a coffee I wouldn't have needed but for his call, I was visited by a thought. Or maybe, more accurately, a scene. I pictured Mrs H, alone in her well-appointed lounge with so many ornaments it took half an hour to dust them all. And this Mrs H, from the comfort of her armchair, picked up a tablet and put through a video call to Mr H, ostensibly at a high-level conference in Dubai, but actually wrapped in the arms of a lady Mrs H knew nothing about, a lady wearing very little, if not nothing at all. How would that work, Wyness? What would happen then? His clients couldn't keep on refusing to take personal calls without attracting suspicion. Parallel Lives wouldn't work.

18

IN MY EXPERIENCE, clients like to be kept up to date with progress made. My practice is to launch a pre-emptive strike in those cases where I have something to report. That way, the client is assured of our interest and isn't put to the trouble of contacting us. Though I had plenty to report to Mr Chen, I contacted Anna van Leeuwen first because, if she was right, and the indications were that she probably was, her safety was our top priority. Clearing it with her beforehand, I dropped into her place of work. Was Miss van Leeuwen expecting me? She certainly was. And behold, lo, my name was on a list.

The young man who ushered me into her office exuded concern. He wasn't yet wringing his hands, but with minimal practice he'd get there.

'The wellbeing of our staff is uppermost in our minds,' he assured me, in true managerial style. 'Miss van Leeuwen is a valued colleague.' Which she probably was, but concerns for the security of the bank may have been as important to him as the lady's personal safety.

'I'll leave you to it then.'

When he did, I told Miss van Leeuwen the little I knew; my colleagues and I believed she was being stalked, our suspicions falling on a cyclist we had now seen several times.

'I saw him too, on the camera Mr Wyness installed and also here in Conference Square. Oh, and by the way, you won't believe this, but I think I'm now being stalked by a woman as well.' She then described Maureen MacNeil, someone I had yet to tell her about. 'She looked a bit dubious to me, somewhat down at heel.'

'Ah, yes, I should have said. I apologise for that. She's a colleague, Maureen MacNeil. Retired detective sergeant, very experienced.'

'She looked too young to be retired.'

'She wanted to go private, less paperwork.'

Miss van Leeuwen, never slow with a response, was remarkably quick off the mark.

'Worse pension.'

She turned to the screen she'd been studying as I entered.

'Excuse me a moment, I need to send this document off.'

That accomplished, she asked me what I proposed to do. I explained MacNeil's intention to follow the stalker home, at which point we would be able to establish who he was and also, if it came to that, persuade him to stop.

'With a baseball bat,' she suggested, helpfully.

'With reasoned argument, Miss van Leeuwen.'

In the meantime, I gave her MacNeil's number and asked her to put it on speed dial along with my own in case of emergency. Then, having covered the angles, I left the building and phoned Mr Chen, who was happy to have me call in at the Heavenly Garden Market, a mere five-minute stroll away, though most of it uphill.

The Heavenly Garden proved to be deeper than it was wide, an advantage, he explained, when it came to calculating business rates. Very astute, Alison would have taken to him at once. It seemed there had been a recent delivery, since I found him and a helper surrounded by boxes, all with Chinese characters on the sides.

'Ah, Mr Hunter, do come in.'

He wheeled me through to the back office and insisted on pouring green tea from a bone China teapot into matching bone China cups, all adorned with delicate rose petals. I added green tea to my list of groceries to buy and in due course, the social niceties taken care of, he asked how it was going. I began by describing Vellacott's attack on the Body Art Studio and how the manager, Brian Doyle, had ended up in hospital. He looked shocked, as well he might, but had a question.

'And Miss Hennessy?'

'She was there at the time but managed to escape unharmed.'

He was relieved to hear that, having taken a shine to her on the flimsiest acquaintance. But isn't that how instinct works, don't we all operate that way?

'We are dealing with a man of violence, a dangerous individual.'

'That we are, Mr Chen.'

When he asked about our progress identifying Vellacott's current whereabouts, I was able to report that we'd tracked him down to a tenement off Lady Stair's Close but had yet to identify the flat. Given his violent nature, I couldn't advise Mr Chen to knock on his door when we found it, though that decision was his. Bailiffs would be safer all round.

'Very well, Mr Hunter, so what would you consider the best way forward in such a case? I have to say it isn't clear to me.'

'Well one option is to sue him, have him served with the necessary papers while we still know where he is. People like him are given to what we sometimes refer to as sofa-surfing. He may not remain at his present location for long.'

'I see. What we might call a fly-by-night individual.'

'Exactly. But thanks to Vellacott himself there is another course of action open to us now.'

Mr Chen was happy to hear that, very pleased indeed.

Following his attack on Body Art, the police were currently preparing a file for the Procurator Fiscal. He would be charged with aggravated assault and vandalism. A major witness in the case would, of course, be Linda Hennessy, who was also a witness to the moonlight flit, his previous act of vandalism at Mr Chen's flat, and the theft of goods from the flat.

'Ah, I see. Then a second charge can be added to the sheet.'

'Indeed. His crimes against you.'

I considered this very neat, though there was one caveat.

'Of course, this can only occur if you report what happened with respect to your flat. Provided you do that, together with the photographs we already have and Linda Hennessy's testimony, then we have a watertight case. I'm sure the investigating officer will be happy to help.'

'And who is this officer?'

'Detective Sergeant Anastasija Cook.'

He wrote that down on the side of a packing case and not, I couldn't help noticing, in Chinese characters. Then, after a moment's reflection aided by green tea, there was something he wanted to know.

'Tell me, Mr Hunter, are these courses of action mutually exclusive?'

This was a tricky one, to be answered, if at all, with great care. I crafted a reply to indicate that any view I might have should not be relied on.

'There are people out there who know much more about the law than I do, Mr Chen.'

A practical man who owned five flats, Mr Chen didn't doubt that for a moment.

'But Mr Hunter, that could be said of us all.'

'Anyway, bearing that in mind, and knowing I'm not a lawyer, I can't see that they are. You could probably choose to pursue the matter on both fronts, though civil action against Vellacott might prove expensive.'

'Of course, but I believe such an action would damage

his reputation, subject him to the scrutiny of the public gaze, alert others to the danger of having anything to do with the man.'

There was a certain logic to this, always assuming Vellacott had any reputation left to lose. But what did it mean that Mr Chen was returning to the same idea several times in differing guises? Either he was given to rhetorical flourishes or, possibly more likely, he was betraying a strong underlying emotion without knowing it. Whatever the explanation, he had to realise that any sum awarded by way of compensation would never find its way to his pocket.

'Please tell this detective sergeant of yours I will be happy to cooperate and will shortly be in touch. And may I give you this,' he said, producing a frosted glass bottle from a desk drawer.

'Kwai Feh Lychee liqueur. Very good.'

According to Mr Chen, and he would know, Emperor Ming of the Tang Dynasty had supplied his consort with this potion and, said with the hint of a smile, was richly rewarded for his generosity. Though what form this reward took was not recorded in the histories, it was open to us all to hazard a guess.

As I left the Heavenly Garden, I wondered why it was that of the two environments I had visited that morning I was so much more at home in a market full of boxes with Chinese symbols I didn't understand than in the concrete and glass workplace where Miss van Leeuwen and her colleagues interrogated screens I didn't understand either. The office atmosphere seemed sterile by comparison, though having read analyses of computer keyboards at the microbial level, I suspected it was not as sterile as it looked. The boxes, on the other hand, didn't pretend to be what they were not, and their contents were useful.

19

THAT EVENING I was alone with my thoughts, one in particular. When I'd been with the police my working hours were defined. There were occasions when overtime was required, but apart from that my life was straightforward. When I made it back home of an evening my time was my own. But things had changed. No longer working for an organisation paying my wages and setting my working hours, I couldn't clock off. Working for myself I couldn't, if I can put it this way, leave me at the office when I came back home.

Since she also worked for herself, I'd discussed this problem with my business partner, Alison. After all, she'd been self-employed much longer than I had. And not wishing to type-cast the lady in any way, I felt my accountant friend had come up with a singularly spreadsheet solution to the problem.

'You must learn to compartmentalise, Douglas, it's the only way.'

She advocated setting aside hours for myself, hours which she termed "me time". For obvious reasons, these would typically occur during evenings and weekends.

'And I can't stress this enough, your me-time must be sacrosanct. However tempted you may be, you should allow nothing to erode it.'

She recommended setting aside seven till midnight, weekdays, plus Saturday afternoon after one o'clock, Saturday evening, and all-day Sunday. These hours, she maintained, would be necessary for regenerative growth, recharging the batteries and, just as important, detoxification – terms which, while having an undoubted resonance, lacked clarity for me. When pressed, she said that by detoxification she was referring not to the body but to spiritual cleansing. Had an accountant ever come so close to sounding like a guru or swami? I couldn't help but notice, though, that no form of relaxation came into her plan. Nonetheless, she clearly had a point. I must strive, as she had done, to separate the business and personal in my life.

These wayward thoughts were interrupted by my phone. MacNeil. Since it was after seven, this was a call I shouldn't have taken, but I did.

'You realise you're intruding on my me-time?'

What was I on about now, she wondered.

'Have you been drinking?'

She knew how unlikely this was and carried on regardless, a road-roller in human form.

'Will van Leeuwen be at work tomorrow morning? Because, if she's not, we could deal with that bastard Vellacott then.'

Anna van Leeuwen worked alternate Saturdays and wouldn't be at work the next day.

'Right, good, well the camera can take the strain.'

I'd told her which building Vellacott was living in but also that I'd no idea which flat. She wanted to join me in finding out.

'You really think it takes two?'

I couldn't safely do this on my own, Vellacott was violent. Without saying so directly, Maureen MacNeil was offering to protect me. Both of us knew that her skill in unarmed combat far exceeded mine so I agreed to meet her at Lady Stair's Close the following morning at half past eleven. Vellacott should be up and about by then. And something else Alison had taught me; if you're offered help, and in the unlikely event you have any left, swallow your pride and take it.

No sooner had the call ended than my phone rang again. Alison.

'I've been trying to get through but the line was busy.'

A bit of fancy footwork got me out of that one.

'John Banks.'

'I see. Well, I just wondered how things were going.'

She probably did wonder that, but it wasn't why she'd called. Hotel rooms were all very well, there was nothing wrong with hers, but it just wasn't the same. I could picture her in her room, bed with a light at each side, wall-mounted TV, minibar. In my mind's eye she was perched on the edge of the bed in that slinky kimono of hers, mobile phone clamped to one ear. But she'd be much happier at home. Who wouldn't be? Added to that was the fact that though she'd been speaking to many people in the course of the week they were, at best, nodding acquaintances, nobody she could let her hair down with.

In the months I'd known her, even when we'd been a lot closer than we were now, one thing she'd never done was let her hair down.

'It's just an expression, Douglas, you know perfectly well what I mean. Really,' she sighed, 'you must try to take things less literally.'

The Alison I knew was coming through loud and clear, almost as if she was with me in the room. And then she revealed that something was worrying her. Her employer, Ergonomica, had taken over two smaller companies but were finding it much more difficult than anticipated to streamline, as they hopefully put it, the differing accounting systems used across the group. In order to sort this out, she had to look at the accounts of all three companies. Where could they integrate, where would changes be necessary?

Would a complete package have to be junked and replaced? She didn't see my eyes glaze over as she ran all this past me, but she probably guessed.

'But Alison,' I said lamely, 'you're good at this.'

'That's the trouble, Douglas. I am, and I'm picking up a problem.'

It was early days yet, much more work would be required, but she now suspected that the value of Edwards Interiors had been inflated prior to purchase. As a lay person, without an accounting bone in my body, I couldn't see how this was possible.

'Well, there are a number of ways; for example, booking projected sales as if they'd already been made. I could go on.'

I was sure she could, but still didn't get it.

'Surely Ergonomica checked all that before buying?'

'I believe you're referring to due diligence here and, yes, they employed a well-known firm of accountants to check the books before making an offer.'

'What are you going to do?'

'Keep digging, that's all I can do. I must have a solid case before taking this upstairs.'

I didn't like the sound of it at all. If there was evidence of fraud, I could see this ending up in court with the blameless Alison being grilled for hours as an expert witness.

'Do you miss me, Douglas?'

'Of course.'

'Just thought I'd ask.'

Though I was missing her less than I'd expected when she set off for the west, I felt the absence of a steadying presence. And lying on my mattress later that night, on my sleepless pillow, as the poet might have it, I found myself wondering how close anyone can get to someone else. How close had I really been to Alison? How close could I ever have been? And if I'd fallen short in that department, was it down to me or an inevitable consequence of the human condition?

I fell asleep without resolving any of these issues which, looking back, was probably just as well.

20

It was raining that Saturday morning, not heavily, but a light penetrating rain, what they call smirr where I come from. MacNeil had her faults, but being late wasn't one of them. I found her standing in the courtyard wearing a dark green waterproof jacket with its hood up. Her new improved hair would be protected from the rain. She was holding a small packet.

'My birthday's not till August.'

'Get real, Hunter. The only gift you'll get from me is a bill for services rendered.'

The packet, clearly a prop, was addressed to Mr Charles P Vellacott and I have never discovered what, if anything, was in it.

'So how are we going to do this?'

'Follow me.'

We faced a steep flight of moss-stained stairs which branched into two more flights at right angles to the first before reaching a landing. You had to be fit to live here; if your knees were shot, forget it. At each end of the landing was a door, one giving access to twenty-one flats, the other to the seven.

'Which door is it, Douglas?'

I didn't know, a fact she took in her stride.

'Ok, we'll start with the seven, we might get lucky.'

Of the flats listed, all were even numbers and all but one had names. We couldn't be sure, of course, but the nameless flat 8 was possible. The key safe on the wall suggested transients and might be for that flat. MacNeil strode up to the entry phone and pressed button 14, Desjardins.

'Yes?'

'I have a delivery for 2 but there's no reply. Could you let me in to leave it?'

'Do you realise how often this happens?'

The put-upon party complained in a French accent but buzzed us in anyway.

'This stair's better lit than some,' MacNeil said, but switched her phone light on and started examining the walls.

'Checking the paintwork?'

Keeping track of occupants in blocks of flat was difficult. Some posties dealt with this by writing the names of current occupants in very small writing on the wall near each door. Otherwise, it was too much to remember. It might say McLintock on the nameplate, but the people who actually lived there were Davies, Henderson, Macintosh, and Sykes.

'So it pays to look.'

Though not on this occasion. Who would be mailing Vellacott here when he could only have been in residence a few days and was keeping a low profile anyway? The old MacNeil would have contested this with some vigour, probably laced with expletives, but the new MacNeil, MacNeil Mark 2, took it in her stride.

'True.'

She decided that no French person would have anything to do with Vellacott, scratched Number 14 from her list, and with it the fourth floor. Following her up the stairs to the third, I noticed that flat 12 had a doorbell, not often the case, but no one replied, so we tried flat 10. The occupant assured us that she'd never heard of anyone called Vellacott. Since she was well over sixty, we believed her. Then, about to descend the spiral stairway to the second floor, we heard the main door open and someone come in.

'Stay here, don't move. It might be him.'

This was good advice. When Vellacott entered the building, he saw MacNeil coming down but didn't see me. If he had, he'd have recognised me from Body Art, gathered his gear, left at speed and imposed himself on someone else. Our effort would have been wasted. When I heard the door to Number 8 shut behind him, I joined MacNeil on the ground floor and we left the building.

'You're sure it was him?'

She was, the red burgundy cords a sure-fire give-away.

'Right,' she said, when we'd made the main courtyard. She checked her watch. 'Ten to twelve, early lunch.'

She took my arm and led me the short distance down George IV Bridge to Nando's. She was hungry and not just for my company.

'This do you?' I asked, as a waiter pointed us to a small table by the window.

She looked round the room as if the restaurant harboured secret agents whose sole purpose in life was keeping an eye on her, a fleeting reversion to her previous coke-induced paranoia, a lingering after-effect not so easy to shake off.

'Have to do, I suppose' she said, pulling out a distressed turquoise chair and sitting down, 'make mine a Mozambique.'

'What's that when it's at home?'

'A beer, Douglas, an alcoholic beverage.'

She ordered a quarter chicken breast but reacted with outrage at the suggestion of a side-salad to go with it. Had the memory of her mother just been insulted? I didn't think so.

'Never liked lettuce,' she said, 'strictly for the rabbits.'

Then, with the aid of the menu, she turned her fire on my apple juice.

'An orchard in a glass, what a load of crap!'

It was marketing-speak alright but the juice was refreshing, which couldn't be bad. She'd heard me order and hadn't said a word, but when my mushroom and halloumi pitta arrived, she couldn't help herself.

'You do realise, Douglas, that however hard you try you'll never be a card-carrying member of the middle class.'

'Healthy eating, Maureen, a balanced diet. You should try it. Live longer if you do.'

All the experts said so, dieticians and the like, but pointing this out opened an unexpected trapdoor in the mind of Maureen MacNeil which she duly fell through.

'Live longer! Who in their right mind would want to do that?'

I was visited by the thought that death might be something she would welcome, an impulse kept at bay as best she could by constant activity – which worked well for her during daylight hours but was surely a problem when she returned to her flat of an evening since, like me, she lived alone. Then I remembered that this same Maureen MacNeil was heavily into video gaming, an activity alien to me but which, I knew, could take up many hours of her time and probably did.

But back in the land of the living, we had decisions to make and the sooner we made them the better. We now knew where Vellacott was staying, though not who he was staying with. We knew, too, that he wouldn't be staying there long; he was on the move to avoid being caught and who could put up with him anyway? If he didn't leave of his own accord, he'd soon be shown the door.

So we agreed that I should tell Mr Chen immediately, at which point, having done what he hired me for, I could bill him for our trouble. We also agreed that I should inform DS Cook, but tomorrow rather than today, giving Chen a chance to confront Vellacott before she arrived to arrest him. And it was during this discussion that it struck me how easily we agreed on such things, how well we worked together.

'I have a question, Maureen.'

'You would.'

'If you'd chapped on a door with a parcel for Vellacott and he'd answered. What then?'

'He'd know he'd been rumbled and leave as fast as he could. And yours truly,' she added with a smile, 'would have followed him.'

'At a safe distance.'

'Of course.'

21

SUNDAY, ACCORDING TO some a day of rest, so why not give resting a try? I hadn't done much of it lately. But lingering in bed had never been for me, so when I rose, I rested my bran flakes and popped across the road to the Breakfast Club for an all-day breakfast, in my case a coffee and a bacon roll.

'Any sauce with that?'

I was tempted by ketchup but decided to forego it on health grounds. Susan, my ex-wife, still had a lot to answer for. Then Bob came in, a regular it seemed.

'Morning, Robert.'

He didn't like that at all, preferring to be addressed as Bob.

'Robert's my Sunday name, folks.'

'Ah, but you're forgetting something.'

'What?'

'This *is* Sunday.'

The badinage was still under way when I left; Robert didn't stand a chance.

Back in my flat, I sat at the kitchen table and addressed the question of how, exactly, would I go about resting? I could adopt the lotus position and meditate, clearing what was left of my mind of anything still in it. But I wasn't sure I'd be able to unwrap myself from that position if and when I succeeded. It had been brought to my attention, again by me ex-wife Susan, that I left a lot to be desired in the flexibility department. As I sat there considering this, I began to wonder if Susan, now fled the scene physically, would ever extend me the same courtesy between the ears. Was I doomed to go through life accompanied by this shining role model for the healthy life for ever and a day, or would she gradually fade, granting me some peace at last? Knowing her, I didn't think it likely.

If not meditation, how about reading? Having recently unpacked, I knew there were only two books in the house. One was The Casebook of James McLevy, an Edinburgh detective of the Victorian era whose handle on character was matched by his way with words. The other was a book entitled *Feel The Fear and Do It Anyway*, a self-help manual thrust into my unwilling hands by John Banks when Susan left. This was a book I'd never opened, firstly, because I had failed to identify any fear and, secondly, because I had no idea what the "it" was I was supposed to be doing anyway. And coming from John Banks, this title provoked a wry smile – a man who'd been engaged for seven years after which nothing. No tying the knot, no moving in together. It could safely be said of John, well-meaning though he was, that he hadn't done it anyway himself.

Then I remembered a third book. *Scran for the Single Man* had been given to me by my neighbour Patricia back in Laurieston before I left and was sub-titled *Unique Meals Just For You!* This was another well-intentioned gift, and potentially more useful to me than feeling the fear, but leafing through it I couldn't help but notice that I'd have to shop for ingredients like flat leaf parsley and balsamic olive oil, then subject them to knives, colanders, spatulas, whisks, pots, pans, ladles and the like. I wasn't into cooking. Enough of it on television to last a lifetime. The sainted Susan hadn't been into cooking either. Give her a carrot and she'd eat it raw, commending as she did so its beneficial effects on night vision.

I could have watched Songs of Praise on television. But I didn't have one, a fact glossed over by TV Licensing, who seemed to think that anyone with a laptop must be watching BBC1. And it was true, I had a laptop, but never used it to watch TV programmes of any sort, on any channel. Research, that was another matter, and making entries in my journal. When I retired, if I ever reached that point, leafing through my journal would prove to me that, yes, I really had lived once.

Feeling restless and ill at ease, I decided to go for a walk or, as Wyness put it, stretch my legs, though stretching them was often as far as he got. Standing up was asking too much. Susan had said to him once, *don't sit when you can stand, don't walk when you can run.* He could barely conceal his astonishment. *Well,* he'd replied, *that's not going to work.* But behind it was the perfectly sensible thought that keeping active was good for the heart and lungs and, according to her, the digestive system as well. *Sedentary people like you,* she said, pointing to his stomach, *are much more given to constipation than those of us who choose to remain active. Why do you suppose,* she asked him before he could reply, *that Dulcolax is used so much in care homes?* And being a sharp mover, she'd left the room while he was still looking up the medication in question.

I walked through the entry from Gifford Park to the main road, after a week in residence still admiring the murals on either side, and strolled north towards the city centre, a route which took me past St Patrick's Square. Mindful of the deal I'd struck with Anna van Leeuwen, I loitered there for a while to see if there was any sign of her stalker. I must have been there for twenty minutes or so when my mobile rang. Anna. Did we still have her under observation as arranged? The timing could hardly have been better.

'As a matter of fact, we have. I'm in the vicinity now. Look out your window.'

I walked round to her basement flat and gave her a cheery wave before moving on to a safer distance where I might spot the stalker without being seen myself.

'That's very reassuring, Mr Hunter. You'll keep me posted.'

I assured her I would, and I meant it. What I didn't know, but would soon find out, was that while this was happening Mr Chen and a friend, presumably there for protection, gained entry to the tenement containing flat 8 and rapped several times on the door. It was eventually opened by a bleary-eyed young man who worked as a DJ in the Liquid Room, just the sort of person Vellacott might know. He'd been scratching vinyl till four in the morning and the least he could expect was an undisturbed lie-in to compensate. Mr Chen apologised, as he would, but demanded to speak to Vellacott at once. This request being refused, he left the building threatening to call the police which, unfortunately for me, was exactly what he did. Because, later that afternoon, I was visited by DS Cook and DC Robertson, Hector of that ilk.

'So,' she said on the doorstep, 'I have a bone to pick with you.'

I ushered them into my living room and could tell they weren't impressed.

'Have a seat, Mr Hunter.'

Invited to sit on one of my own chairs, I did so, but there were three people and only two seats.

'I noticed a couple of chairs in the kitchen on the way past.'

She said this to Robertson, meaning that he should bring one through, which he did. A year before he'd been taking orders from Maureen MacNeil, now he was taking them from DS Cook, but he didn't seem to mind so why should anyone else.

'We were contacted earlier today by a Mr Chen, who attempted to speak with our friend Charles Vellacott.'

'I see.'

'Well the thing is, Mr Hunter, your client knew where Vellacott was because you told him. What I'm wondering is why you didn't follow up on your agreement to tell us. You knew perfectly well that he was wanted in connection with serious offences. I take it you agree that putting someone in hospital is serious?'

'I do.'

'So?'

I gave her the only explanation I could, namely, that if I had informed her at the same time as Mr Chen, Vellacott would have been taken into custody before my client had an opportunity to confront him, and that had been the whole point of him hiring me in the first place.

'What you're saying, effectively, is that your deal with Mr Chen took precedence over the public good.'

I couldn't deny that, but since she hadn't asked a question, I stayed silent.

'Now here's the thing, Mr Hunter. When we arrived in response to your client's call, we gained access to flat Number 8, searched it thoroughly, and I'm talking under beds and the interiors of broom cupboards here and – surprise, surprise! – Vellacott was nowhere to be seen. The bird had flown. According to the occupant, a young man who styles himself DJ Dailly, Vellacott had packed up and left when he realised his whereabouts had been discovered. What do you make of that?'

DS Cook was understandably annoyed, I had compromised her arrest of Vellacott.

'That's too bad, I'm really sorry to hear that, especially when you think we'd actually managed to track him down.'

'As fulsome apologies go, that one left a lot to be desired, wouldn't you agree, DC Robertson?' Hector nodded. He agreed. 'Oh, and by the way, when you say "we", someone was with you at the time, one of your associates perhaps?'

She leant on the word ever so slightly, as if to suggest that any associates I might have were fictitious, for marketing purposes only. And though DS Cook was polite by nature, I knew I had jeopardised any possible cooperation from that quarter and the only way out of it, if there was one, was to be as open as possible. I wasn't sure she was entitled to know this, but I told her anyway.

'Maureen MacNeil.'

Robertson, normally impassive, was so shocked that he broke the habit of a lifetime and spoke.

'You have to be joking!'

'Sorry, Hector, but there it is.'

DS Cook paused for a moment, not to draw breath but to marshal her attack.

'Right, so you inform an officer dismissed from the force for serious misconduct, but not the serving officer who replaced her.'

'I didn't need to inform her; we'd tracked him down together.'

'Well, for your information, we believe some of his belongings are still in the flat, so for the time being we're keeping a discreet eye on the building. As for you, I am instructing you to keep well away from it.'

She looked across to Robertson, still recovering from the shock of hearing about MacNeil.

'We're not getting off to a good start with this man, are we?'

'You can say that again.'

'I'm genuinely sorry about this, DS Cook. It's entirely my fault.'

'Well at least we agree about something.'

She looked round my sparsely furnished quarters.

'As for this flat of yours, it seems to me you're taking Nordic minimalism too far.'

When Alison phoned that evening, I told her about my run-in with DS Cook, omitting only any reference to

Maureen MacNeil. She was sympathetic. After all, I'd simply been doing everything I could to honour a contract with a client, which was just good business practice.

'And you should perhaps remind this Cook woman that if it hadn't been for you, she wouldn't have known where Vellacott was in the first place. So really, she had nothing to complain about.'

22

MacNeil had deliveries to make the next morning so keeping an eye on van Leeuwen reverted to me. I waited about fifty yards from her front door till she appeared, pretending to study houses for sale in Warner's window, an innocuous activity, but one which reinforced my belief that buying a new flat was not possible. They cost too much.

Anna always walked to work, so I'd abandoned my car and gone to St Patrick's Square on foot. Alison would have approved because I was saving on petrol but, as I'd pointed out in the past, there were downsides. Surveillance was much better sitting in the comfort of the car when it was raining, much to be preferred to lurking in doorways getting wet. And the older I got the more I started to stiffen up when standing, something which didn't occur so much in the car or on the move. But since these arguments only concerned my comfort, they didn't interest her at all. Lastly, and most importantly, I was much less evident to the eye in the car than I was when hanging around on my feet, and so less likely to be spotted. *Good point, Douglas*, she'd said at the time, and it was.

I followed van Leeuwen to her work without incident, but as she entered the bank, I noticed our cyclist on the other side of the road. He was standing between billboards announcing the forthcoming visit of the Manic Street Preachers to the Usher Hall. I was sure it was our man: the same diagonal yellow band across his jersey, the helmet-mounted cam, the mirrored goggles. Identifying his gear would be easy, identifying the wearer would not.

He hung around for a while, but knowing by now that the object of his interest would be in the building for hours, he disappeared in the direction of the fitness centre. After twenty minutes or so I followed him in and pretended to an interest in the facilities, equipment, terms of use and so on. As a member of staff was laying it out for me, complete with leaflets, I realised that something was wrong. The shouting was probably a clue. A personal trainer appeared from the interior and joined us. She'd been working with a resident of the Sheraton when she heard raised voices. She didn't pay much attention at first, but as the volume increased, so did the aggression.

'You ought to have seen them, Farhad. Neanderthals the pair of them.'

As far as I knew, Neanderthals weren't notable gym users, couldn't afford the subscription. In any case, I had yet to see evidence that they were any more aggressive than those of us who came after. I found that hard to imagine.

'One of them picked up a barbell and hit the other one over the head.'

'It wasn't loaded, I take it.'

'Of course not. Witold tried to separate them while Sally phoned the police. There was blood on the floor by the time they arrived.' Though keen to continue without pausing, she had to stop for breath.

'I had to give a statement.'

According to which, one of the men had taken exception to the other hogging a leg press and words were exchanged.

'Such as?'

'I can't bring myself to say, not in polite company. The policeman was nice, though.'

Aware that I was still standing there taking it all in, Farhad turned from his colleague.

'I'm sorry about this, sir. An incident like this is very

unusual.'

And none too good for business, I thought, as two men were escorted from the premises. I saw them both as they left, but since I'd yet to see the stalker's face, I'd no way of knowing if I was looking at him now. The older one I could rule out, middle-aged, balding, shorts too tight for his body. The younger one fitted the bill when it came to age and height, but that proved nothing in itself.

Across the road again, in a coffee outlet, I sat for a while mulling it over. The young man hadn't been wearing a black jersey with a yellow diagonal, but our cyclist friend would have a locker and change for training. I fired off a text to my man on the inside, John Banks, asking for any information he might have on the incident, only to receive the unwelcome reply *Sorry, no can do. See you later.* Cook had put an embargo on any member of the force telling me anything at all, including the time of day. I hadn't cooperated with her, she wouldn't with me. I couldn't blame her, really.

Then I phoned Maureen. I could hear she was on the road, but how far away?

'If you must know, I'm taking a bookcase to Carrington.'

But she'd still be able to pick up our cyclist friend on his way home and follow him in her van. Even assuming he'd been involved in the fitness centre fracas, he'd be back in circulation by the time van Leeuwen left work. Which left me free for a pencilled-in meeting at the bank.

I strolled down the main road to South Clerk Street, entered the bank, and was shown into a small office. The financial advisor introduced herself. Fiona MacIntyre. She still had the bloom of youth on her cheek, I could have given her five years at least, so how had it come about that she knew more about money than I did? Where had I been all this time? She offered me tea or coffee, both of which I declined on the grounds that I'd just had one.

'So, Mr Hunter, the reason we wanted to speak to you

was that you have rather a lot of money languishing in your current account at the moment. Just under one hundred thousand pounds to be exact.'

'It's safer there than under the mattress.'

Miss MacIntyre allowed herself the flicker of a smile.

'That's true, of course, but it's not doing anything. As you may be aware, the current inflation rate is at the unusually low level of zero-point-five percent. But even at that, if you were to leave a thousand pounds in your current account, it would shrink to nine hundred and ninety-five over the course of a year.'

'I see.'

'But the amount presently in your account is one hundred thousand pounds in round figures,' Miss Macintyre would know, she had a pleasantly round figure herself, 'which means that the value of your money would reduce by five hundred pounds over the same period.'

'But I'd still have the hundred thousand.'

'Of course, but it's value would be less by five hundred pounds. To put it another way, if you were to spend this money after a year, you'd be able to buy five hundred pounds less because the cost of what you were buying would have gone up by zero-point-five percent, but your money wouldn't have followed suit.'

Alison had run this one past me recently and pointed out the same problem.

'Another factor to consider is that inflation is not expected to continue at this low level indefinitely. In another few years, two thousand and twenty say, it might have risen considerably and the effect on your capital would be very much more damaging.'

I looked through the glass door separating us from the main floor of the bank, Chinese students, local pensioners, and everyone in between sorting out their affairs. And here I was separated from them by one hundred thousand pounds, with hardly a sound getting through the divide. What did money get you? Among other things, special treatment. I knew from experience what a problem lack of money could be, but this was the first time I realised that having too much could be a problem too. What to do with the stuff?

'So what are you advocating, Miss MacIntyre?'

'Well, to begin with, I have to inform you that I'm not an independent financial advisor, so the only products I can advise on are those offered by the bank. But I can suggest possible strategies for dealing with this sum in general terms.'

She began by saying that she didn't want to tell me what I probably knew already, but she was now obliged to do so because of past mis-selling. That said, she explained the difference between having money on deposit and investing it.

'So, if you have money on deposit, it's safe but might not be earning so much.'

'Exactly. And if you invested in stocks and shares the potential profit would be considerably greater.'

'As would the potential loss.'

'Indeed. Ultimately, it's a question of risk. How much are you willing to take? How much *should* you take? For example, some people regard property as the best hedge against inflation because, historically, it's been less volatile than the stock market.'

This to a man who'd just been checking house prices in an estate agent's window.

'As things stand right now, I can't afford to buy a house for myself to live in, let alone anyone else.'

But this didn't put her off mentioning buy-to-let mortgages which, I suspected, she would be able to advise on. Given the capital sum available to me now, she was sure I'd have no difficulty getting one. She was probably right, but to put this suggestion in the bin where it belonged, I produced my phone and showed her the damage wreaked upon Mr Chen's flat by his departing tenant. As a tactic, it worked a treat.

'Oh dear, this is absolutely appalling.'

She looked at her screen for a moment or two, the source of all information in the world as presently constituted, and moved on.

'I see you also have a business account with us, Mr Hunter.'

'That's right.'

'And your turnover's so low you don't have to register for VAT.'

That was also true. Hunter Associates could not be described as a robust concern, though I liked to think we would get there in the end.

'Mm. Interesting. Commercial banking isn't my area, but if business doesn't pick up, you might have to consider lending some of your money to yourself.'

23

MacNeil came to see me that evening and not by prior arrangement. She wanted to update me but could easily have done it by phone. Was it sharks which had to keep swimming or they'd die? If so, MacNeil was a shark. She'd certainly had that reputation in the force.

'Parking here's no joke. I'm on a double yellow.'

'Not a good idea, Maureen, even at night.'

But it gave her a reason to keep going over to the window and checking the street below.

'So, how did it go?'

'Worked like a dream.'

She'd waited as planned in the car park of the Salisbury Arms. When our suspect appeared, having cycled up Salisbury Road the wrong way, just as she'd predicted, she tailed him in her van; turning right onto Dalkeith Road then left onto Prestonfield Avenue.

'He went into a tenement, three floors. But the bottom floor's a shop so it has to be the second or third. He took his bike in with him.'

'Didn't want it stolen.'

'Would you?'

Settled in my living room on one of my directors' chairs, she thought we probably had enough to go on now for Wyness to follow it up. And before I could stop her, she phoned him in his eyrie and filled him in.

'I didn't know you were on the case,' Wyness said. 'Does her nibs know about this?'

He was referring to Alison Eadie, the other named partner of Hunter Associates, a woman he knew to be critical of his lifestyle and currency trading both.

'I doubt it,' she replied, giving me a hard look, 'he's been keeping me a well-guarded secret for some reason.'

'I wonder why that would be,' Wyness said, 'something to do with you accusing her of bumping off her husband?'

'I know, ridiculous isn't it. How touchy can you get!'

I didn't like the way this was going. Between them, Wyness and MacNeil were threatening to ruin what was left of my relationship with Alison. Either that or they were noising me up for the hell of it. I wasn't sure which but hoped it was the latter.

'Ok, Maureen,' Wyness said, 'have to go but I'll get onto it straight away.'

Since this conversation had lasted a good minute, MacNeil rushed to the window and looked out.

'Not a warden in sight.'

She was turning back into the room when something she'd seen but failed to register till then came to the forefront of her mind.

'My God, I don't believe it. Salvation is at hand. You've got religion!'

She'd finally noticed the True Jesus Church some thirty yards down the road. I'd seen it before I'd moved in, with Chinese characters above the door, but had yet to find out anything about it. For example, did Mr Chen attend? His market wasn't so far away.

'The eighteenth spiritual and evangelical convocation!' She was reading from a large banner on the wall. 'These people really have it bad.' Turning from the banner to me, she couldn't resist it. 'I'm beginning to think you've got religion on the brain, Douglas. Your last house was opposite a convent and next door to a church. What's going on here?'

'Sheer happenstance, doesn't mean a thing.'

'A bit like your life then.'

And with those few kind words she upped and left leaving my front door open behind her.

Raiding the fridge, I removed a lamb hotpot and let the microwave take care of it. And when it had, I sat down at the kitchen table with open laptop and fork. Whoever said males couldn't multitask should have seen me then.

We were making some progress with the Vellacott and van Leeuwen cases, but none whatsoever with Dan Drysdale and his image problem. Maybe because there was no progress to be made, but I thought I'd do a modest search myself. Yes, believe it or not, I now had a wonderful shooting script to hand, replete with zombies, witches, and broomsticks with built-in satnavs; all I needed was the money to make the film. Financial backing. Where should I turn? It would have to be a third party; there was no way I was risking my own hundred thousand. After an hour chasing down links, I was none the wiser. Chester H Burt, executive producer to the Born Again film franchise, was nowhere to be found. Not by an amateur like me. Yet in that hour, my associate David Wyness accomplished a lot, as he told me, breathlessly, over a video link.

Our cyclist was one Leroy Gaines, twenty-four years of age. According to the voters' roll, he lived with a woman of the same surname, probably his mother, on Prestonfield Avenue. Their flat was on the second floor of a three-storey tenement set off from the road and near to a bus stop. There was reason to believe he was of mixed race, his mother English, his father Jamaican, hence the natural tan, but he'd have to do more work on that.

'And what do you know, he has a blog!'

'In which he admits to his stalking activities,' I suggested hopefully.

'Very funny, but what he does do, he takes his health and fitness very seriously.'

He showed me Gaines' latest post, in which he revealed to the world that he didn't use anti-perspirants because sweat was a necessary bodily function which should not be inhibited. For example, salt was released through sweat which helped keep blood pressure down. He did, however, use an aftershave splash in preference to an eau de toilette since it was more diluted but still effective while being discreet.

Reading posts like this and looking at the pictures he'd posted of himself in full cycling gear, complete with muscles, I felt this was a man who admired himself in mirrors. Wyness had found out a great deal, no doubt about it, but we were still no closer to knowing if Gaines' motive was personal, in that he'd taken a fancy to Anna van Leeuwen or, for want of a better word, commercial, to do with her role at the bank.

'What do we do now?' Wyness wanted to know.

'Confront him, tell him we know who he is, where he lives, and what he's up to. That should be more than enough to put him off.'

'And if he's one of these obsessional types and carries on anyway, what then?'

'Good question, David.'

'Right, but what's the good answer?'

I said it in jest, but no one can tell the future.

'Set Maureen on him.'

24

THE FOLLOWING MORNING I contacted Anna van Leeuwen, who asked if I would pop into her place of work at lunchtime to update her. I was happy to do that and was shown into her office after a visitor's ID badge had been hung round my neck on a beaded lanyard, something which hadn't happened on my previous visit.

'Sorry about that, Mr Hunter, we neglected our own procedure last time. Do take a seat.'

She listened intently as I ran through what we'd discovered, then she put me on the spot.

'Where does he live, this Leroy Gaines?'

'I don't think I can tell you that.'

'Whyever not? Do you really think I'd go there with pepper spray and a shotgun?'

I explained that my reluctance was a matter of policy and in no way a reflection of her character, but I could tell she didn't believe me.

'You do realise that now I know his name I could probably work it out for myself.'

As long as the information didn't come from me, I was happy with that; at which point she accused me of fireproofing, and she was right, that was exactly what I was doing.

'Alright, so what *do* you advise? Inform the police, legal action of some sort?'

Informing the police, definitely, though there wasn't much they could unless Gaines' activity became more oppressive and threatening than it was at present.

'Am I right in thinking he hasn't contacted you via your mobile phone or email?'

'You are.'

He probably didn't know her number, which was good, though if he'd sent her texts and emails we'd have concrete evidence against him.

'Legal action, then. There must be something we can do.'

Legal procedures taking as long as they did, I couldn't recommend that, and I could see that beneath her polite exterior she was becoming frustrated at the prospect of inaction. Neat as ever, she slipped off one shoe with the toe of the other, opened a desk drawer and removed a transparent plastic box.

'I'd offer you some, but as you can see it wouldn't stretch to two.'

She was referring to her lunch which, as far as I could tell, consisted of couscous, cashew nuts and dried apricots. Just as well MacNeil wasn't there to see it.

'I often bring a packed lunch to work; the outlets round here are unduly crowded at lunchtime. Anyway, Mr Hunter, what, if anything, do you recommend? There must be something I can do!'

'You should do nothing at all. This is really important, Miss van Leeuwen. Do not engage with this person in any way. You should leave that to us.'

Though these were words which would come back to haunt me, the advice was good.

She smiled. 'I don't play ball.'

'That's it.'

'So what's the way forward here? Correct me if I'm wrong, but I don't seem to be hearing that.'

'We'll contact him. We'll make it clear we know his name, where he lives and what he's up to. That will put his gas on the peep.'

She hadn't come across this expression before, so I translated it into English. She got the idea.

'The sooner you tackle him the better. I'm tired of looking over my shoulder all the time.'

On behalf of Hunter Associates I promised to do exactly that.

'Oh, and by the way, we're pretty sure he spotted you in the Fitness Centre. We've seen him there on two occasions so far.'

'Okay, so in your opinion which is it, my body or the bank?'

'We can't be sure yet, but you're body's more attractive than the bank.'

She looked round her office, then through the windows to the rest of the department, a series of desks with monitors and mice.

'Some might say that wouldn't be difficult, but I guess you've taken this as far as you can.'

'Short of confronting him, yes, we have.'

At this point, accustomed to moving in banking circles, she came up with an incentive.

'Let me know when you've done that, then I can pay you.'

I left with the ID still round my neck. Destined to become a souvenir, I decided to keep it. There was a mild breeze in the street outside, pleasantly fanning the face, giving the impression of fresh air; natural, compared to the stale atmosphere of Anna's office. But whether I wanted to or not, I had to know it wasn't as fresh as it seemed, being heavy with exhaust emissions on what was, after all, a main thoroughfare. But since we couldn't see them, they weren't there. Which was how we behaved and why the problem was still to be faced.

Acting on impulse, I made my way home via the Meadows. And sure enough, there they were: dog-walkers, cyclists, exercise groups, tai chi for seniors, and joggers with rectangular devices strapped to the upper arm. All activities which got you nowhere in the end. However hard you tried, entropy would set in, your bodily systems failing one by one till you pegged out.

I attempted to counter these negative thoughts by walking a little faster, making a modest demand on my muscles, heart and lungs. And I can't deny that it had a beneficial effect, which lasted till I got home, opened the front door and found a card behind it. SORRY YOU WERE OUT WHEN WE CALLED. An attempt had been made to deliver a set of legs for my bed. I could arrange a new delivery time or drive out to Benjamin's Beds and collect them.

25

THE REST OF the day I expected to be quiet. I had a brief chat with MacNeil to agree on a division of labour. After a delivery of a Victorian fender and fire irons to an address in Canonmills, she was free all afternoon. She would follow Gaines home as before, jangle his doorbell and tell him – and with any luck his mother as well – that we at Hunter Associates knew exactly what he was up to, and it had to stop. If it didn't, she would warn him that there would be consequences, without being specific as to what these might be. After all, we couldn't be seen to be threatening the poor young man.

'Right, so that's me sorted. What about you?'

I told her about the card behind the door. But I could never be sure when I'd be at home to accept a delivery, so I had no option but to drive out to Benjamin's Beds "where sleep comes easy and dreams are delivered to your door".

'They don't actually say that, do they?'

They did, and I didn't believe it either. As though it required a degree in engineering, she wished me luck fitting the legs to the base.

'And then you'll be ready to go.'

I didn't ask her what she meant in case she told me, drove out to Straiton and duly collected the legs.

'I'm sure they'll do you proud, sir.'

Whatever that meant, I hoped they would and drove back home to fit them.

While I was doing this, I noticed that my duvet cover, a

131

rather nice teal and yellow job bought by my ex, could do with a wash. This was particularly noticeable on the yellow parts, but the teal sections had to be as bad. Memo to self: buy a dark brown cover next time. And then I discovered, as many must have done before me, that cramming a double duvet cover, pillowcases and a bath towel into a small washing machine left no room for water. This wasn't going to work.

I stuffed the offending items into a black bin bag, again with some difficulty, and walked down to the Ace Cleaning Centre, where the lady in charge assured me that I could wash the lot in one of her larger machines. She pointed to a row of industrial sized JLA washing machines, one so large she could have got into it herself.

'This'll do you fine.'

I was sure it would and asked if they did service washes, to which the answer was yes, for a modest additional charge. They would even deliver the finished article on the same basis.

'Want it dried as well?'

I should have thought of that but yes, I did, and left the Cleaning Centre with two spare hours on my hands. I could hardly believe it. Things were starting to fall into place at last. Even the bookshop café had a spare table for a wandering soul on his own. Because, and I couldn't help noticing this, when couples came in, one would go to the counter to order, leaving the other free to bag a table. It could be the last one, you were there first and had your order in to prove it, but that was your tough luck. Nowhere to sit when you got it. Yes, couples were at an advantage alright, I was really missing Susan now.

Given the location, I should have spent some time checking out books. Instead, I sat nursing a coffee and a slice of lemon tart, continuing my search for the elusive Chester H Burt on my phone. Perhaps if I masqueraded as a film producer myself, after all I did have money in the bank, our paths would cross. Come to think of it, why hadn't my youthful financial advisor, Fiona MacIntyre, thought of that? There had to be tax breaks for risking your life savings in the film industry. I looked the subject up and there were. Get with the programme, Miss MacIntyre!

The rest of that Tuesday I frittered away in fruitless research on the film industry, relaxing in cafés and shopping for groceries. And that at least wasn't fruitless; I came home with bananas, grapes, and Deglet Nour dates. That evening, on a bed raised from the floor and under a duvet in a clean cover for the first time in years, I dozed off surfing stations on my radio and slept till nine o'clock the next morning.

After a day in which I'd succeeded in putting no pressure on myself at all, I was ready to wake on the Wednesday to a new day in better shape. I woke to a new day alright, but the shape took a turn for the worse. I'd just finished breakfast when the entry phone rang: the lugubrious DC Robertson wanted to collect me.

'And why would that be, Hector?'

True to form, he was short on detail, but issues had arisen which his boss, DS Cook, needed to discuss. It was a matter of some urgency. As we retired to an interview room at St Leonards, I couldn't help but notice the lady had been working on her roots. If we're going to pretend to be blonde, we might as well do it properly. Attention to detail got a girl there in the end.

'Good morning, Douglas. Have a seat.'

'Good morning, Anastasija.'

Normally I wouldn't say a word I couldn't spell, but feeling the need to reciprocate first name terms, I made an exception in this case.

'Good news or bad, which would you like first?'

'Good.'

She looked up at me from the papers she'd put on

133

the desk. I had replied too quickly, without a second's hesitation.

'Well,' I said, spreading my hands outward in what I took to be a gallic gesture worthy of a mime artist on a bad day, 'what can I say? If I hear the good news first, the Grim Reaper might save me hearing the bad at all.'

DS Cook didn't do disconcerted, but she made a stab at it now.

'In saying that, it seems to me you're striking an attitude.'

'One informed by adverse experience.'

'I see. Then we may say you're a pessimistic individual.'

'We may.'

'Not without reason, in this case.' What did she mean by that? I didn't like the sound of that at all. 'Very well, I shall start with the good. You may remember we thought we had noticed some of Mr Vellacott's belongings still in flat 8. We decided to keep an eye on the building for a day or two, which we might not have done but for his violent tendencies.'

And the tactic had paid off. The previous evening, an alert constable had noticed a light on the fifth floor. Good for him, though I had a problem with that.

'But DS Cook, the building only has four floors.'

'Ah yes, when you went there, you didn't ascend to the fourth.'

'That's correct.'

'If you had, you'd have noticed that the spiral staircase continued upwards, not to a flat, it's true, but to a large communal storeroom. When we returned late last night, we discovered Vellacott in that storeroom, which is large enough to have electric lighting and a sizeable window in the wall facing the street outside.'

I could have pointed out that, just like us, the police hadn't gone to the fourth floor on their first visit either, yet sensing trouble ahead kept that thought to myself.

'So he's in custody.'

'Yes, and a most unsavoury character he is. But now that your client's come forward and we have Miss Hennessey's statement, we're charging him both with the attack at Body Art and trashing the flat.'

'That's excellent news, DS Cook.'

'We think so, yes. Though because of a previous spot of bother with the law, he was represented as recently as three years ago by criminal defence lawyers. You may have heard of them. Cartwright and Considine.'

'Spot of bother?'

He attacked a man he thought was making a move on his girlfriend.'

'Linda Hennessy.'

'Don't be ridiculous. Three years ago. He has trouble keeping a relationship going for three months.'

'He'll apply for legal aid.'

'No doubt. Now to another matter, which is really why I asked you to come in.'

As if by a signal, though I didn't detect one, Hector Robertson entered the room with a laptop open at the page.

'You managed.'

He looked pleased with himself. 'I did.'

He pulled up a chair and sat down beside Cook, who was watching me closely. How would I react to what they were about to show me? Robertson turned the laptop towards me and played a short video. To say it was badly shot would be an understatement.

'What do you make of that?'

'Not a lot. Could I see it again?'

It looked as if someone had shot video footage at road level, the camera at ninety degrees to the vertical. But it didn't mean much to me.

'To explain then, Douglas, this footage was captured by a helmet cam belonging to a Mr Leroy Gaines. DC

Robertson here,' round of silent applause for Robertson, 'has transferred it to his laptop.'

'Right.'

'The reason for the strange angle of view is that Gaines, while cycling back to his home, was struck from behind by a vehicle which we take to be the white van seen fleetingly towards the end of the clip. He was lying on Prestonfield Avenue at the time.'

'I see.'

I also saw that the registration of the van was impossible to read.

'Now we can't prove this as yet, but the indications are that your colleague, Maureen MacNeil, may have been driving that van. Can you shed any light on this for us?'

Quick thinking was required here but not forthcoming. I knew Maureen intended to visit Gaines' house but had no idea what had transpired when she had. As for the collision, I knew nothing about it.

'Feel free to respond. We're on taxpayers' time here.'

'Sorry, but this incident comes as news to me.'

'I thought it might. So why don't I fill you in a bit.'

According to Cook, MacNeil had gone to Gaines' house to warn him off. Gaines hadn't taken kindly to her visit, not with his mother in the hall hearing what he'd been up to. Words had been exchanged, including expletives which Mrs Gaines, a well brought up woman, had heard but refused to quote. The altercation ended with Gaines threatening to call the police and MacNeil encouraging him to do just that. Mrs Gaines did confirm, however, that MacNeil had called her son a pervert and shouted at him as she left that he hadn't heard the last of this.

'I would call that a threat, wouldn't you?'

'I would. To take the matter further. Which doesn't necessarily mean mowing him down on a public highway.'

'We see part of a white van in the clip. Your associate,

Maureen MacNeil, owns a white van.'

Both of these statements were true, but where did that get us?

'Unfortunately, being a helmet cam, it was facing the road ahead and Gaines was struck from behind, so we have no footage of the impact itself.'

'Excuse me, DS Cook, but don't you the think the person you should be speaking to here is Maureen herself?'

She did. But the said Maureen was currently delivering a bulk consignment of cat litter to Eyemouth and wouldn't be back in the city for three hours at least.

'Meantime, we're putting things together as best we can by talking to yourself and Mrs Gaines.'

'And Gaines himself, I assume.'

'Ah yes, now we find him surprisingly reticent. Why would that be, do you think?'

'That would be because he's been stalking someone and doesn't want it to come out.'

'Then you do know about that.'

'Of course. The victim is a client.'

'Anna van Leeuwen. Yes. You advised her to report the issue to us and she did.'

'And there's that other matter,' Robertson reminded her.

'Thank you, Hector. Yes, it so happens that we recently came across Gaines in another connection entirely, an altercation at the fitness centre behind the Sheraton.'

'So he has form.'

Cook nodded. 'A little, maybe. Not a lot so far. But he's certainly worth keeping an eye on.'

While that was probably true, who was going to do it? I doubted they had enough slack to cover such a job. And then DS Cook, thanking me for my cooperation, now and in the future, escorted me from the building. And as she did so she said something totally unexpected.

'I'll be in the bookshop at eight.'

26

BACK IN THE relative safety of my own home, I brewed up the better to think and considered what Cook had said over a mug of chamomile tea, an infusion I didn't much like but was said to promote a calm state of mind. I failed to detect an increase in serenity as I drank, but in a time of healing crystals, singing bowls, and Hopi ear candles I wasn't surprised. On the face of it, what she had said was a simple statement of fact, but why did I need to know when she would be at the bookshop? There could only be one reason; I was expected to be there.

Very much on the back foot now, I knew I should go, but before that I should get my facts straight. And the starting point was finding out from MacNeil exactly what had happened, because it didn't look good. I called and texted, then called and texted again, but she ignored my calls. I considered driving out to her flat in Roseburn but decided against. If that was the way she was playing it, and even assuming she was there, she wouldn't let me in. MacNeil had gone to ground, and it didn't much matter where that ground was, the effect was the same wherever it was.

Jim Cook, Anastasija's husband, owned and ran the shop. Popularly known as Cook the Books, he'd nevertheless chosen to call his business Ruby's Ready Reads. When asked why, he replied that his granny had got him reading where his primary school had failed. To honour this lady, now departed the scene, he named it after her. A framed picture of Ruby hung on the wall just inside the front door.

She was knitting. *I couldn't find one of her reading; this is the best I could do.* And everyone thought that was fair enough.

I made my way from the Grassmarket up the West Port past yet another tattoo studio, three cafés and two second-hand bookshops till I reached Cook's establishment. As I opened the door, a simple lever rang a bell to alert Mr Cook, often to be found in the basement, that a customer had arrived. But on this occasion, he wasn't on the premises.

'He's at the bowling club,' his wife explained. 'And before we have any wisecracks, it's not just an old man's sport.'

Jim was ten years older than she was, a fact which was drawn to her attention too often, though the word on the street was that Jim was more taken with the clubhouse bar than rolling woods from one end of the green to the other.

'We're downstairs.'

She led me to the top of the stairs, under a lintel consisting of a board bending under a load of books, and on down threadbare carpet to the basement; three more rooms full of books, a toilet, and a small pantry with a sink, fridge and portable hob on the counter.

'Coffee?'

I was expecting instant, but she filled a percolator and lit the gas under it. Confident I would come, the basket was already loaded with ground beans.

'Red Brick.'

Seeing that meant nothing to me she explained.

'Fifty-three percent Peruvian, forty-seven Brazilian.'

'Right.'

'Scone?'

I'd had a bowl of soup and a ham sandwich for tea, but that had been two hours ago. The prospect of a scone appealed to me.

'Thanks.'

'Help yourself.'

Apart from a plate of fruit scones, she provided a lump

of butter on a saucer (presentation could have been better, DS Cook) and a little white pot of apricot jam. As I was spreading these on the two halves of a scone, I saw her pour milk into an electrical device and switch it on.

'Milk frother. Just love them, don't you?'

I'd never heard of them and thought it best to say so.

'Never mind, Douglas, your day will come.'

No doubt it would, but the question was when.

Sitting at a table in one of her book-lined rooms with coffee and scones, I knew she had all the cards. I'd be in deep trouble if I wasn't straight with her.

'Has she contacted you?'

'No.'

'But you've contacted her.'

'Tried to, several times.'

'We need to discuss this.'

'Off the record?'

'That's why we're here.'

As DS Cook saw it, Hunter Associates was in trouble. As far as she could tell, Wyness had his uses, though who knew what he got up to in that garret of his. I'd just found out one of the things he did in his garret, but I wasn't going to mention Parallel Lives to Anastasia.

'He bets on currency movements.'

'Not much help to your agency, I would have thought. And Alison Eadie. Now I have every reason to believe Ms Eadie is an upstanding citizen. She certainly has excellent credentials when it comes to accounting but, again, how useful is that to a detective agency like yours?'

'Not very, when it comes to handling cases, but Alison deals with our accounts, submits our tax returns and so on. She's brilliant at that. Never misses a trick. I couldn't begin to do it.'

'I believe you.'

She believed me alright; she said it without missing a beat.

'More coffee?'

'I'm fine with this, thanks. Great scone, though. Did you make it yourself?'

This drew a wide smile from her.

'I'm completely lacking in domestic skills, Douglas.'

'You make good coffee.'

'That aside. Ok, cutting to the chase. Maureen MacNeil. You have better reason than most to know why she left the force. Now we have this RTA and she's refusing to answer your calls. More to the point, she's refusing to answer ours, and this could have been a very serious incident.'

'How is Gaines, by the way?'

I realised too late I'd forgotten to ask, shown no concern because stalkers like him merited none.

'Bruised but nothing too serious. Our road traffic people estimate that the van was traveling slowly at the time, no more than ten miles an hour.'

'So it could have been an accident.'

'Yes, but if it was, why is she suddenly off grid? That's hardly the behaviour of an innocent party.'

She was right of course. I had to assume that MacNeil had been warning him off, tailgating him maybe, and got too close. But given the words they'd exchanged the previous day at his house, it was possible that the red mist had taken over. It might have been deliberate.

'What's Robertson's take on all this?'

She smiled wryly. 'Hector, yes, either he's a man who keeps his opinions to himself or he has none start with. I'm edging towards the latter. Anyway, Douglas, you have to ask yourself if you can safely employ Maureen MacNeil.'

At that point the bell jangled; someone was entering the shop.

'Dammit, I forgot to lock the door.'

As she went upstairs and explained to the disappointed customer that, sorry, they were closed, as per the opening hours posted in the front window, I had a wander round the room, wondering, as I took an old copy of Miller's Antiques Guide from a shelf and blew the dust off it, if there were people out there allergic to book dust. There was no one it seemed who wasn't allergic to something these days, from peanuts to life itself.

'Sorry about that,' she said as she came back down. By which time I'd moved on to a glass-paneled bookcase with locked doors.

'First editions.'

'Valuable?'

'Some are. Others are just rare. We have to be careful.'

'Of course.'

Resuming our armchairs, which had also seen better days, she continued where she'd left off.

'You should ask yourself if you can safely employ someone as volatile as MacNeil. We both know it was her.'

'Her reputation precedes her.'

'Yes, and on that subject, to take but one possible scenario, let's say she has to appear in court as a witness for the prosecution. What does the defence lawyer do? Demolishes her credibility by revealing why she had to leave the force. You can't afford to run risks like that.'

Anastasija, as I was thinking of her now, had a point.

'Ok, but wouldn't you agree,' I asked, adopting a suitably Thought for the Day tone, 'that everyone deserves a second chance?'

She looked at me as if I had a screw loose, which I probably had.

'No.'

'You wouldn't.'

'Of course not. Would you have given Hitler a second chance? Stalin? Pol Pot?'

'But these are extreme cases.'

'The human race,' she assured me, 'inhabits the extremes.'

I wondered if her thinking was influenced by the history of her country, Latvia having endured decades of Soviet oppression. Or maybe she was making a point at the philosophical level where I was ill-equipped to follow her. Thinking the occasional thought cannot be compared to philosophy.

'You'll be telling me next she's a reformed character.'

Though I couldn't honestly say that I believed she was trying; hard enough to have kicked the coke habit, not an easy thing to do.

'All very well, but bear in mind, Douglas, that a person can try and fail. A man of your experience must surely know that by now. By the way, I have something for you.' She handed me a print. Attributed to Sir William Allan, it was thought the original had been painted in the period 1806 to 1810 when the artist was living in Ukraine. Entitled "The Hunter by Himself", it showed the gentleman in question, faithful Irish setter by his side, holding a firearm and looking resolutely into the distance.

'I thought it might strike a chord,' she said, 'and grace your wall at the same time.

The gift was not surprising from a woman whose husband's shop contained a selection of prints in boxes, many of interest but none of great value.

'There's a bit of foxing round the edges, but it's otherwise quite good.'

And the lady wasn't done yet.

'Oh, and this.'

"This" turned out to be a CD of Latvian kokle music. Until that night I had never heard of the kokle, an instrument like the box zither, whatever that was. But it was that same sleeve note which really got me going, the music "evoking images of beautiful blonde-haired maidens in traditional folk dress, dreamily strumming the kokle as they sang their songs".

Sounded good to me. The closest I could hope to get to a blonde-haired maiden.

27

THE FOLLOWING MORNING, while waiting for MacNeil to make contact, as she must surely do soon, I started to compose an email to my image-conscious client Dan Drysdale, explaining that tracking down the Edinburgh home of Chester H Burt was proving difficult, stating how much he'd already clocked up by way of a bill, and asking if, in the light of these facts, he wanted us to continue with our efforts. Fortunately, I had great difficulty calculating exactly what he owed us. How many hours had I spent on the case, how many had Wyness? And while I was still wrestling with this problem, which Alison would have solved in five minutes, I noticed that a message from Wyness had come through at three thirty-four in the small hours. Headed "Drysdale", it contained information which at last suggested a way ahead.

A Born Again Convention, complete with psychic Leandra, was taking place here in the city in May. Tickets were available through Eventbrite. The Franchise had never attempted this before, so they'd been cautious in booking a venue – not the International Conference Centre but the South Hall Complex in the grounds of Pollock Halls. The hall would accommodate three hundred, but also attractive were the two hotels in the grounds, right on the doorstep for delegates coming from further afield. Advance publicity indicated that the director of Born Again 3, John Purkiss, would be there, as would the stars, Jason Summerlee and Desirée Donahue. Two unnamed producers were also expected to attend, but from a trawl of Burt's info on IMDbPro, there were indications he might be one of them. Burt was represented by the United Talent Agency, which had an office in London. Wyness would follow this up during daylight hours.

Reading this news, I junked my draft email to Drysdale and composed an altogether more positive one. Tricky though it was, we at Hunter Associates were now making real progress on his case, outlining what that progress was. On the downside, I reported the reaction of my legal advisor, Louise Galbraith, to the effect that suing Burt would be both costly and difficult, since identifying the legal basis for such an action was challenging to say the least. I concluded the email by stating that he had now run up a bill totalling two hundred and fifty-nine pounds, a figure plucked out of the air as having a likely ring to it. Did he wish us to continue?

Having a sense of achievement after firing off this message, I felt I deserved a coffee, but when I made it using my humble filter jug, I noticed that the result couldn't compare with Cook's effort of the evening before. Since my beans were reasonably good, the difference had to be down to the little device she had used, her milk frother. Maybe I should invest in one, and a percolator while I was at it. I'd just started researching these must-have items for the modern man about town when my mobile rang. MacNeil was outside, could I let her in?

She burst through the door as one pursued by baying hounds, headed straight for the kitchen, sat down where I'd been sitting a moment before, closed my laptop for me, very thoughtful, and started drinking my coffee.

'This is ridiculous, Maureen.'

'What is?'

Although she had the nerve to ask, she knew perfectly well. Taking her jacket off and throwing it on the floor, she admitted she was in a spot of trouble. I went to the window and looked out, but there was no sign of her van.

'Didn't bring it. Came by bus. That woman Cook, she'll be keeping an eye on the place.'

That seemed unlikely to me, she had better things to do with her time.

'I heard she had you in for questioning.'

'Where did you hear that?'

'A little bird told me.'

'Aye, right.'

Bit by bit I got it out of her. She'd been tailing Gaines, as I thought, but for no good reason; thanks to her efforts the day before, she already knew where he lived.

'That guy really gets on my tits.'

She meant this figuratively, of course, but being afflicted with a literal cast of mind, an unwelcome image appeared to me unbidden. Though I did my best to dismiss it, it lingered too long for my liking.

'To hear him tell it, he'd every right to follow any woman he wanted to and there was nothing I could do to stop him.'

It was too bad Gaines had said this, because MacNeil took it as a challenge and rose to it big time. There *had* been something she could do to stop him.

'He'll think twice about stalking her now.'

That was probably true, but she'd forgotten the helmet cam.

'You saw the footage, I hear.'

When I described what was on it, she was visibly relieved, but that didn't help me at all.

'Cook knows it was you.'

'But she can't prove it.'

'No.'

'There are plenty of white vans out there.'

'True, but only yours had a motive.'

'It took skill you know, bringing him down without running him over. I had to clip his rear wheel exactly right.'

We sat in silence for a moment then MacNeil asked for another coffee.

'I'm stressed out.'

I made her another then confronted her with the dilemma as I saw it. Cook knew it was her, Hector Robertson knew it was her, I knew it was her. So either she came clean, or she claimed it had nothing to do with her because she knew they couldn't prove it. But that wouldn't look good. Playing fast and loose with the law would antagonise DS Cook and we couldn't risk that without sinking our business.

'OK, I could admit it was me but say it was an accident.'

'Admit you were tailing him two days in a row.'

'To establish a pattern of behaviour.'

I was considering whether she could get away with that when I noticed she was more dishevelled that usual. Her hair, neater of late, was all over the place as if she'd just come in out of a gale, and it didn't look like she'd changed her shirt either.

'Great thing about vans, Douglas, you can sleep in them.'

When I'd last checked, MacNeil wasn't on the FBI most wanted list or any equivalent nearer to home. The fact that she'd slept in her van suggested to me another slight regression to the paranoia which had afflicted her the year before, and that wasn't good.

'You didn't need to do that.'

'Cook was looking for me, and that robot Robertson.'

They'd tried to contact her, that was true, but had been far too busy looking for two missing girls from Kirkliston to be actively searching for Maureen MacNeil, a woman they knew they'd catch up with without breaking sweat.

After some thought, I came to a conclusion. I couldn't compel MacNeil to admit it had been deliberate, she might just get away with her accident explanation, but I couldn't safely keep using her. Unless. . .

'I have a suggestion.'

I ran it past her as diplomatically as I could but, as it turned out, not diplomatically enough.

'An anger management course? Me? You've got to be fucking joking!'

28

As soon as she left, I messaged Cook to tell her that MacNeil had made contact and would be calling in to see her soon. This was acknowledged with a graphic thumbs up and I put the matter on the mental back burner for the time being, though I later learned that when MacNeil reported to Cook as agreed she fed her the accident version, which both of them pretended to believe. But by way of a warning, Cook pointed out that one more "accident" could kill not only the victim but her delivery business too, and she wouldn't want that, would she? Strangely, this hadn't occurred to MacNeil, whose tunnel vision approach had led her to focus only on stalking, a crime against women which made her blood boil and, in this case, boil over.

Cook later told me that she, too, had recommended an anger management course. MacNeil assumed, as she would, that I had put her up to it. Though we hadn't exchanged a word on the subject, she was wary of me for a while on the grounds that I was trying to stitch her up. But she had to tread carefully with Cook. When she offered to enrol on an online course for troubled individuals wishing to better regulate their emotions, Cook would have none of it. *We'd never know if she was following through. She could tell us anything. There has to be someone we can ask for a progress report, or at least the assurance that she's actually showing up. Don't you think?*

I tried not to, but I did. As a man who'd lost his wife then his home, I had to question where thought had got me in the past.

Of more pressing interest to me at that point was the Born Again Convention, due to take place in two weeks' time. Would tickets still be available? As it turned out, they were, so I ordered and paid for two, knowing I could charge them to Drysdale. If he wanted to attend, he was welcome to buy his own. I noted that one-to-one sessions could be booked with psychic Leandra, these taking place in the VIP room. Reading that these cost thirty pounds for a fifteen-minute session, I couldn't help considering a change of career. Assuming our resident psychic fitted in four hopefuls per hour and that she devoted six hours to these sessions, she could rake in a cool seven hundred and twenty pounds over the course of the day. Not bad for a profession with no qualifications and no accrediting body either.

As I was entertaining these wry thoughts, a message came through from Alison asking me to contact her. Where had I been these last two days? But when I did, she asked me to hang up, she would phone me right back. And she did, by video. Not long out of bed and even more untidy than usual, I felt wrong-footed by this move. Alison had got one past me. She, on the other hand, having arrived at an office in an outlying industrial estate, taken her jacket off and hung it on a hook by the door, looked suitably professional in a white blouse with mother of pearl buttons fastened all the way up to the neck. As usual, every hair was in place.

'Well,' she began, in her typically direct way, 'you look as if you've been dragged through a hedge backwards.'

'Why thank you, Alison. Kind of you to say so.'

'Show me round, then.'

She wanted me to walk her through the flat, letting her see how much progress I'm made since moving in.

'Looks a bit bare to me, even your living room. Wait a minute, that print? I haven't seen it before.'

151

'That,' I said, 'is The Hunter by Himself. Sir William Allan.'

Alone on the wall, in solitary splendour, he was as much by himself as I was.

'Never heard of him.'

I feigned astonishment.

'Dear me, Alison, where have you been? Sir William was Limner to the Queen in Scotland!'

'That's as may be,' she said, clearly unimpressed, 'but I have to wonder what impression your present décor will give a visitor.'

I didn't see why; I wasn't expecting visitors.

'These director's chairs of yours, they're all very well but really quite inadequate for a living room where a man in your position might be entertaining guests. We'll have to do better than that.'

I couldn't help noticing the "we" in that last statement. And that was the difference between the Alison Eadies and Maureen MacNeils of this world. MacNeil was quite capable of invading your space and drinking your coffee without so much as a by your leave. Alison would never dream of behaving like that, she was much too correct, but she wasn't above attempting to improve your domestic arrangements. She always had a reason, of course, but the threat remained.

'Douglas, really, I can't emphasis strongly enough that now you're in business for yourself, your home is also your office. You must learn to project a more business-like image.'

This was a point she'd made in the past, even asking me to designate a room in my previous residence as my office for tax purposes.

'Ok, but I haven't had much time to cover an angle like that.'

I had just made a serious mistake and quickly reaped the consequences.

'Really? So what *have* you been doing?'

I explained that our financial position was looking up. Mr Chen had paid on the nail, as I thought he would, and so had Anna van Leeuwen. Still on the search for brownie points from that quarter, maybe even a gold star, though that was probably aiming too high, I reported these facts to Alison Eadie, friend and accountant. And I managed to tell her about MacNeil's "accident" without disclosing that she'd been working for me at the time. It would all come out eventually, but it didn't need to come out now.

'That woman's a menace.'

She probably was, and Alison would usually have taken considerable interest in any dirt I could dig up about MacNeil, but on this occasion she wasn't fully engaged. Something else was on her mind, her ongoing investigation into the accounts of Edwards Interiors.

'I don't know if I told you this, but before being taken over by Ergonomica, the business was owned by Alastair Edwards. His wife worked in the office but that was it. On the payroll but not a director or anything like that.'

'A wage slave.'

Alison laughed, a rare occurrence.

'I doubt that very much. She probably amounted to little more than a cosmetic expense against tax. Anyway, Edwards was in total control of the business, so he was behind any false accounting there has been. As for his wife, she might have been aware of it, but maybe not. As I can testify from personal experience, wives are often kept in the dark.'

She was referring to her late husband's dubious activities over the years, which only his death had brought to light. And I couldn't help noticing as she developed this subject, that she was showing signs of agitation. Normally a picture of repose, she was now moving within the confines of my screen, almost like a graphic Alison colliding gently with the sides of the picture area. I knew this effect might not have been so evident on my laptop, but on the small screen of my mobile phone it was striking.

'Is something worrying you, Alison?'

She was sure that someone had been in the Edwards Interiors office and rifled through her papers. She also suspected that the same person had tried to access the office computers and failed because she'd changed the passwords.

'There was no sign of forced entry so whoever it was had a key.'

'Alastair Edwards?'

'Or someone acting on his behalf. Anyway, I can't have that, it really won't do.'

'You should have the locks changed. Where is this office?'

'Hillington Park, where I'm speaking from now.'

She swung her phone round the office; two desks, computers, filing cabinets and a large year planner on the wall. Not a potted plant to be seen. It had a distinctly Portacabin look to it.

'It's nothing to write home about as you can see. When the takeover's complete, it won't be needed any more. The lease runs out in two months anyway.'

'Good. Sounds like the less time you spend there the better.'

'Douglas?'

'Yes?'

'Do you miss me?'

I hadn't seen this one coming and was slightly slow to respond. After all, since we'd shared a bed several times in the recent past, the answer should have been obvious.

'Of course.'

Which was true. Of all of us, she was by far the most stable, if slightly conventional with it. She was, as Cook had realised in no time flat, an upright citizen. And that was good as far as it went, though I now realised it might have gone just a bit further.

'You don't sound very sure.'

'I am.'

'OK, so what I was wondering; could you come through at the weekend? I'm out on a limb here, I would welcome your support.'

29

MARKETING STRAPLINES ARE usually absurd, but one of the few I like is COACHING BEATS TRAINING. My ex-wife Susan was, and doubtless still is, into physical training, only to be expected in a professional ski instructor. Though she gave up encouraging me to ski after I told her it was downhill all the way, she was right in thinking my fitness level could be improved. But however you go about it, training involves working up sweat with a consequent increase in laundry bills and outlay on deodorants. And even though Leroy Gaines left a lot to be desired, he was surely correct in thinking that anti-perspirants are not a good idea. We sweat for a reason. But not if we stand on the side-lines with a stopwatch encouraging others to pump the iron, spend another ten minutes on a treadmill, execute a further fifty bench presses or whatever. Coaching is altogether more relaxing.

And so I sank into my seat on a coach from Edinburgh to Glasgow, to be met at Buchanan Street Bus Station by the lady herself, Alison Eadie. And I could tell she was pleased to see me. She smiled, only to be expected, but the hug was something else. There was an element of clinging on for dear life about it, a search for reassurance. But for her hairstyle, not to be tampered with, I would have given her a comforting pat on the head. Wondering where else I could safely pat her, I settled on the left shoulder. We were in a public place, after all, and even an elder of the kirk could not have taken exception to that.

A great one for taking control, Alison led me on a short walk to Cineworld, not far away.

'What's on?'

'Don't be ridiculous, Douglas.'

We were heading for a branch of Starbucks, also within the building, to take on food and drink and talk through the issues of the day. Which really meant exploring her concerns. Feeling the need for something more substantial than tea or coffee, she ordered hot chocolate and a triple chocolate muffin.

'The thing is,' she said, guiding me to a table near a window to ensure there wasn't a tail on the street outside, 'I feel really uneasy about this. I mean, I'm out there in a small office in a huge industrial estate, all on my own. I wouldn't mind that so much, but something's definitely going on. I might be in danger. Who knows what this Alastair Edwards might do to prevent his jiggery-pokery coming out.'

'We're assuming he was the one searching through your papers.'

'We are.'

'You've asked for the locks to be changed.'

'I have, but it hasn't happened yet.'

Her concern was justified. Most people involved in fraud didn't engage in violence, the preferred approach being to destroy as much of the evidence as possible so that much could be suspected yet nothing proved. But on occasion, when someone had stood in the way of destroying the evidence, or worse, was actively engaged in bringing it to light, that someone had come to a sticky end, and she was mindful of that.

'I mean, just think of Roberto Calvi.'

The name rang a bell but I couldn't place it.

'For heaven's sake, Douglas, the Banco Ambrosiano business. You must remember, surely.'

Realising her command of this subject greatly exceeded

mine, she filled me in on the trial of Calvi for money laundering and other crimes, and I had to admit the sum involved – twenty-seven million dollars – was large.

'But we're not talking about sums like that here.'

'Oh no, nothing like. But are we remembering what happened to the man?'

Since we were not, Alison, with a sad shake of the head, reminded me that in nineteen eighty-two he'd been found hanging under Blackfriars's Bridge with bricks in his pockets.

'And not to put too fine a point on it, Douglas, it's hard to see how he could have accomplished that by himself.'

As Alison explained all this, I did remember hearing about it at the time, but it had since slipped from my mind. I had to agree with her though, there was reason to believe that Calvi had been strung up.

'I assume there's no Vatican involvement in this case.'

'Of course not.'

Two young men in sharp business suits sat down at the table nearest us and Alison sized them up out the corner of her eye. Were they concealing bricks in their briefcases? Probably not, but for all she knew her movements were being closely observed by two of Edwards' hired hands posing as filmgoers. In recognition of their proximity, she lowered her voice.

'And let's not forget Graziella Corrocher.'

But you couldn't forget what you hadn't known in the first place.

'Graziella Corrocher?'

'Calvi's private secretary. She jumped to her death from the fifth floor of the bank's headquarters in Milan. Or so we are led to believe.'

'You don't.'

'Of course not. She knew too much. She was pushed.'

I'd allowed my coffee to cool somewhat and took a couple of mouthfuls while it was at least lukewarm and

Alison was still talking.

'In situations like these, it's often the woman who takes the fall.'

As Miss Carrocher had in more ways than one.

'And in this case, you're that woman.'

'Well done, Douglas. I do believe we're singing from the same hymn sheet at last.'

I could see that where very large sums were involved such a fate might befall a person, but how much was at stake here? Alison estimated a ballpark figure of some two hundred and sixty thousand pounds and rising, though she still had some work to do establishing a final figure. And I couldn't deny that people had been bumped off for less. So what did she want to do?

'Well I'm not giving up, if that's what you think. No one should get off with this sort of thing. I just wish I felt safer, that's all.'

'I could come out to this office with you.'

'What, every time I go? I don't think that would work. No, I'll just have to wrap this up as quickly as I can and never set foot in the place again.'

Well, it was an idea, if not a very good one. And I had another.

'This venue has sixteen screens, guess what's showing on one of them.'

But even in the interest of research, nothing could persuade her to take in Born Again 3, which left us with a decision; what to do with the rest of the day. I pointed to my bag, which I couldn't deny had seen better days, though black insulating tape was holding it together quite well.

'Dear me,' she said, giving it a narrow look. 'You should consider a knapsack. Much better. Leaves both hands free.'

'What for? Playing the piano?'

'I didn't know you could.'

'I can't.'

I unzipped the bag and took out two items, still boxed: a webcam and a motion sensor alarm.

'I brought through a couple of things for you, Alison.'

Methodical as always, she studied the wording on one then the other.

'Where did you get these?'

'Maplin.'

'They come recommended?'

'Yes.'

'And you're capable of installing them?'

According to Wyness, they were both idiot-proof, so the likelihood was I'd hit a snag or two. But if so, I could always contact him for advice.

'It's good to know you're thinking of me, Douglas. I appreciate that. But I really don't feel like driving out to Hillington right now so you can set them up. I was looking forward to an hour or two relaxing with one of the few friends I have left.'

I could understand that. She had grown increasingly tense as one day followed another in her hotel room of an evening and the office in a business park by day, neither conducive to relaxation. And now there was the added worry of someone invading her space and going through her notes. But since she wouldn't be able to deal with this technology herself and I was here now, the logic was inescapable. I made a weak attempt to sugar the pill.

'If someone had done the same for Graziella, who knows, she might still be with us today.'

So we went to Edwards Interiors, I set up the web cam and the alarm, which took me longer than someone more tech savvy, Wyness for example, and having nowhere better to go we ended up back in her hotel.

'Have I time for a shower before we eat, I need to freshen up?'

She had time for two.

30

HAVING DONE MY duty by God and the Queen on Saturday, Sunday found me alone with my thoughts in the flat. At first these centred on Alison, partly because she might be at risk, but also because of her deft handling of what had been, in the recent past, Alison and Douglas. When she suggested the thing to do for an evening meal was follow the line of least resistance and eat at her hotel, she knew at once what my suspicion would be and allayed it in her usual, business-like manner.

'Don't worry, Douglas, I don't have designs on your body.'

After that it went well, even down to her pan-fried fillet of sea bass garnished with asparagus spears and herb crushed potatoes. I went so far as to share a bottle of Pino Grigio with her, and it wasn't too bad.

'I realise you're breaking the habit of a lifetime in joining me with this,' she said, raising her glass. 'Here's to success.'

I wasn't surprised when she moved the conversation on to my future, a subject she'd artfully introduced in her liquid wish for success.

'I sometimes wonder if you know how much you'd have to salt away each month if you hope to subsist on anything more than potatoes and gravy when the time comes?'

'The time comes?'

'To cash in your chips, to leave the field, to retire.'

The last time she'd brought this up I'd mentioned the sum I had coming in – half the value of the house I used to share with my wife – as if it represented a permanent solution, a financial get-out-of-jail card. She'd demolished my argument with figures illustrating the erosive effect of inflation. And they hadn't come out of nowhere, these figures, she'd prepared them just for me.

'So, this famous money of yours, what are you going to do with it?'

How many people were going to confront me with this before I came to a decision?

'My financial advisor asked me that.'

'Good for her, but what did she propose?'

'Not to put all my eggs in one basket.'

'And that was it?'

'Yes.'

'Wonderful!'

Realising that Alison would continue to harp on this string till I did something about it or it broke, I made a suggestion.

'I could always ask Anna van Leeuwen.'

Her jaw dropped. If she'd had false teeth they'd have fallen out.

'Anna van who?'

'The woman who works at the bank, the one who's being stalked.'

She could hardly believe her ears; as if a wealth manager would be interested in a hundred thousand pounds from a client with minimal income who might have to draw on some or all of it at a moment's notice. And why would I turn to a stranger anyway when she, Alison Eadie, chartered accountant of this parish, was frequently asked for investment advice by those few of her clients making enough to need it? Then a possible explanation occurred to her.

'Is she blonde, this van Leeuwen woman?'

'No. Why do you ask?'

'But she's attractive.'

'I would say so, yes. Very trim. Petite. Wyness was close to salivating when he saw her.'

'Was he indeed. Why am I not surprised!'

Though finding the lines can be difficult, we must learn to read what we can between them. In Alison's case it was easy: they furrowed her brow, otherwise smooth, when something bothered her. As it did then. Her problem was me and she'd hinted as much before. As far as she could tell my ambition for our relationship had been as limited as it was for our business. We'd only stayed together as long as we had because I was too indolent to stray further afield. A dating app would be the last thing she'd expect to find on my phone. So why this twinge of jealousy? What woman in her right mind would be jealous of a man like me? The conclusion was sad but obvious. She had yet to find someone better.

'We're not going anywhere, are we.'

It was a statement, not a question. She already knew the answer.

'I wouldn't say that. Word gets round. Clients keep knocking on the door.'

Sensing one of the characteristic evasions I trotted out to avoid confrontation, she fixed me with an icy stare.

'You know perfectly well what I mean. I think in future we should confine our relationship to business, though I hope and believe we'll always be good friends. Let's face it, Douglas, we hardly set it on fire between the sheets.'

I silently agreed with her stark assessment by not taking issue with it and moved the conversation on to her safety at the industrial estate. Was there on-site security? No? Too bad, but never mind. One thing people who break and enter can't stand is having attention drawn to them when they're on the job. Hearing an alarm go off, they make their escape as quickly as they can. That was my hope, and I said as much to Alison by way of reassurance. But by that time,

I couldn't tell if it was the burglar alarm or the wine which was making her more relaxed.

Rehearsing these memories in my living room that Sunday, still with only its two directors' chairs, I noticed the CD Cook had given me lying on the windowsill, and for the first time it occurred to me that I'd no way to play it. I had a laptop, but it lacked a DVD drive. Not having a TV, I had no DVD player either. My car had a cassette player so I couldn't turn to that. At a loss, I contacted Wyness, who was his usual accommodating self.

'What is it this time?'

If I brought the CD to his place, he'd rip it for me provided I came with beers and pastries. I'd soon be able to hear the complete shebang on my phone. He liked to think I'd have a reasonably well specified one of those. On my way down to Leith Street, I popped into Tesco for two bottles of beer and cinnamon whirls, neither of which would benefit a sedentary individual like Wyness. But his philosophy was to give people what they want even if it kills them; they were going to die anyway. Already overweight he was sure to be unfit, though I'd no way of assessing that. A cartoon image entered my mind; Wyness' stomach entering the room closely followed by Wyness.

Sitting in what he liked to call his Command HQ with three large screens, computers, webcams and who knew what else, I looked round the room for any sign of Parallel Lives, the side-hustle I wasn't supposed to know about. From what I could discern through the fog of cigarette smoke, there was nothing incriminating to be seen. I was sure he wouldn't mention it, and I was right. But he did mention other things.

'This phone of yours, the camera's good but it doesn't have a headphone socket. I assume you knew that. It does have Bluetooth, though, so get yourself Bluetooth cans and you're off.'

'Cans?'

'Headphones, Douglas. Headphones! Those things you put on your ears.'

By this time, I felt the need to fight back.

'I have a radio, you know.'

But he couldn't resist it. 'Steam?'

In fact, it was digital, but there was no point telling him that; since all his technology was digital, he wouldn't be impressed. Opening a bottle of Peroni and demolishing the first of two cinnamon buns he knocked off in quick succession, he gave me the benefit of his insight into what was left of my character.

'You're not exactly at the cutting edge, Douglas. If you're not careful, life as we know it now will pass you by.'

Wyness assumed, which I did not, that this would be a bad thing.

31

Monday. The start of a new day, a new week. But the start of a new life? Unlikely. Not having a nine-to-five job anymore, I found that my work had become a series of peaks and troughs.

The weekend visit to Alison had been a modest peak with plenty to keep me busy, from installing security to redefining our relationship without recrimination, a task made easier by the lady herself. But now I was at a loose end till the Born Again Convention, or was until the bell rang. My unexpected visitor introduced himself.

'Good morning, Mr Hunter. Albert Reynolds, Cartwright and Considine.'

He worked for a firm of criminal defence lawyers not much liked by the broader profession.

'I'm afraid so, yes, I'm a precognition officer to trade.'

I couldn't help noticing as he spoke, that his teeth were unusually white. Estimating his age at the late fifties, early sixties, either he'd had work done in Istanbul or Budapest, or he was sporting unduly white dentures. I felt sure I'd seen him before but couldn't place where till he confirmed my suspicion. He was a retired police officer.

'Out to grass now, you might say.'

And so you might if, as he was, you were paid to eat it. I asked what his visit was about, though I knew perfectly well.

'We're acting for a Mr Charles Plumstead Vellacott, no fixed abode, who is facing serious charges in relation to an incident at the Body Art Tattoo Studio on the High Street on, let me see now,' he took out a notebook and started leafing through it, 'on Monday the sixth of April this year. I understand you were present at the scene.'

I confirmed that I was, now knowing exactly what to expect.

'Good. So all I'm asking you to provide is your account of what occurred. That's to say, what you saw and what you heard, details you may be called upon to confirm in court.'

I told Mr Reynolds that I'd be happy to do that but would first like to know how Vellacott intended to plead. With any luck he'd plead guilty and I wouldn't be called as a witness.

'He's intimated to us that he proposes to plead not guilty, though he may well have second thoughts as the trial date approaches.'

Mr Reynolds was a tidy enough man in his dark three-piece suit, but surely he was wasting his own time and mine. Three people had seen Vellacott launch his attack, one of whom, Brian Doyle, had ended up in hospital as a result.

'You may well be right there, Mr Hunter, but if this case goes to trial it would be helpful to establish your recollection of what took place before the memory fades. Hence my presence here at such an early stage. Oh, and you should know that what you tell me here, what I write down in my notebook, will not be admissible as evidence.'

If that were the case, and he was correct in law, what was the point in writing it down at all?

'Yes, I'm often asked that, but the legal luminaries at Cartwright and Considine assure me that having witness accounts ahead of the day greatly assists them in preparing their defence. Now I know what you're going to say, Mr Hunter: the last thing you want to do is render assistance to an undesirable character like Vellacott. But in this case, it may be that when faced with the evidence against him in what we might describe as bald terms, he will think twice about pleading not guilty and save us all time and money.'

Since this was an outcome devoutly to be desired, I described what I'd seen and heard in as graphic detail as the facts allowed and Mr Reynolds wrote it down. Closing his notebook, he thanked me and said that he was now going on to interview Miss Linda Hennessy, or would do if he knew where to find her.

'A hard person to track down, this girl.'

That was hardly surprising. Vellacott had gone to Body Art with the express intention of cracking her skull. If it was easy for Reynolds to find her, it would be easy for Vellacott too, which had to be the last thing she wanted.

'Right enough, when you put it that way.'

'If I give you a steer as to where she might be, it's on the strict understanding that the information doesn't reach Vellacott.'

'That goes without saying, Mr Hunter.'

As it would have done if I hadn't said it. There are times when you can't be too careful.

'So don't write this down but you might try Pins and Needles. West Nicolson Street.'

'Another tattoo studio, I take it.'

He took it right and thanked me as he left.

After the strain of talking with someone I'd never met before, it was a toss-up between going out for coffee or making one myself. Opting for the latter, I'd just made it and settled down at the kitchen table to study THE BEST BLUETOOTH HEADPHONES 2015 when the entry phone rang again. As requested, RG Plumbing were paying me a visit. How had I forgotten that?

I showed young Callum into the bathroom and he sized it up at once.

'Not a lot of room here. Not enough for a separate shower and bath.'

That was so true I'd already figured it out.

'What we could do, though, is replace your hot and cold taps with a bath/shower mixer unit.'

It would sit where the current taps were. All he would need to add was a vertical wall bracket for the shower head, allowing the user, me, to adjust for height.

'I could do you one for seventy quid.'

'But?'

'It wouldn't perform so well when the water pressure was low.'

'So what would you suggest?'

'We recommend an excellent unit which still works well at low pressure and,' he added, clearly impressed himself, 'comes with a five-year guarantee. It's a hundred and sixty, though. It's up to you, obviously.'

I put the toilet seat down, sat on it, and looked round my little bathroom. I didn't like baths. For one thing, I sometimes fell asleep in them and woke up in lukewarm water with fingers like prunes. And for another, I'd never relished the feeling that stretched out in the bath I was lying in a suspension of my own epithelials. How hygienic was that? In my opinion, not very.

'It would make washing your hair a lot easier,' Callum pointed out.

And he should know, he was a plumber. But he was right, especially when it came to rinsing out. And there it was, my current shampoo, sitting at the back of the sink, boldly claiming to impart the fragrance of sun-kissed raspberries, more than could be said of me even after I'd used it.

'Where's your stop cock, Mr Hunter?'

The question threw me, I hadn't the faintest idea.

'Probably under the sink. Let's take a look.'

And there it was, though it came as news to me.

'If I could just ask, are you the owner here?'

'No. Why do you ask?'

'Well, this isn't like a chest of drawers you could take

169

when you leave. You'd be spending your own money to improve someone else's property.'

But that was the way of it when you rented. It couldn't be helped.

'And unless you want to flood the floor, you'll need a partition at the shower end. We could do you a nice one, white with a blue porpoise pattern. Actually,' he added as a parting afterthought, 'it would match your ceramic chain handle quite well. They turn out fake ones now but yours is the genuine article.'

He left, promising a quote by email before the day was done, and I returned to my research; headphones, milk-frothers and percolators, three must-haves of modern life, but my research was interrupted by a video call from Alison.

'You'll never guess where I am.'

I could see she was in a warehouse somewhere. They all looked the same to me but I played along.

'In a warehouse.'

'Yes, Douglas, but where?

'Crianlarich?'

A wayward guess, just what she wanted to hear.

'No young man, I'm in Clerkenwell.'

I'd heard of Clerkenwell, it was in London somewhere, but that was the extent of my knowledge. I asked her why she was there.

'Edwards Interiors, they have warehouses here, and until recently a showroom as well.'

'Did you have to go there in person? Wasn't there someone local?'

'I felt I had to, yes. I'm no longer sure who's involved in what.'

I was pleased to see that she wasn't alone. Lukasz, a forklift driver, was with her to check out the higher shelves.

'You may remember I told you I'd uncovered some forward invoicing, well hold onto your hat here, Douglas, but this is something else.'

Inventory lists showed the warehouse held a considerable stock, and when Alison and Lucasz went there to check they found boxes and crates to match alright, some of them piled high on metal shelving. They were only part of the way through their check so far, but it looked like most of the boxes were empty.

'I was astonished.'

'I can imagine.'

It was a question of value. Had the boxes contained what they were supposed to, their value would be considerable, but it looked as though Ergonomica had shelled out a lot of money for artfully packaged air. She swung her mobile round the shelves to give me some idea of the number of boxes involved.

'And there are two other warehouses.'

I could tell from her tone that Alison was excited, an investigator in her own right tracking down wrongdoing or, as she sometimes said for added gravitas, fiscal malfeasance. But there was also a sense of outrage. Although she was five years older than I was she still felt outraged by events. Very endearing, really. I, on the other hand, though younger, could no long rise to outrage. I had to think that I'd become too world-weary for that. Human nature being what it was, bad things happened; it was only to be expected.

'Where are you staying?'

'The Premier Inn Hub. It's in Clerkenwell too. Very handy. I'll have more to tell later in the week.'

Interesting as this was, it shot out of the water my cunning plan to invite her through for the convention. Even if he agreed to come, Wyness would be unlikely to arrive before noon, so I was left with MacNeil for the second ticket, the one I'd bought with Alison in mind. It's often said that you can't win them all, but it would be nice to win some.

32

THE DAYS TILL the convention passed slowly. For no reason I could justify, I was looking forward to it as though it was a major event in my calendar, which probably showed that, as Wyness put it, I should get a life, though he was a fine one to talk. I helped MacNeil with a delivery or two, one to Abernyte taking the best part of a day. Moving vintage chiffoniers and Georgian bow front sideboards proved to be a challenge, but by way of a thank you MacNeil, observing that I could do with more muscle, stood me a cauliflower soup in the Café Circa.

When I arrived at the grounds of Pollock Halls on the big day, the day when it was all going to happen, I passed groups of students on their way out from their various halls of residence, and Born Again hopefuls making their way in. A small group of devotees had already arrived and were waiting outside the doors, due to open at nine. I was soon joined by MacNeil, whose restless nature meant that she was either on time or early, and in that sense at least totally reliable.

'Can't wait,' she said, which was not what she meant. 'I've seen one of these films. Absolute crap. And,' she added in disbelief, 'they're actually developing a Born Again video game! It's at the beta test stage. Who in their right mind would waste money on that?'

I had no idea. But people had bought tickets for the convention so there would be some. And when the doors opened, in they poured, looking anxiously from left to right to see where the action was. It was immediately clear from the signage that Kirkland Hall would be dedicated to the refreshment of those attending and the action would take place in the South Hall itself. Flashing our e-tickets to the greeters, we were about to go in when I overheard MacNeil asking a young man behind the table where the VIP room was. I wondered why she wanted to know.

'I've booked a session with Lady Leandra. Quarter to eleven.'

'You've what!'

'You heard. Call it research.'

I knew what I'd like to call it but kept that to myself until I could establish what she was up to. She'd told me she was down on her uppers, or up on her downers, but really, someone strapped for cash giving thirty pounds to a psychic, however beguiling her name, didn't seem a good to move to me. She caught this vibe off me immediately and changed the subject.

'Chester H Burt, do we know what he looks like?'

We did. He'd appeared in a photograph taken at a red-carpet event in Los Angeles, and there he was, making up to our very own producer of motion pictures, Charlotte Wells. He was of average height, neatly turned out, and sported a beard and a moustache, both dark brown and neatly trimmed. His shoes shone so much in the powerful lights set up for the occasion he called to mind a professional ballroom dancer.

'Send that to me,' Maureen said, a little testily, I thought, 'I can't be looking at your phone all the time.'

First impressions of the event were that the average age of the conventioneers was much lower than would have been the case at a similar Star Trek gathering. The Born Again series had only been going since 2008. Star Trek had been spinning off sequels, prequels and animations like a spiral galaxy since 1937, or so it seemed to me. And then there was the merchandise, where Star Trek had the edge big time, a wide range of outfits being available from the original Star Trek, through the Next Generation, Voyager and Picard. Not forgetting inflatable Seven of Nines and that staple item, sets of Mr Spock's ears designed to peek through even the thickest hair. Born Again couldn't hope to compete with that.

I hadn't seen any of the three films so far, but learned that when a character was born again, he or she sported impressive amber eyes, copies of which were available as soft contact lenses – with the caveat that they were not prescription. For those whose vision left something to be desired and wouldn't see a thing if they popped them in, drops were available, though colouring the entire cornea rather than the iris alone, fans hadn't taken to them much.

Nonetheless, looking round the large South Hall, there were many tables selling Born Again T-shirts, Born Again DVDs, and Born Again books, both conventional novels and graphic versions for the visually literate. And members of the growing throng were queuing up to buy them in the sure and certain knowledge that our two stars, Jason Summerville and Desirée Donahue, would be present in person from eleven o'clock to sign them. At which point the resale value on eBay was expected to increase, though few of those attending would want to sell such treasured items. MacNeil, who'd been reading up on the subject, informed me that Desirée Donahue was known to her male admirers as Double D, and not just because of her name.

As the number of delegates increased, the noise they made reflected more and more from the hard walls of the interior and the equally hard glass of the windows. As if this wasn't enough, scenes from all three films were showing on large wall-mounted screens, their soundtracks adding to the noise. I couldn't help noticing that the excerpts chosen often featured a scantily clad Ms Donahue, whose image had already spread far and wide on social media and to which many young girls aspired.

In their efforts to look exactly like this model of the body beautiful, and I had to admit she was far from ugly, they were assisted by an extensive range of Double D lipsticks, glosses and other cosmetic products, none of them the result of animal testing. This was a good thing, of course, and tailored to the belief of many devotees that rats and rabbits, cats and dogs were born again too. And after all, what did I know? I lacked the theology to argue with this view and, unhelpfully in this case, scripture was silent on the point. Surely Habakkuk or Nehemiah could have spared a moment or two giving us their thoughts on the subject.

MacNeil may have said something to me, I saw her lips move, but had no idea what it was. She took me by the arm, led me outside, and had just asked me about following Burt as he left the event, when the noise ratcheted up a notch.

Cordoned off by members of the management team, a young man with a megaphone was shouting towards the hall, the event, and its organisers. Though we couldn't know this at the time, he was a fan of a Hungarian film of the same name who felt that the Born Again franchise was not only scraping the barrel of invention but eating into any box office success his film might have. MacNeil and I looked on in amazement. However Hungarian the production may have been, the amplified insults were audibly in English.

'You couldn't make this up.'

I had just agreed with her when DS Cook and DC Robertson arrived. Since detectives wouldn't be there for a minor public order offence, it had to be something else. I saw Cook spot me and direct Robertson in my direction. He sidled up and spoke into my left ear.

'Keep your hands in your pockets, Hunter. Pickpockets. Professionals.'

They'd arrived by train that morning from Birmingham

and been spotted on CCTV at Waverley Station.

'Easy pickings with this lot,' he added, indicating the assembled delegates, before moving on into the hall. 'Airheads all.'

So the enigmatic Robertson entertained opinions after all. But as the hour of the stars' arrival neared, Cook and Robertson disappeared into the hall, as did MacNeil, anxious to keep her appointment with Lady Leandra, for which she'd already parted with thirty non-refundable pounds she couldn't afford. For my part, I was keeping an eye out not only for Chester H Burt but Daniel Drysdale as well. I'd alerted him to the event, so where was he? Had he been too tight-fisted to stump up the money for a ticket? That didn't seem likely in someone who was contemplating the heavy legal fees associated with litigation.

Suddenly, as if at a pre-arranged signal, a crowd of conventioneers ran from the entrance hall up the footpath to the nearest car park, where the stars and their minders had arrived in a small fleet of limousines. Too bad the limos couldn't make it right up to the main entrance, but it at least it wasn't raining. And the pair emerged, Double D deftly displaying a length of leg as she left the vehicle, and slowly made their progress into the building, smiling and waving to the excited throng. Both had inserted their amber contacts in advance, and both looked the part, especially the lady, who had one of the most bountiful heads of hair I'd ever seen. Several press photographers took as many shots as they could from as many angles, something they wouldn't be allowed to do in the hall, where official photographs were already on sale. Yes, this was an event, no doubt about it.

And who should be bringing up the rear but Chester H Burt, dapper as ever, together with a colleague I took to be the director, John Purkiss. The crowd were less interested in them than the stars, but they counted too, and those few more interested in process than personality, stopped to talk to them. The thrust of their questions concerned a possible Born Again 4. Was this film really in the pipeline, as rumoured in the trade press and, if so, would some or all of it be shot here in the city? Both Burt and Purkiss used quite a few words to answer these queries but left their questioners none the wiser. Perhaps they would be born again as politicians. Stranger things had happened.

I followed the official party into the hall and observed the stars, each at a separate table, signing T-shirts, baseball caps, DVDs, photographs and books. Despite the efforts of the minders, large groups of delegates were eager for selfies and the actors obliged. Plainly star material, both were remarkably good at producing winning smiles with total strangers. At this point the house lights were dimmed, prelude to a moving head disco light display, reds, greens, and blues flashing all over the hall, which may have energised some but made surveillance even more difficult than it had been.

In due course, MacNeil emerged from her consultation with Lady Leandra and tracked me down in the hall. I was standing at the back, the better to eyeball the crowd.

'Any sign of him yet?'

But Drysdale was nowhere to be seen.

'Odd.'

It was. Very. 'So how did it go with your psychic?'

'Tell you later.' Then she noticed DS Cook. 'We could do without her.'

'She's not so bad.'

'Glad you think so.'

I pointed to Double D. 'Check the hair on that.'

MacNeil gave me a look of utter disbelief verging on contempt.

'For God's sake, Douglas, you don't actually think it's all hers!'

It was obvious to everyone except me that Ms Donahue used woven extensions to bulk out her flowing locks, adding length and volume to whatever was there to start with. Then another change of tack.

'I'm getting a bit peckish.'

We fought our way through the crowd to Kirkland Hall, where she tanked up on a Born Again Burger and guacamole dip and I settled for a modest mixed berry platter. MacNeil couldn't resist poking fun at the continued influence of my all-too-healthy ex-wife.

'Fine, but you haven't a clue what's in that burger.'

Neither she had, but she didn't care. Life was too short.

'Even shorter if you eat junk like that.'

Not according to Lady Leandra, who'd predicted that MacNeil would live a long life.

'Great, Maureen, but will it be a happy one?'

We went back to the main hall and not a moment too soon. While the stars were obliged to remain, Chester H Burt was not. He was already making his way towards the exit.

'Where's your car?'

'Commie car park.'

The Commonwealth Pool was quite near but MacNeil, anticipating the need to get on Burt's tail quickly, had parked her van on a double yellow line not a hundred yards from the hall.

Keeping up with Burt proved easier than it might have been, his progress impeded by a group of evangelicals outside the hall with placards and whistles keen to assert their ownership of born again as a concept. They had come prepared with leaflets explaining the significance of the phrase as recounted in the Gospel of John and offered them to all who might want to know. I took a copy, folded it and slipped it in my back pocket, an offering MacNeil refused with a brusque gesture of the arm. But Burt made it through without incident and headed for a Beamer with a woman at the wheel ready to whisk him away to who knew where. But that was exactly what we needed to know.

'With me,' MacNeil said, as if she were still a detective sergeant with me as her sidekick.

And for the time being, that was exactly what I was.

33

IN THE TIME it took me to reach my car, Burt and his companion would have gone, so like it or not I was a passenger in MacNeil's van. She didn't rate my car anyway.

'You can always collect it later, what's left of it.'

MacNeil was an excellent driver. She'd kept it to herself, but I knew she'd passed the police Advanced Driving Course at Tulliallan, so except when she decided to take out a cyclist like Gaines, I was in safer hands than mine. But if I was expecting an exciting chase across half the city, I was disappointed. Burt's vehicle turned right onto Dalkeith Road, continued down to St Leaonard's, then slowed along much narrower streets till it reached the comparative backwater of Haddon's Court.

MacNeil followed it and stopped opposite the houses just in time to see Burt and his friend park and enter the communal garden to the front of number four. Neither of us saw him ring a bell because he had a key to the main door. So now we knew he was living in one of these apartments, but which one? Fortunately for us, there were no dwellings on the opposite side of the street, just goods entrances to shops which fronted on the main road beyond. So unless moved on by a warden, we could wait in the van and look out for any action we might see. If we were lucky, Burt might appear at a window and give away his exact location.

Waiting in vans can have its longeurs, but waiting in one with MacNeil was something else again. Reaching over me as if wasn't there and wouldn't care if I was, she opened the glove compartment, produced a bag of soor plooms and offered me one. I wasn't into sweets at the best of times and eyed them suspiciously.

'An alternative to coke?'

'Suit yourself,' she said, putting them back where they came from before I had a chance to take one.

'You'll find I've moved on, Douglas.'

So saying, she produced a pack of Orange County Disposable CBD vapes, put one in her lipstick-free mouth, breathed in and exhaled.

'I know what you're thinking, just keep it to yourself.'

Evidently Lady Leandra's psychic powers had rubbed off on her. She knew I was thinking that when they died, these five disposable vapes of hers would end up in landfill or the ocean. Multiply that by all the five-packs used by millions of vapers and we had a problem.

'You're thinking I'm moving on from cigarettes, and you're right.'

I had noticed, though, that as her head passed close to my mine when she reached for the glove compartment, MacNeil smelled fresh and healthy, something I couldn't have said a few months before. And the odour wasn't out of a bottle, it was natural. If my nose was any guide, she was turning her life around in one area at least. But as The Wanderer put it in his poem, keeping your thoughts to yourself is a smart move, especially if you want to live longer. Unfortunately, I didn't want to breathe in the clouds of vapour she was exhaling.

'Mind if I open the window?'

'Be my guest.'

It occurred to us after half an hour. Wyness had failed to trace Burt before, but at that time he'd been searching the whole city. Now we knew it had to be one of four flats and could give him a street name and number.

'Try him again, might get him out of bed.'

Since it was already early afternoon, Wyness was up and agreed to try one last time with our new information. And it took him ten minutes at most. Burt lived in flat one. He'd paid £125,000 for it in 2007. He was somewhat coy about how he knew all of this but apart from checking house sales on ZOOPLA, admitted that one of his contacts worked as a canvasser for a political party – he wouldn't say which one, but other parties were available. Canvassers like his friend, using the electoral roll, went door to door amending entries to show, for example, that Mr A was a supporter, Mrs B was hostile, and Miss C subscribed to the widely held view that how she voted was between herself and the ballot box. So Wyness was not only able to pinpoint which flat Burt lived in, but also to report his claim to be a member of the Worker's Revolutionary Party.

'That would be a wind-up, of course.'

I was sure he was right; canvassers are natural targets for leg-pulls like this.

Moving off the single yellow line and on to a legal parking place, MacNeil and I went through the pend to the nearest café, which was unusual on two counts; it had shortbread worthy of the name, and it had no wi-fi. The management didn't say why, but everyone knew it was to discourage students buying a coffee and stretching it out for three hours as they worked on their dissertation on the role of the differential and integral calculus in society at large, or some such topic well beyond the understanding of the average bear.

For the greater privacy it offered, we settled into one of the booths towards the back, MacNeil with a cappuccino, insisting on double shot, and me with a flat white. I talked her into joining me with a shortbread, which turned out well. She liked it.

'Right, so now we have the information Drysdale wanted. You can bill him and pay me.'

'You haven't submitted an invoice.'

'For God's sake, Douglas, you're turning into Alison Eadie.'

I'd said it in jest, of course. I was paying her off the books, from my own money.

'I had another letter yesterday. I'm seriously thinking of jumping before I'm pushed. The more the arrears mount up the worse it'll be.'

We figured out together how many hours I owed her, and it was more cash than I had on me. I left her to her own devices while I went to a nearby ATM for paper money. When I came back, I found that she'd put the saucer on top of my cup in an attempt to keep my coffee warm. She was studying notes she'd taken that day. They concerned Lady Leandra.

'What did you make of her?'

'Your coffee will be cold by now. Want another?' she asked, brandishing one of the twenties I'd just given her; a delaying tactic if ever there was one.

'What was she like?'

MacNeil, in defensive mode, wilfully misunderstood, describing her as short, around the five-foot two mark, plump, brown hair tinted with henna, and heavy make-up round the eyes.

'Brass earrings from a curtain rail?'

'Don't be daft.'

According to the woman herself, Lady Leandra, guided by spirits, had access to the past, present and future. And what were these spirits? The archangels for a start, followed by Pallas Athena, Sappho and, bringing up the rear for welcome added weight, Hypatia of Alexandria.

'I had to have a single question ready, something I really wanted to know.'

'When would you meet Mr Right?'

Though the rumour in the force had been that MacNeil

was lesbian, I'd never believed it, but my crude attempt to flush her out fell flat on its face.

'I sometimes wonder about you, Hunter.'

I couldn't blame her, I sometimes wondered about myself. Her immediate concern wasn't men, it was money. She wanted to know whether she'd keep her house.

'She had this loop of twine on the table between us. I had to put my hand in a bag of crystals, take some out and let them fall on the table. Quartz, amethyst, citrine and so on. With me so far?'

I'd never heard of citrine but took her word for it.

'So that's what I did. Stones that fell outside the loop, they didn't count. The stones that fell nearest to me were the most important, the ones farthest away referred to the dim and distant.'

'Past?'

'Future. Ok, so then Leandra interprets the significance of the stones in relation to which stone fell where. There's a name for that.'

I was sure there was, I could think of one right then.

'It's a form of divination, lithomancy by sortilege. Now I know what you're thinking, it's all a load of crap.'

This was the second time today MacNeil had known what I was thinking, so maybe she was qualified to divine her own future without assistance and hand her thirty pounds to herself for the privilege. But not knowing the extent to which she had signed up to Lady Leandra and her abilities, this was another thought I kept to myself.

'Right, so cutting to the chase here, Maureen, what was the prognosis?'

'Ah, well there's more than one way of looking at that. It's not as if each stone carries only one association.'

'Ok, but will you be able to keep your flat? Yes or no?'

The issue, not being entirely clear cut, MacNeil had been left in some doubt, but the answer, on the balance of probabilities, was a qualified yes.

'Probably.'

Which sounded to me like having the Delphic Oracle as your financial advisor.

'You must be relieved.'

But I could tell from her expression that she wasn't. She looked round the café, quite full at that time of day and noisy.

'I think I should plan for the worst-case scenario. If it turns out better than that, fair enough. If it doesn't, I'll just have to meet it head on.'

Sound though this policy was, it could easily have been arrived at without Lady Leandra and her stones and MacNeil had to know that.

'There's a row of charity shops near here.'

There was, just the job for a woman low on cash.

'I think I'll have a rummage for something more lightweight. Summer's round the corner and this thing,' she said, touching her winter jacket, 'is warm enough to grow tomatoes. Join me?'

She had to be joking.

34

THE FOLLOWING DAY promised to be less intense than the convention and certainly less busy. I was sitting at the kitchen table composing my invoice to Drysdale when I realised I'd yet to update him. Payment for services rendered only works if you actually render the service. I sent him an email telling him briefly about the convention, stating that we'd hoped to see him there, and describing how we'd tracked Burt down to Haddon's Court. He replied at once, reinforcing my belief that mostly working from home he came close to living online, much like Wyness but closer to office hours. He'd hoped to attend the convention but his employers, Linton Legal, had landed him with urgent work he couldn't get out of. I pointed out that if Burt was only in town for the convention he probably wouldn't be staying long, so the sooner he arrived at the door to document his grievance on video, the better his chance of success.

Just after I'd sent this message, a fresh one came through from Wyness. He couldn't be absolutely sure, but further digging suggested that the lady who'd collected Burt from Pollock Halls wasn't his fancy woman, as MacNeil liked to think, but his sister Lenore, currently over from the States on a two-year postgraduate course in artificial intelligence. In his opinion, MacNeil and I needed all the intelligence we could get so this had to be a good thing.

Allowing a polite time to elapse before following up my report to Drysdale with an invoice, I was just preparing to relax when I remembered: Alison hadn't given me keys to her house for nothing; a week had passed since I'd watered her plants. It wasn't so long a walk from my place to hers, but fighting my way through crowds on the Bridges was harder going than I liked.

Making it to the relative calm of Royal Terrace and climbing the steps to her massive front door, I was struck yet again by how palatial her home was, a feeling reinforced when I let myself in. The hall was spacious, furnished with an old-style stand with mirror and an item she particularly liked, a glazed ceramic umbrella holder with a tastefully understated umbrella design. Why she needed so many umbrellas was anyone's guess. There was paper behind the door on the runner; advertising for take-aways, laser eye surgery and a furniture sale, all destined for the bin, and several letters, two in brown manila envelopes. I'd call her later and take her advice on those.

My first port of call was the kitchen, and the watering can under the sink. Memories came flooding back; watching Alison and her husband living separate lives together shortly before he died, observing her attempt to cook an omelette and ending up with scrambled eggs. She couldn't cook, but so what? She was delightfully unabashed by the fact and, in any case, her formidable talents lay elsewhere.

I headed for the cheese plant in the lounge, a large specimen close to four feet tall and still growing. To my relief there was no sign of a setback through lack of water, though I'd always felt that the wicker container it lived in gave off an unpleasant odour of damp as if, despite the waterproof material lining the interior, parts of it were water-logged. *I don't know what you're talking about,* she'd replied when I mentioned it, *I can't smell a thing.* The matter was not to be raised again.

I sat on her sofa for a while wondering how anyone could hope to dust the many crystals of her chandelier.

Some could be lowered for cleaning but hers wasn't one of them. This was the sofa we'd sat on while MacNeil, then a detective sergeant, had questioned her about her husband, suspecting among other things, that Alison and I were involved not only with each other but also in his death. She'd yet to apologise for this ludicrous suspicion and, being MacNeil, never would; except, perhaps, through her actions, which she would like to think spoke louder than words. Well maybe they did. Given time I might hear them, I believed I was hearing them already, but Alison never would.

I climbed the stairs to the upper floor, two large bedrooms and a spacious bathroom, the bath with ornate plumbing and shower head calling to mind an antique telephone. There was a window to the outside world, but not content with your standard frosted glass, Alison's was stained glass and attractive with it. Linton Legal would have described it as an original feature, as no doubt it was. More memorable to me than all this, though, was the floor, the place where Desmond Fintan Shaughnessy, the predatory colleague of Alison's husband, having broken into the house, bled to death on her laminate. We all make mistakes, but dying in a pool of blood on her Arctic Oak was bigger than most.

It had upset her so much that even after the floor had been cleaned by specialists recommended by the police, she'd considering having it ripped out and replaced. It was less the thought of any remaining blood, there was none to be seen, but the innocent Arctic Oak reminded her of unpleasant events. A change of colour would help erase the memory, Norway spruce, perhaps, or something entirely different.

In addition to watering the plants, she'd left her heating on at low to prevent any freezing of the pipes and tasked me with making sure everything was fine. Stepping over the spot where Shaughnessy's body had been, I turned on hot and cold in the bath and wash hand basin both and left them running for a minute. Everything was in order, not to be wondered at in May, and then went so far as flushing the toilet in case she asked about that, something she was quite capable of doing.

On my way back down, I took a quick peek in the master bedroom. No plants there, of course. She'd ruled that out on health grounds, claiming they breathed out noxious fumes in the night. Orderly as ever, Alison had made the bed before leaving for the west and laid fresh nightwear on it against her return. Some people have photographs in their bedroom, Alison had none and I could understand why. Nobody in her right mind would want pictures of a cheating husband, now dead, and Alison was definitely in her right mind. Every picture of the once happy couple had been junked for the fictions they were.

Back in the kitchen I turned my attention to the spider plants, one on the table, the other on the counter near the microwave. Both had produced healthy offshoots. Alison could have planted them out for an independent life but preferred to leave them hanging, signifying, she said, the endless dependence of offspring on their parents. This was accompanied by a reference to the bank of mum and dad which I didn't entirely get, but accountants will have their little jokes. I offered each some water, which they soon soaked up, decided I needed watering myself and put the kettle on.

I rested my brew on the front room coffee table beside back numbers of New Accountant and a ladies' clothing catalogue. Noticing an empty envelope marking a page in the catalogue, I found that it referenced "control underwear". Was it possible that Alison, by no means fat, was exploring the possibility of constraining the few excess ounces she had to boost her appearance? If so, why? Could it be preparatory to entering the flesh market again? For her sake, I hoped not, still clinging as I was to my new motto – stay single and count your blessings.

I leafed through Alison's mail. One was stamped HMRC and might well concern taxation relating either to herself or a client. So I called her.

'Hello, Douglas.'

'Hi Alison. You'll never guess where I am.'

'In my house watering plants.'

Extending her record of winning every round, she was right again.

'You have mail, one from the Revenue.'

She asked me to open it, but it was nothing urgent, a change of tax code for one of her clients.

'Everything in order through there; plants, pipes?'

Assured that it was, she moved on.

'I'm having a spot of bother here, Douglas. I would have called you if you hadn't called me first.'

When she and Lucasz had gone to the other warehouses of Edwards Interiors, the locks had been sealed with superglue. They'd called out a locksmith to gain entry, and when they had, both had proved to be the same as the first, stacked with empty boxes pretending to be full. She'd also done more work on the company accounts and discovered several folders, one within another. When she'd finally made it through to the last it contained fifteen encrypted files which she thought might be the accurate trading figures for the company rather than the inflated ones provided to Ergonomica.

'I've' never seen anything like it, Douglas, it was like a series of digital Russian dolls. But no one at Armstrong seems able to decrypt them. I hate to say it, but this might be a job for that Wyness character of yours.'

As Alison saw it, the character defects of David Wyness were something to do with me, which didn't seem fair. But life didn't either, so that was alright.

She now she had reason to believe Edwards was onto her, concerned that if she continued on her present course his false accounting would be revealed.

'Someone's being trying to wipe files.'

'In person or online?'

'Remotely. A hacker of some sort. In person and I'd be out of there sharp, believe me. Oh, and I've had two threatening emails, both of them very unpleasant. In a graphic sort of way, if you know what I mean. What would happen to me if I didn't back off. I wouldn't want to repeat some of the words.'

I didn't like the sound of that at all.

'No texts?'

'Not as yet, no.'

So at least they didn't have her number, but being in business as an accountant she had to include a contact email address on her website or she couldn't expect any takers.

'Forward them to me, I'll check them out.'

By which I really meant I'd have Wyness check them out, but the less I mentioned him to her the better.

'Enough of me and my troubles. Any developments at your end?'

In fact there were two, but I'd yet to catch up with either.

35

LATER THAT DAY, in the comparative quiet of my flat, I sat down to a bowl of packet soup and checked my incoming mail. Apart from the usual junk, there were two items of interest. The first was from a client I'd worked for in the past, Mr Cameron of Albion Assurance, a big fish in a small pond down at Thistle Street. He had another case on offer, full details available to view on a secure shared folder. When I'd recovered from choking on croutons I'd forgotten were included in the soup, I checked it out.

Joyce Abercrombie ran a business in Dunblane, a small jewellery shop on the High Street. In addition to the usual range of bracelets, necklaces, earrings and broches, she specialised in amber. I hadn't realised till I read the notes that quality amber was so expensive. Some of the quoted prices amazed me. And the reason they were quoted at all was that her shop, Jezebel, had been robbed. I found myself looking at a beautiful Baltic amber ring in an elegant eighteen carat solid gold setting. Price? A cool four hundred and forty-five pounds. For added value, it contained a spider, trapped while the amber was still liquid. Was this a con? Apparently not. Its authenticity had been verified by the National Museums Scotland no less. And this item was just one of many. Reading on, I came across an amber necklace priced at an eye-watering eleven thousand pounds.

As I read through Mr Cameron's file, I began to have misgivings. Jewellery was an area Hunter Associates were ill-equipped to handle. I knew nothing about precious stones, settings and so forth, MacNeil wasn't into personal adornment of any sort and since jewels weren't digital, Wyness knew nothing about them either. Alison would know more than the rest of us put together, but she was otherwise occupied and likely to stay that way for several weeks. If I'd had any other work in the pipeline I'd have thought twice about this one, which promised to be tedious with little likelihood of success. Even knowing where to start was far from obvious, but beggars can't be choosers.

I was only halfway through Cameron's folder when my attention was taken by a notification from Wyness concerning Drysdale. It contained a link which I should follow, a video posted by the lad himself, which Wyness claimed was hilarious. I watched it and had to admire the lad's chutzpa; he handled it well.

He approached Burt's door and rang the bell. When Lenore opened it, his frustration was only evident for a fraction of a second.

'Good morning. I'm actually here to see Mr Burt.'

'And you are?'

'Daniel Drysdale.'

'He's expecting you?'

'I'm afraid not, but I'm sure he'll appreciate what I have to say.'

Lenore called for Burt, who arrived at the door clad only in shorts, a rumpled T-shirt and carpet slippers bearing a fake baronial crest.

'Yes?'

'Good morning, Mr Burt, my name is Drysdale. You don't know me as yet, but I appear in one of your films.'

Burt looked unconvinced.

'Good for you, but I can't be expected to remember every single extra.'

'In this case you don't have to. I am not now, and never have been an extra.'

'So what's your beef, buddy?'

'Simply put, I appear in Born Again 3 without my permission being sought, thus infringing my image rights.'

Burt looked suitably surprised.

'You're well-known? A celebrity of some sort? Famous?'

'Don't have to be. It's a well-known principle of jurisprudence that everyone is equal in the eyes of the law.'

'Get real son. If you believe that, you'll believe anything.'

Burt was turning back into the house preparatory to shutting the door, but Drysdale wasn't finished.

'I appear in your latest film walking down the street, clearly visible and easily identifiable, going about my lawful business.'

'Without a care in the world, right?'

'Until caught by your cameras, yes.'

'Ah, I get it. Side-walk celebrity's not good enough for you, you want your fifteen minutes of fame.'

'Just shy of ninety seconds in fact, but the principle applies. I did not give my consent to appearing in this motion picture. Further to that, at no point was my permission sought.'

Burt considered this briefly before rejecting it out of hand.

'Listen, Drysdale, what you're suggesting just isn't practicable. I assume you were one of many.'

'Again, however true that may be, it has no bearing on the principle.'

'You think? So how could any filmmaker go about identifying all the people appearing in the background of a scene? And even if he could, what if just one out of fifty didn't consent to a guest appearance? What then?'

'I was brought up to believe that if you create a problem it's up to you to solve it.'

'Oh, great. Well have a good day. Mr Drysdale. Anything else you have to say on this subject should be directed to my agents.'

'UTA.'

Surprised that Drysdale knew this, Burt was about to shut the door on this troublesome young man when he was joined by his sister in protective mode.

'I don't know who you think you are, but we must ask you to leave.'

'I know exactly who I am, Lenore, and I'm prepared to take this all the way to the top.'

Hearing her name taken in vain, Lenore realised that Drysdale had done his homework and could prove troublesome.

'Wonderful,' she said, pointing due east to the nearest peak, 'if it's the top you want, you'll find Arthur's Seat over there. Goodbye.'

She pulled Burt inside and slammed the door in Drysdale's face.

'You haven't heard the last of this!'

In the meantime, a small group of onlookers had gathered, including two passing vagrants who found the whole thing vastly entertaining, and the owner of a mobile phone, who'd transformed himself into a citizen journalist with one touch of his screen.

And shortly thereafter, all of this appeared on YouTube, the full version posted by Drysdale himself, who linked it to his crowd-funding appeal, *Justice for All, Big or Small*, which now stood at a cool £37,000 and with the added publicity likely to rise still more.

Having been entertained by all this, I should have returned to Cameron's file but, mea culpa, I did not.

36

As was only to be expected from such a punctilious individual, Mr Cameron called me at nine o'clock the following morning, not a minute before, not a minute after, exactly on the stroke of nine.

'Good morning, Mr Hunter, I trust you are well.'

After a brief exchange in which each pretended to care how the other was faring, he got to the point.

'I see you've joined our shared folder – excellent – and you will doubtless have given your attention to the documents it contains.'

'I have, and I must say, Mr Cameron, I'm astonished at the value of some of items in the list, especially the ambers. But tracking them down could prove difficult. Ninety-seven items of assorted jewellery couldn't be sold on in one place at one time.'

'We can agree on that, Mr Hunter. You'll have noted that Miss Abercrombie has proof of purchase of all except three of these items, but our emphasis here is not primarily on recovery, as I'm sure you will have realised.'

If I'd read on, I might have, but when he said this, I was at a loss and had to freewheel somewhat in an attempt to conceal the fact.

'True, but forty thousand pounds is a large sum.'

There was a brief pause while Mr Cameron wondered whether I had yet to wake up properly or hadn't given enough time to the documents in his folder. Knowing him, he could live with the first but would take a dim view of the second.

'But Mr Hunter, you must surely have noticed that Miss Abercrombie's stock is insured by another company and so not our immediate concern.'

So what *was* our immediate concern? I had no idea.

'Good point, Mr Cameron. I suppose I have a one-track mind when it comes to dealing with stolen property, the urge to track it down.'

'Your bloodhound instinct certainly does you credit, but on this occasion our concern here at Albion is the income protection policy taken out by Miss Abercrombie some five years ago.'

'Of course. Yes.'

'It might be advisable to renew your acquaintance with the details, you not being an insurance professional yourself.'

'Agreed.'

Since taking out her policy, Joyce Abercrombie had been meticulous in meeting her monthly premiums, so no problem there. The policy granted her cover in the event that her business, Jezebel, went into administration, provided she didn't fall foul of any of its exclusions.

'For example, she couldn't just wind it up because she wanted an extended break in the Caribbean then expect us to foot the bill.'

'Of course, not. No.'

On the face of it, there was no such problem. Her shop had been broken into, most of the contents stolen with only some minor items left. Though the stolen items were insured, settling a claim of this nature could take an extended period of time. In the meantime, the loss was so large she couldn't hope to make it up and so had entered voluntary administration.

'And here at Albion we can quite see why. Her overheads remained – business rates, utility bills and so on – with her only means of meeting them taken from her by theft.'

That was all very clear, so what was the problem?

'This is a delicate one, Mr Hunter, so bear with me please.'

I have seldom been so glad a call was audio only. I could picture Mr Cameron on his captain's chair behind his double-pedestal desk, his propelling pens and pencils neatly aligned on the tooled leather, but he couldn't see me, still stretched out in bed trying to make sense of what he was saying.

'Sad to say, her trade has been falling off in recent years. How do we know this, I hear you ask? The answer is simple. The terms of her policy oblige her to submit audited accounts on a yearly basis and this she has done. These accounts are, of course, open to inspection.'

'So the business was straight up.'

'Not a term we recognise in the industry, but yes. Up till now very much so.'

'Let me get this straight, Mr Cameron. You suspect Miss Abercrombie may have been behind the break-in.'

'It's a possibility we must consider, however unlikely. The lady is a graduate of St Andrews University, after all.'

What that had to do with it wasn't obvious, well-educated crooks were by no means unheard of.

'I assume the local police were called to investigate.'

They had been and spotted nothing amiss, but Mr Cameron then introduced a point which he was pleased to call Cameron's Caveat. Though no longer in the first flush of youth, Miss Abercrombie had a way with her and probably charmed them out of due vigilance.

'You'll have seen the accompanying photographs.'

'I have.'

'Most comely, I'm sure you would agree.'

She was attractive, no doubt about it, her ash-blonde hair piled up on her head and held in place with decorative hardwood skewers.

'A handsome woman, yes.'

At last realising what was bothering me, I sat up in bed the better to think. If the local force was on the case, what did he expect me to do about it?

'As you will have read in the documentation, the policy will not pay out in the event of fraud. But failing evidence of that, the costs to us would be considerable. Her income protection insurance would pay out until she returned to work, retired, or died. The lady is only forty-three years old now and might live till, who knows, eighty or ninety.'

'You want me to investigate the possibility of fraud.'

'Discreetly, yes. On the same footing as before.'

'How long have I got?'

'Three months.'

This was longer than expected, but for a reason. To reduce her monthly premiums, Miss Abercrombie had agreed to a three-month deferral before any payments due would be received. So I agreed to take the case on, and since I hadn't the faintest idea how best to go about it, fired off messages to Wyness and MacNeil concerning procedure and Alison on the subject of amber. Like it or not, we'd have to put our heads together on this one to stand a chance of getting anywhere at all.

37

I WAS BEGINNING to wonder about David Wyness, not so much about his state of mind, eccentric as it was, but more concerning his body. It seemed to me that he'd become more reclusive of late, reluctant to leave his flat, and there were several possible reasons for that. The most obvious was that going up the four flights of stairs to his door was taking it out of him more than before. Smoking so much, his lungs were labouring now, so by the simple expedient of not going down to street level in the first place, he didn't have to climb back up again. But knowing the connection between heart and lungs, this could only be bad. *Why would I go out when I can have it delivered?* That's what he'd asked me the last time I'd brought the subject up. My reference to healthy living fell on deaf ears.

I couldn't be sure, but it was possible his last outing had to been to fit the security camera in Anna van Leeuwen's front room. Though the device belonged to him, he'd asked me to retrieve it on the assumption that she didn't need it anymore; Leroy Gaines had surely been put off stalking for the time being when MacNeil knocked him off his bike. But why not reclaim it himself? I knew he'd noticed van Leeuwen sizing up his midriff, something she could hardly fail to do when he was perched on her windowsill with camera and gaffer tape. Perhaps he was starting to feel self-conscious about his body on public display. If that was the case I couldn't blame him, he was a sorry sight.

So I wasn't surprised when he declined my suggestion of

a brain-storming session with MacNeil and myself, offering instead to do what digging he could from home into the affairs of the comely Miss Abercrombie.

'She's in business. There's bound to be something out there.'

As for MacNeil, instead of replying to my message she headed straight for my flat, rang the bell then pounded on the door. I could understand that in a way. With Wyness' reluctance to go out, the only place we could have met was his flat. But she'd have taken in more smoke second hand than she'd have inhaled directly in a week. So she refused to go there for any reason at all, and no one but Wyness would blame her for that.

'Got your message,' she said, walking past me and dumping a black bin bag in the hall.

'It wasn't an invitation.'

'Too bad. I'm here now. Like it or lump it.'

So she was, and not bearing croissants this time. Since all I had to offer her was bread so tired it would have to be toasted, I settled her at the kitchen table with my laptop open at Cameron's folder.

'Read carefully and inwardly digest.'

She made it clear that when it came to digestion what she needed was something she could chew and swallow, so I left her reading and went out for the croissants she'd failed to bring.

'Sorry about that, a bit short right now.'

I walked further than necessary to give her adequate reading time, and when I returned the first thing I heard was my washing machine in action. She shrugged. That was life, apparently.

'On my way to the laundrette when I got your message.'

She had two mugs ready, the kettle boiled, plates and knives laid out together with butter and marmalade. As she set to work at the kitchen counter, I noticed she was better turned out than usual; her denim skirt actually matched her jacket, a first in my experience. Neither was distressed, though both had lived a life before she bought them.

'I scrub up well, right?'

She had eyes in the back of her head.

'I'm impressed.'

'You should be.'

But after she'd eaten, she plunged right into it.

'The police report indicates a break in, but if it was an inside job they'd make it look like that anyway, so it doesn't help much. No mention of CCTV. I assume there was none. Oh, and the burglar alarm was awaiting repair.'

'Doesn't look good to me. So on the assumption it was her?'

'She'll want to move the stuff; the question is how.'

As MacNeil saw it, Abercrombie had three options. The first was private sale on platforms like eBay, Gumtree and so on, but if the lady was as smart as Cameron seemed to think, she wouldn't do that. Too easily traced back to her.

'Failing that, then?'

'Craft fairs. They sell everything.'

MacNeil and craft fairs didn't get on. She had no time for hand-painted ceramics, Fair Isle knitwear, wooden toys with articulated joints, glove puppets and vegan confectionery. And there was always a jewellery stall or two. She listed the articles they sold as if they were items on a charge sheet.

'Silver pendants, earrings lovingly crafted by mermaids on Tiree. You know the sort of thing.'

I didn't really but nodded sagely. MacNeil was on a roll.

'She wouldn't try that in the Dunblane area, of course, but she might risk it farther afield. Aberdeen, Inverness. If she was really careful, she'd get a friend to take some of her stuff. Try tracing that!'

On the verge of entering deep into negative territory,

she took a couple of swigs of coffee and out of the blue was overtaken by a distant look.

'I have a sister in Inverness.'

This was the first time in the several years I'd known her that she'd mentioned family at all. As far as any of us knew either she didn't have one or, if she did, they were estranged, probably due to one of her many intemperate outbursts, giving it to them straight, as she would have it.

'A half-sister, actually. Chloe.'

'Still in touch?'

'She married a taxi driver, a total pillock. Wouldn't take him in a lucky bag.'

Maureen and Chloe shared the same mother. The lady had been unlucky in love and gone through a string of boyfriends after her husband left her, one of these liaisons giving rise to Chloe. Then, as suddenly as she'd opened this window into her world she closed it again.

'Know what I'd do? Set up an entirely new business and sell through its website.'

'She'd have to know how.'

'Even if she didn't, there are people out there who'd do it for her.'

The doorbell rang for the second time that morning.

'Who could that be? Expecting someone?'

Without a second's hesitation, she went to the door – my door, the last time I'd checked – came back with a packet and slapped it down on the table.

'For you.'

We went over Cameron's documents till the washing machine finished its final spin.

'You don't have a drier, I suppose.'

38

I'D ALREADY GIVEN Wyness enough work to be getting on with, so for the rest of that week I decided to do some research myself, starting with craft fairs due in the near future, where and when. Going to most of them wouldn't have been practical but given that many of Abercrombie's items were high value it made sense to discount small church hall and community centre events and concentrate on the large ones. I liked griddle scones and homemade raspberry jam as much as the next man but there had to be a limit.

But whenever I opened my laptop, I was confronted by a problem I'd been aware of for some time and done nothing about. No wi-fi. I'd had it in Laurieston, but not here in my new des res at Gifford Park. I'd been side-stepping the issue, connecting to the internet through my phone, a tiresome process involving a cable and venturing into menus to change settings, for me a risky business. Wyness would have felt even more secure in his technical superiority if he'd caught me at it. There was an alternative, though, taking my technology to a café with free wi-fi. And this had other advantages. I found that the buzz of people talking helped me concentrate, though I couldn't help wondering why. On the face of it, it didn't make sense.

And so I found myself on several occasions that week, ensconced in the café at Blackwells surrounded by customers chewing the fat at great length and others who, with crablike and sideways motion, appeared to be making a move on each other. There was even the occasional tutor going through work with students. *Turning to your chapter six, The Question of Style in the Writings of Cicero and Sallust; excellent in most respects but I can't help but feel we could do with some restructuring here.* Yes, well we could all do with some of that.

Life as we know it today. My search threw up a remarkable number of craft fairs. I noticed one due shortly at the Eden Court Theatre in Inverness. Perhaps MacNeil could have her sister drop in. She might even visit her and they could go together. But a better bet was surely the Merchant Square Craft & Design Fair in Glasgow. Since it ran every weekend, this would be an ideal venue for Abercrombie to move her merchandise. I didn't know how much it cost stallholders, but for private investigators entrance was free. And as an added bonus, Alison, who knew a thing or two, was already in the city.

I was sitting in the café later that week comparing broadband deals when two messages came through in quick succession. The first was from Daniel Drysdale, who reported that Burt or his agents had retained a certain Aphrodite Clutterbuck-Smith, partner at the law firm Ingold Lumb. Aphrodite specialised in media, privacy and reputation management and advised that he, Drysdale, hadn't a leg to stand on, but if he chose to stand on it nonetheless it would cost him big. This was plainly Burt's summary of what she had said, rather than a direct quotation of the lady's legal language. But Burt had been delighted to pass on the gist of it, adding that if Drysdale persisted in publicly airing his complaint and posting the results on YouTube, he would find himself on the thick end of a legal action he couldn't hope to win and certainly couldn't afford, crowdfunding notwithstanding.

I replied to Drysdale's message at once, asking him what he intended to do in the light of this development and he replied very quickly, all this, be it noted, in his employer's time. He wasn't going to be intimidated by some woman with letters after her name, no way, and I should expect further developments. This was so vague it could have come from Lady Leandra herself, but I was confident the two had never met, so she was not alone in taking a broad-brush approach when it came to predicting future events. What, if anything, would he do? Do dreams tell the future? As Xenophon so rightly put it several years ago, if you really want to know, the best thing to do is wait and see.

The second message was from Wyness, who'd been researching Joyce Abercrombie, alumna of St Andrews university and seller of amber on Dunblane High Street. He hadn't found anything untoward about this lady, who'd been in business for over five years and submitted audited accounts to Company's House for each of them. She was active on social media, but only when it came to reporting her activities as a member of what he was pleased to call the bauble brigade. Pictures of her abounded at social gatherings, often with glass in hand, and even Wyness noticed she was attractive. *Wouldn't kick her out of bed I can tell you.* Apart from the fact that he'd never have the opportunity, I doubted if he now had the physical ability to kick anyone anywhere. He had discovered one thing, though.

I probably didn't know this, but Joyce had a brother called Torquil, a crime in itself, he thought, and this brother was dodgy to say the least. He'd been convicted of breaking and entering on two occasions, and charged with reset on five occasions, being found guilty on two. Since I had been a police officer, he assumed I knew but told me anyway that reset was the dishonest possession of goods obtained by someone else, by way of theft, robbery, fraud or embezzlement, in the knowledge that they were obtained that way.

I read all this with astonishment. It shed an entirely new light on the matter and, in doing so, made it very much harder to establish whether the sister, Joyce, was involved. To clarify what passed for thoughts on the matter, I listed the possibilities on a napkin. 1) The robbery had nothing to do with Joyce or Torquil but was committed by a third party or parties as yet unknown. 2) The robbery had been committed by Torquil, Joyce having no part in it. 3) Torquil had committed it with Joyce's knowledge, the business being on a downward trend with no prospect of improvement. If either of the first two was the case, then Cameron should pay out on Joyce's policy. But if it was the third, then she wouldn't get a penny and serve her right.

This was going to be tricky, to say the least. I phoned MacNeil and asked her if she was busy, a stupid thing to do as she was always going to say yes. But she agreed to meet me provided I paid for her parking. She arrived twenty minutes later, dumped her belongings on the chair opposite me, and in one easy movement I pressed a ten-pound note into her outstretched hand. MacNeil was neither greedy nor grasping, just desperate and we both understood that.

'What'll it be?'

She scanned the menu and plumped for a blueberry muffin and an Earl Grey tea. Before I could explain anything, she spotted the napkin and read it.

'Torquil!'

I sometimes wondered if the names our parents give us influence our lives – going forward, as they say in management circles. Charles Plumstead Vellacott might have turned out differently if he'd been called Harry Smith. He couldn't have turned out much worse. As for Torquil, it was too soon to say, but I had my suspicions. To me the name positively reeked of entitlement. *There are valuable amber items in my sister's shop to which I, Torquil Delahunt Abercrombie, am plainly entitled. Since the po-faced inadequates among us may not agree, I shall acquire them in the dead of night with no one to see me but the moon.* Because those bound by convention may well have included his sister, he would keep such thoughts to himself.

MacNeil was waving her muffin in my face in an attempt to get me back to planet Earth, not necessarily the best place to be but there was little choice. And having returned, I gave her all the background I had.

'Right, well here's how I see it. You go to Glasgow and check out the next craft fair. Seeing your fancy woman's there, that should suit you down to the ground. Kill two birds with one stone, one of them being her.'

Contesting this version of events would just have added fuel to the fire, so I took The Wanderer's advice and held my own counsel.

'Meanwhile, I'll go to Dunblane and see what I can dig up. I have a contact there, could be useful. I might even manage,' she added, hopefully, 'to fit in a delivery while I'm at it.'

So she wasn't above killing two birds with one stone herself. There was, however, a problem. All but one of her tyres had failed her recent MOT, so to stay legal she had to replace them. The mechanic had pointed out that the fourth didn't have long to go either, so the smart move was to replace all four which would, he said, result in a better balance. If anyone needed a better balance it was Maureen MacNeil, but this would involve handing over money she didn't have. With retreads she could keep the cost down to two hundred and forty pounds.

'After all, we have money coming in from Chen, van Leeuwen and Drysdale.'

True, we had, but now we were out of cases except for this one, so we had to make headway somehow. I decided to go with her to the dealer and sort it out.

'You do know,' MacNeil said, with a faint smile, 'that you

weren't the worst of them.'

She was referring to the years we'd spent together on the force. As the worst of them were misogynistic in the extreme, this was good to know. It was also as close to a compliment as I was likely to get.

39

ALISON WAS PLEASED to hear I'd be joining her in Glasgow that weekend, and probably relieved as well. I'd had the feeling, when we last talked, that she wanted to ask me through but was reluctant to do so, perhaps because she didn't want to seem weak. When we met at the bus station, she treated me to an unexpectedly warm embrace and we headed straight to the venue.

'Makes a change from combing through accounts.'

And so it did, because when we arrived the place was heaving with people brandishing fiddles and other instruments, many of them resplendent in kilts.

'Where's the craft fair?' I asked, already fearing the worst.

Though normally occupying the whole weekend, on this occasion the fair was restricted to Sunday, Saturday given over to a major event by the Glasgow Fiddle and Accordion Society.

'Well that's great,' Alison said as we retreated to the entrance, 'nothing quite like forward planning.'

'I'm really sorry about this Alison. What can I say?'

'Nothing that could make the situation any better.'

This was true but not very helpful.

'Anyone can mistake a mistake.'

'Yes, but you make more than most.'

She may have had other mistakes in mind, but probably not; it was simply a verbal slap in the face.

A helpful steward pointed out that the weekend's

schedule had been well publicised in advance, on the venue's website, for example. Although I was sure this was true, it was an intervention I could have done without.

'And you call yourself a detective!'

The sounds of reels and jigs was audible from the interior, several being played at the same time at various speeds and in different keys.

'They're just tuning up,' he told us as he walked by, a passing enthusiast in tartan trews and bow tie.

We idled away the rest of the day in shopping centres, coffee shops and a lunchtime restaurant, which was where I learned how concerned Alison was for her personal safety.

'They keep coming, Douglas, three yesterday and another this morning. Threatening emails.'

So they did, and most unpleasant they were. Threatening to rape and strangle wasn't on for anyone, let alone a law-abiding citizen like Alison, a woman who was simply following a legitimate line of enquiry into the dodgy dealings of an undoubted chancer.

'Has Wyness got back to you yet, I take it you have him on the case. No offence, Douglas, but it's not the sort of thing you're capable of investigating yourself.'

She was right. On the other hand, even I had suspected that emails purporting to come from Cruella de Vil concealed the identity of someone less fictional and much closer to home.

'We need to know who's behind this.'

At Alison's insistence, I phoned Wyness, who surprised me by picking up at once.

'Yo, Hunter. What is it this time, buddy, more technical advice? My rate is a hundred pounds per hour, fractions of an hour rounded up.'

Quick though he'd been when investigating Chester H Burt, he admitted to dropping the ball on this one. He'd start on it right away.

'Tell her I'm on a holding pattern,' he said, ending the call.

I could hardly tell her that, it didn't mean anything.

'He'll get back to us within the hour.'

'So I should hope.'

She was eating a prawn salad at the time, with spinach, avocado and cucumber. My chicken fricassee was less impressive.

'In all the time I've known you, Douglas, you've never gone for seafood. These prawns are excellent.'

She couldn't stand the feel of food on her lips and was always very active with the napkin. As for prawns, as far as I could tell from what I'd read, they lived out their lives in an unsavoury suspension of raw sewage and plastic so, no thanks. But telling her that wouldn't have gone down well, not nearly so well as the prawns.

'I don't know, Alison, I've just never fancied them much.'

Alison had just offered to pay the bill, *you're visiting me, after all*, when Wyness got back to me. Tracking the source of the poisonous emails was next to impossible, the sender had gone to great lengths to conceal his true identity.

'You say "his", but Cruella was a woman.'

Astonished at my naivety, Alison challenged this remark at once.

'For heaven's sake, Douglas, that tells us nothing at all. In online circles men pretend to be women all the time, young girls even. You've come across grooming, I take it?'

I had, but couldn't help wondering if Edward's wife Rachel was behind it.

'She worked there, after all.'

'Well, maybe so, but you really can't infer a thing like that from such scant evidence.'

Wyness thought the same, the first time in living memory my associates had agreed about anything, so I was dead meat. He promised to keep digging but didn't hold out much hope.

'Besides,' Alison added with some point, 'how would this woman go about raping me? Exactly?'

I had to admit she had a point there, but I preferred not to dwell on the mechanics of the thing. In particular, I didn't want to visualise it.

'Tricky one.'

'So, Douglas.'

'Alison?'

'What do we do? We need to do something.'

We ordered coffees and thought it over. Alison was a threat because of what she knew and might reveal. But the moment she made it public, silencing her would achieve nothing and the threat would be over. The information would be out there.

'You've got to tell these people at Ergonomica what you've discovered and hand over all the evidence you have.'

'I haven't quite dotted the I's and crossed the T's yet.'

'Ok, but from what you've told me you have a lot. What more do you really need?'

'I've still to estimate a final amount lost to this fraud. I can hardly report back till I've done that.'

I could tell from her expression she wanted to hold off till she'd tied the job up with ribbons and bows, but the time for that was past. From what she'd already told me, she had quite enough to go on.

'Alison, seriously, do you want to achieve perfection or live longer, what's it to be?'

'Well, when you put it like that.'

'You don't want to be the next Graziella Corrocher.'

Not wanting to be thrown from a fifth-floor window like poor Graziella, she agreed to arrange a meeting with the Ergonomica board the following week if I would come along as moral support. At which point she changed the subject.

'The fair will be on tomorrow.'

'True.'

'There's not much point you going all the way home today just to come straight back again.'

I knew what she was driving at. Her room at the hotel wasn't a double, it had two single beds. She only needed one so I could use the other. I pointed out that I'd nothing with me, no pyjamas, for example, no spare socks. But that wasn't a problem.

'We'll pick up a sweatshirt. You can sleep in that.'

And so I did, uneasy at first in case the lady had other things on her mind, but if she had she did nothing about it. Alison and I had reached the full platonic, an excellent place to be and the best prospect of having a friend for life.

40

AFTER BREAKFAST, WE tidied ourselves up, Alison improving her face in front of mirrors with her travelling cosmetic kit, and left for the fair in her car. Parking was hard enough on a Sunday, so I could only imagine what weekdays were like. But this time, arriving at the entrance, we were at least assured of being in the right place at the right time. On Sundays, doors usually opened at noon, but to make up for the Saturday lost to music, they were opening earlier today. Finally in the hall, we were confronted by a bewildering array of stalls: prints and photographs, cards, clothing, ceramics, glassware, mugs, cupcakes, artisan cheeses. And jewellery.

'My goodness, it's absolutely packed.'

It was, so we agreed to split the floor area between us and meet up afterwards to compare notes. In my half, I tracked down two stalls selling jewellery. The first I could discount at once, mostly wooden bangles, large and nicely decorated, but hardly a precious stone in sight. The second, Jade's Jewels, was a different matter. In addition to a display of items by a silversmith from Barra, some including stones, there were several individual pieces, a few of which were amber. The stallholder, an older lady with unusually large earrings, spotted me taking a picture of the items in question and approached me.

'Anything catch your eye, young man?'

"Young man", I liked that.

'I'm interested in amber but don't know much about it.

Some of these items seem competitively priced.'

She smiled. 'There's a reason for that.'

This came as no surprise. There's a reason for everything, even if we don't always know what it is.

'I'll let you into a secret. There are quite a few synthetic ambers out there. Look like the real thing but they're not.'

I didn't like the sound of this at all. How did we know that the items stolen from Joyce Abercrombie's shop weren't synthetic? If the break-in was a scam, it might have been even cleverer than we thought. But by this time, a small crowd had gathered round me, hoping to benefit from the lady's expertise. I was reminded of scenes from one of the many antiques shows on the box.

'Right, so how can you tell the fakes from the real thing?'

'Oh, I wouldn't call them fakes. They're normally marketed as exactly what they are. Synthetic amber.'

'Ok, but supposing they're not?'

There were several ways. Jade didn't want to bore me with the details, but she recommended one simple test. I should dip my amber in a glass of salt water. Glass or plastic epoxy amber would sink but natural amber would rise to the top because its density was less than salt water.

'Just add three teaspoons of salt to a glass of tap water. Nothing to it.'

A man standing behind me, clutching what looked like several catalogues, hit the unsuspecting Jade with a supplementary.

'Fine, but what about copals?'

'Ah now,' Jade said with a smile, 'that's something else altogether.'

I suspected the man was a dealer, though maybe he was just rehearsing for a pub quiz. Who knew? I didn't, but I noted the word "copal" just in case and moved off. There were tables round the periphery for food and drink. I sat at one and compared Jade's items with pictures of those which had been stolen. While a couple of necklaces looked similar, they didn't admit to closer inspection. I'd drawn a blank, but Alison might be luckier.

After a few minutes she appeared beside me with coffees and pastries.

'Hot in here, don't you find. All these people breathing out!'

She offered me a choice, a cinnamon pastry neatly coiled or another which looked as if it had a poached egg in the middle, though I took it to be apricot. I went for the coil, less messy, knowing full well that Alison always travelled with a pack of disposable wipes and could take the apricot in her stride. I noticed she had a bag with her now, which she hadn't had when we arrived.

'Hemp,' she assured me, 'environmentally friendly'.

I'd heard that one before and would hear it again. She slung her jacket over the back of her chair, took a swig of coffee, then fished an item from the bag and handed it to me.

'For you.'

'Why thank you, Alison. Very thoughtful.'

'Think of it as a house-warming gift.'

She'd bought a wooden cutting board at one of the stalls, correctly assuming I wouldn't have one.

'Lovely, isn't it. He had all sorts of things; cutting boards, rolling pins, Lazy Susans, all in beautifully finished wood.'

Before we got down to business I thanked her again, wishing the board was just a little less heavy. She looked up at the gallery, an eating area with tables and chairs.

'We could always go up there, keep an eye on proceedings from above, though I'm not sure it would be worth it. I couldn't find a thing.'

'Neither could I, and no sign of the beauteous Miss Abercrombie.'

'I beg your pardon? You never called me that, not in my hearing anyway.'

In case her outrage increased, I explained.
'It's Wyness. He finds her attractive.'
'He would.'

41

THE FOLLOWING DAY, I looked back on a less than productive weekend. A lot had happened, but it was only too easy to confuse activity with results. The best we could say was that Joyce Abercrombie had not been attempting to sell valuable artefacts from a stall at the fair and no one else had been doing it for her. But though the Glasgow event was well established and high profile as craft fairs went, there were many others throughout the country, and we couldn't hope to check them all. Which left the us with Maureen MacNeil and her efforts on the ground at Dunblane. I was about to contact her when I was beaten to it by the first of two incoming calls, Mr Cameron, from Albion Assurance.

'Good morning, Mr Hunter, I trust the day finds you well.'

I was beginning to wonder if the man had strayed from the nineteenth century.

'And to you, Mr Cameron.'

'An unusual one, this, I expect you can shed some light on it.'

He'd just been approached over the phone by a woman identifying herself as Maureen MacNeil. Prior to departing for Dunblane in pursuance of an ongoing investigation, she was looking for some form of credential from Albion which, she hoped, would open doors and, once through them, tongues as well.

'I assume that this person is one of your associates, but it would reassure greatly me if you could vouch for the lady in question before I accede to her request.'

I had heard MacNeil referred to as many things, some of them unprintable, but never before as a lady. If anyone had called her that to her face she'd probably have been offended, regarding it as forced inclusion in an effete social stratum she had no time for. She'd called Alison Eadie a stuck-up bitch for a reason.

'Maureen MacNeil is one of my associates, yes.'

'Ex police like yourself, I trust.'

'I can reassure you on that one, Mr Cameron, Miss MacNeil was a detective sergeant before joining me in the private sector.'

'Excellent. Pleased to hear it. So to expedite matters, the requested credentials will be available here at our Thistle Street office from eleven this morning. Should I be unavailable for any reason, they will be collectable from Miss Clarke at reception. On sight of the requisite ID, of course.'

'Of course.'

Before hanging up, Mr Cameron felt obliged to establish a protocol for any such requests going forward; they should come from me on behalf of the associate in question, rather than the associate him or herself. That way, he assured me, clarity lay. For me, clarity also lay in the need to collect the said credentials myself; if Cameron came face-to-face with MacNeil, he'd think twice about handing them over.

Barely a minute had passed before the next call came in, this time from DS Cook, who was seeking clarification on this latest case.

'I've been contacted by colleagues in Dunblane. They've been approached by your friend MacNeil, who hopes to liaise with them concerning a robbery on Dunblane High Street. Know anything about that?'

'A jewellery shop. Jezebel.'

'She said she'd been a detective sergeant with us but failed to mention she'd been shown the door, or why.'

Well, no, she was hardly going to ruin her chances doing that.

'Are you happy with her involvement in this? We've already discussed the risks involved.'

'I believe the danger is past but I'm keeping an eye on her.'

'Forgive me, Douglas, but wouldn't that entail being in the same place at the same time?'

She had a point.

'Let's just say I'm keeping a watching brief.'

'From a safe distance.'

'Yes.'

'Fair enough. You make your decisions, I'll make mine.'

There was a hint of a threat in this but what could I do? I'd no one else to call on and whatever else you could say about her, when it came to investigation MacNeil knew the ropes.

'How will you respond to Dunblane, DS Cook?'

'Anastasija to you.'

'Right.'

'Until I arrest you, anyway.'

Cook intended to give her Dunblane colleagues a qualified yes, but MacNeil wanted fingerprints from the shop and they didn't feel the expense was justified, which suggested to me that they didn't know about Torquil.

'Who the hell's Torquil?'

I told her everything I knew about Joyce Abercrombie's brother, and she conceded at once that fingerprints would be justified. With a record like that, his prints would be on record. At which point she turned social.

'How's business?'

'Could be better. This is the only job on our books right now.'

'I may be able to help.'

I was pleased to hear that but didn't ask how. If it turned

out that she could pass some work my way, fine; if not, it was only to be expected.

For the next hour or two my way ahead was clear: tidy myself up, collect MacNeil's credentials from Albion, meet up with her to hand them over and screw out of her how she intended to proceed. I'd hoped to walk to Thistle Street, but when I opened the main door discovered it was raining and took the car instead.

Miss Clarke, for it was she, was happy to hand me an unsealed A4 envelope containing two letters of certification, one for MacNeil, the other for me. She invited me to check the contents before I left, which I did. The text was short, to the point and printed on a heavy weight paper with the Albion Assurance logo at the top. Why the logo included a lion I had no idea. Lions were rare in these parts, yet they abounded on logos and coats of arms. As for the text, it was reassuring to know we were fully accredited agents of the company with whom confidential information could safely be shared.

I had just got back in my car intending to call MacNeil and arrange to meet when I was visited by an idea. She thought nothing of arriving at my door unannounced then breezing in as if she owned the place, so she could hardly complain if I did the same to her. With this dangerous thought in mind, I drove out to Roseburn, climbed the stairs to her front door, still with its MacNeil tartan nameplate, and rang the bell.

'For fuck's sake, Hunter, what are you doing here?'

'We need to talk.'

'Not here we don't.'

She let me in with great reluctance and took me to the kitchen.

'I have the credentials you asked for.'

'You have to be useful for something, I suppose.'

She hadn't gone to Dunblane yet. She had delivery

jobs over the weekend and cash in hand was better than the promise of cash to come. Besides, many shops on the High Street would be shut on a Sunday so she couldn't have asked Abercrombie's neighbours if they'd seen anything suspicious.

'Tea? Coffee?'

I declined both and stuck to my guns.

'So when are you going?'

'Tomorrow. A couple of angles to cover here first.'

I assumed these involved the packing cases I'd noticed in that hall.

'Deliveries?'

'You could say that.'

I'd only been in her flat once before and that was at night, so at the time the darkness didn't surprise me. But now, in the morning, albeit on a wet and overcast day, it was striking. I assumed her bedroom was always dark; it was where she slept and played video games like Serrated Edge III. But the curtains in her living room were drawn too, so the kitchen, where we were then, was the brightest room in the house. The window was letting some light in and would have let in more had it been clean.

'I'll go there tomorrow, don't worry. Today there are things I have to move.'

42

As MacNeil led me into the hall towards her front door, I had the sense she was relieved to see me go. Though I tended to have that effect on women anyway, this was something more. She was anxious but trying to conceal it. Why? Looking back into the hall, I was struck again by the boxes. A delivery, she'd said. Yes, but who for? I walked past her into the house and headed for her bedroom; her gaming gear was there alright, but disconnected. If this had been Wyness, I'd have guessed she was upgrading. But MacNeil had never needed the latest of anything. Even if she had been that way inclined, she couldn't have afforded it.

'You're giving up, you're leaving.'

She stood there in the T-shirt she'd slept in, briefs, and socks which doubled as slippers, and rewarded me with a slow sarcastic hand clap.

'Well done, Douglas, got it in one.'

'Right, well I'll have that coffee now.'

'You just want to know if I still have a kettle.'

The coffee wasn't great but the mug was warm in the hand.

'You asked that Leandra person if you'd be able to keep your flat. According to her the answer was a qualified yes.'

'She also said several factors were involved which made it hard to say for certain.'

'There's a surprise.'

'She was hedging her bets, I get that.'

'And she got your thirty pounds.'

'Thirty pounds wouldn't have got me out of this one.'

We sat in silence for a while, thinking our thoughts, before she told me more.

'I had to cut my losses. The longer I stayed here the more they added up.'

'So you went to the bank.'

'Handing back the keys on Friday.'

'What happens then?'

'They put the house on the market, use the money to pay off the mortgage.'

I'd read of cases like this. The profit from the sale might not be enough to pay off what she owed. If that happened, she'd still have a mortgage but no house to go with it. The worst of both worlds. I wondered if she knew that.

'You might make a profit on the deal.'

'Come off it, Douglas. It's unlikely to pay back everything, they warned me about that, but I'll owe a helluva lot less.'

'I'm really sorry this is happening.'

'You did what you could.'

'So where are you going?'

'Rillbank Terrace.'

'Never heard of it.'

'It's not far from you, near the Sick Kids.'

Three empty houses had been occupied by squatters. No one was going to buy them, too near the proposed redevelopment at the hospital. In due course they would probably be demolished, like the other houses in the street. Progress in reverse.

'You know any of these people?'

'Booked a couple of them once. Possession. Harmless, though.'

I didn't like the sound of this one bit. Having an associate living with convicted druggies, how would that go down, with DS Cook, for example? It would probably be the last straw. And being around users there was always the danger that she'd regress and start using again. That would be a shame.

'None of them are dealers, Douglas, not one.'

While this was good to know, there was no escaping the look of thing. And how would she handle her clothing, her laundry and so on? Seeing her now in her night attire, that was fine, I was a sorry sight in that area myself. But it suddenly occurred to me to wonder how she dressed when working for me. Alison laid great stress on how clients, like it or not, judged by appearances before results. She'd forced me to sharpen up my act, bought me a tie, on one occasion ironed a shirt. *You can't go out like that!* What would she make of MacNeil? She could do neat and tidy but elegant she was not.

'I have a problem, though.'

She intended to deliver the boxes to her new home that day, but her computer, monitor and console, that was something else.

'I can't leave them there. People come and go all the time. I was wondering if I could leave them with you till I sort out something permanent.'

I was in two minds about this. It would be churlish to refuse, but if Alison called, which she was bound to at some point, the game would be up. She'd spot them right away. I could hear her even now. *Maureen MacNeil, are you out of your mind!*

'I could throw in a sweetener.'

'What might that be?'

'You still have those daft director chair things in your front room. I have real chairs. You could have them. Save you the trouble of shopping around.'

I went through to her front room to check them out. There were two, both a very light beige. I suppose they'd be classed as armchairs, though the arms were minimal.

'Try one. See what you think.'

I did. It was solid and comfortable as chairs went.

'I'll throw in free delivery.'

'When.'

'Tomorrow, if you ride shotgun. They're heavy. Take them to yours with my gaming gear.'

Though nothing had been farther from my mind when I got up, I spent two hours making repeat journeys to MacNeil's new home and carrying boxes to her room, which was reasonably large with peeling wallpaper and a high ceiling.

'I have it to myself.'

'So I should hope. What's the legal position, by the way?'

'Don't know, don't care, can't afford to.'

If memory served, squatting was illegal, but I made a mental note to check it out, then another problem crossed my mind. There was no lock on the door so anyone could rummage through her stuff when she was out. She couldn't risk leaving anything confidential in this place, her letter from Albion Assurance, for example. When she didn't need it, she'd have to leave it with me. And she was fine with that, why wouldn't she be?

On our last trip of the day to Rillbank, I was lifting a bin bag full of clothes from the back of the van when someone I recognised left the building. I turned to MacNeil.

'Know who that is?'

'No idea.'

And then I remembered that MacNeil hadn't actually seen her.

'Linda Hennessy.'

'Of Vellacott fame?'

'The same.'

It seemed our tattoo artist had found a new home too.

43

THE FOLLOWING DAY we struggled up the stairs to my flat with her surprisingly heavy chairs and more manageable gaming gear.

'What do you think?'

MacNeil hoped to hear that her chairs improved my front room.

'They're good, a great improvement.'

'So you can fold up these slatted things,' she said, referring to the director's chairs, 'and stash them in a cupboard. Just take them out when you have visitors. Or,' she added, 'since we both know you never have any, junk them in the nearest skip.'

She'd piled her computer equipment in a corner of the living room, and I thought how fortunate it was that I had no sofa which could double as a bed. If I had, MacNeil might have moved in too.

'Right, I'll be off.'

'Dunblane tomorrow?'

'Yes. You could come too if you like.'

'No thanks.'

MacNeil on her own was enough for the citizens of Dunblane to deal with. Two of us would come over as a heavy mob and we didn't want that. Besides, I wasn't sure I'd be available. Alison had texted me to be prepared. The subject being of some urgency, she was expecting a meeting with Ergonomica very soon. She added that a certain level of personal presentation would be advisable, kindly pointing out that my shoes hadn't met with polish in several weeks.

Fortunately, from the parking point of view, the location wasn't in central Glasgow but the Phoenix Business Park in Linwood. To avoid arriving late, Alison advised I use my satnav, forgetting I didn't have one. Nearer the destination I trusted my phone and arrived no trouble at all, to find Alison there already, car door open, papers on her knee. Last minute revision, this was a test she had to pass. When she saw me, she put her paperwork in her briefcase and joined me.

'Ready? Shall we go?'

The building occupied by Ergonomica was a two-storey affair of modern design between identical units on either side. A lady identifying herself as Eve saw us arrive and led us upstairs to a meeting room adjacent to the MD's office which, as a nod towards his status, was on a corner with windows giving out in two directions. Despite having a better view than most, he still hadn't seen it coming. Yes, there was a message there for us all. Feeling another Thought for the Day coming on I squashed it at once.

Neither of us had a coat, which was just as well as there was no sign of a stand. We were ushered to one side of the table and joined by two Ergonomica people on the other side with the top spot reserved for the boss. Neatly laid out at each of our places was a high gloss folder with the Ergonomica logo and the address of that company's global headquarters. Possibly a reflection of their coffers, the folders were empty.

'Good morning people, and thanks for coming at such short notice. I'm Frank Armstrong,' he told me, since Alison knew him already, 'MD here at Ergonomica.'

Frank had left his jacket in his office and took his place at the head of the table, sleeves rolled up and ready for action. To emphasise his boundless energy, he didn't sit down, but stood at his place like the conductor of a small band.

'Introductions, gentlemen?'

'Adam Douthwaite, Chief Financial Officer.'

'Eve Applebaum, head of HR.' Though not a gentleman herself, she deployed that well known human resource, the smile. 'We've already met.' And I had to hand it to her, she had an excellent set of ivories, small but perfectly formed.

'And this,' Armstrong said, indicating the man sitting beside Douthwaite, 'is Arthur Bridge. Arthur is not in fact a board member but co-opted on this occasion for reasons which will soon be clear. Before we begin, I should explain that the remaining members were unable to attend at such short notice.' He laughed uneasily. 'Mr Abrahams is in Shanghai even as we speak. Renegotiating. Something to do with castors, I believe.'

Alison handed her documents to Eve Applebaum, who took them from the room to the nearest copier, while Armstrong advised us all to pour ourselves water. We'd be likely to need it, if not something stronger. When Applebaum returned, she distributed copies of Alison's documents and our folders were empty no longer.

'Before we get down to business, some housekeeping. Arthur?'

'Thank you, Frank. In light of these developments, there's a possibility, indeed a likelihood of litigation further down the line. Though this meeting isn't on the schedule it is taking place nonetheless and if it comes to the bit we can't deny it took place. For example, we have all been seen entering the building and will no doubt be seen again when we leave. In due course, therefore, we may be required to produce minutes.'

With that in mind, Arthur Bridge, commercial lawyer, advised that if anything contentious were said it should not be minuted. This was particularly the case when it came to the accountants who had acted on Ergonomica's behalf before the recent take-overs.

'So when the minutes are proposed at the next scheduled meeting, they should be seconded, regardless of what may be omitted, as a true and accurate reflection of our discussions here this morning. That will provide us with a necessary degree of protection.'

'Thank you, Arthur, I trust we're all happy with that. In the absence of a secretary, Eve has agreed to take the minutes. Sensitivities being as they are these days, I should explain that the sole reason for this is that she alone among us has a legible hand.'

Used to the ordeal by soft soap and flannel, Ms Applebaum smiled in acknowledgment.

'So, necessary preliminaries over, I hand you over to Alison Eadie and her associate, Mr Hunter.'

The following few minutes proved demanding. Alison began by referring us to Document 1, which showed in great detail that Edwards Interiors had been booking projected profits as though they had already been made, giving the impression that the company was worth much more than it was. We spent several minutes poring over the rows of figures Alison had thoughtfully provided. In my case, though I understood the principle, the detailed columns of figures were beyond me. With one exception, I suspected I was not alone.

'Ah,' Arthur said, breaking the silence at last, 'a clear case of forward invoicing.'

'Exactly.'

Agreed on that point, Alison referred us to Document 2 which listed, again in great detail, the various crates and boxes found in Edwards Interiors' warehouses, all of which were innocent of their supposed contents. The list was long.

'This is fraud on a massive scale.'

Arthur again, though this time the document was easily understood by us all. Adam Douthwaite, chief financial officer, was appalled.

'For fuck's sake!'

Armstrong and Eve exchanged knowing looks.

'Don't worry, Frank, I won't minute that.'

And there was something about their brief exchange which led me to wonder if there were other things they shared, also absent from the minutes. But if there were, it really didn't matter.

'Any evidence of cookie jar accounting, Miss Eadie?'

According to Arthur, and he would know, this colourful phrase referred to reserves. When a company failed to meet its earnings target, it could dip into the cookie jar to inflate its numbers.

'In this case no, Mr Bridge. To do that, you need reserves to dip into.'

After thirty minutes of bad news, the Ergonomica contingent were looking understandably shell-shocked.

'It just goes to show, doesn't it,' Douthwaite said, 'you can have as many letters after your name as you like, but when push comes to shove they don't amount to a row of beans.'

He was referring to Ergonomica's accountants, who'd been retained to conduct due diligence and been paid handsomely for it.

'I mean,' he continued, reading from their website, 'just get a load of this: ATT, AAT, CTA, ACCA, CA, ACA and FCCA!'

These, he told us, were the tax and accountancy bodies JYD Accounting were accredited by or affiliated to. And he was making a valid point, but I couldn't help wondering why, as chief financial officer and an accountant with letters after his name as well, he'd failed to notice something amiss himself. It had taken the amazing Alison Eadie to see through it all. Yet looking at him across the table, I realised he wouldn't have long to go before he shredded his spreadsheets and headed for the course with his clubs, probably in the Algarve or some such place. He was sixty at least. And trim though he was, I couldn't but notice the beginnings of a double chin and bags under the eyes. After this debacle, his exit might be swift. My musings were cut short by Armstrong.

'First of all, Miss Eadie, please accept the thanks of the board for your work, I'm sure we're all very impressed. We certainly should be. And now, to the question of how best to take this forward. Can you put a number to the loss Ergonomica has suffered through these frauds?'

Alison referred us to Document 3.

'What you see here is a ball-park figure, Mr Armstrong. I've done my best to quantify your losses, but I don't think we can ever hope to come up with anything other than a reasonable estimate.'

'£340,000 and rising!'

'I expect it to exceed £400,000 when everything is accounted for.'

Douthwaite heard this figure with alarm, possibly imagining it might be subtracted from the considerable sum set aside for his pension.

'Two main questions confront us now,' Armstrong said, 'do we report this to the police, and whether we do or not, do we sue JYD? Arthur?'

'That's obvious, I would have thought. What do we want? We want our money back, or as much of it as we can get. Forget the police. Go straight for the jugular. Sue the bastards.' He appealed to Alison on the other side of the table. 'Excuse the legal language.'

'Mr Hunter, from your law-enforcement background?'

'I agree with Mr Bridge. Edwards Interiors has a case to answer but handing it over to the authorities isn't recommended. You can't fail to have noticed the collapse of several high-profile cases pursued by the Serious Fraud Office in recent years. In any case, the procedure is so lengthy that their ill-gotten gains will have been squirreled away long before it ends. If you can't get our hands on the money, what's the point?'

The way forward was to sue JYD Accounting. Alison had shown that their diligence had been woeful. They were a large outfit, they couldn't just skip the country as Alastair and Rachel Edwards might do, and probably had already. In my mind's eye, the couple were sunning themselves on the deck of their luxury yacht, the Monkey Business II, off the Centre Nautique at Balaruc, Sète or Nice. What were they drinking, I wondered?

'If I might just suggest,' Alison said, 'that the simple threat to sue might well be enough. JYD have their reputation to consider. Who would want to do business with these people if their dismal record with us was public knowledge? The damage would be considerable, their bottom line would take a heavy hit. It would be in their interests as much as ours to come to a private settlement.'

'Amen to that.'

I wasn't sure who'd said it, but given the parlous state of affairs, the meeting might better have begun with a prayer.

Having got to the stage where little of significance was left to be said, Eve led us downstairs to a kitchen where coffee and tea were available from large flasks, together with a selection of biscuits and shortbreads. Milk was on tap from a cute penguin flask, the bird being attired in its customary black and white dinner suit, with little yellow feet showing at the base and a matching yellow beak at the top. On the basis of no evidence whatsoever, a well-known technique among detectives, I suspected Eve was behind this blatant subversion of the business ethos.

I approached her as she was pouring a coffee for Armstrong, a coffee he could easily have poured for himself.

'Quite a meeting.'

'It was. Your colleague, Miss Eadie, has done an outstanding job, you know. We're all very impressed.'

I hoped this would be reflected in her fee but wasn't

indelicate enough to say so.

'We're shocked by the threats she's had.'

'That's really why I'm here. Accounts aren't my strong point.'

'Nor mine. So, Mr Hunter, do you think she'll accept?'

What was she referring to, a Bourbon cream, a one-off bonus payment? I must have looked puzzled, so she explained. By mutual agreement, Adam was heading for the exit.

'We've offered Alison a full-time position, chief financial officer.'

44

THERE ARE SEVERAL measures out there to help us drive safely. We shouldn't drive under the influence of alcohol or drugs, nor should we drive with the wheel in one hand and a mobile phone in the other. But no one's come up with a regulation forbidding the distraction of thought. How could they, and even if they could, how would it be enforced?

I was distracted by thoughts all the way back from Linwood to Gifford Park, so much so that I exited correctly at several junctions without noticing I'd done it. It was almost as if the car, like a horse, knew the way home and took it without human intervention. But it wasn't the car but my brain which was on automatic pilot.

Without meaning to, Eve Applebaum had sunk my peace of mind. She'd naturally assumed that Alison had told me about her job offer, we were associates after all, but Alison had not. When I asked her why that was, she pointed out, in case I hadn't noticed, that we were not in fact married. Behind this curt put-down was the idea that husbands and wives always levelled with each other. Both of us knew this was nonsense. She had no idea of her husband's sexual shenanigans till he died, and I had failed to notice that my loving wife was about to depart taking our dog with her. Our border collie, Ben, had later died of complications from the pica, but he was sorely missed, and I couldn't help thinking that what I could do with right now was a collie of the mind to round up my straying thoughts.

And here was another. Though we were associates in the

private investigation business, Alison was an accountant in her own right, a separate enterprise entirely where she operated as a sole trader. What work she undertook in that capacity was no concern of mine. She'd rounded off her defence by stating that no one told their business partners everything. Did I tell her everything? Thinking of my dealings with MacNeil, I had to admit she had a point. In any case, she hadn't decided yet, so there was nothing definite to report.

But if she accepted the Ergonomica offer, there were serious implications, and not just for her. Commuting from Edinburgh to Glasgow every day was possible, many people did it, but over time it would be wearing. So she might end up moving through to the west. In which case there would be small point keeping on her Royal Terrace house and paying for somewhere to live over there as well. And if she did that, where would Hunter Associates be then? She was not only a partner in the business but the one who took care of our accounts without charging a penny for the privilege.

In the hope of halting these runaway thoughts, I turned off the motorway at Harthill Services and made my way to the Wild Bean Café. It wasn't large but there were a few empty seats for the weary traveller. By the look of it, excellent croissants were available, but I associated these with breakfast, and being somewhat hidebound in my thinking, felt they weren't appropriate for two o'clock in the afternoon. So I took my seat with a coffee and a sandwich. Egg and cress on wholemeal bread.

I'd left my Ergonomica folder in the back seat of the car and had nothing to write on, so I listed salient points in an email addressed to myself for my attention later in the day. For example, a high-profile job offer was all very well, but how secure would it be? A stickler for detail, she might fall out with the dynamic, shirt-sleeved Frank. Or the company might fold. Either way she'd be out of a job. What then?

More pressing than this, though, was the question of Alison's safety. There would be no point trying to silence her now that several people, me included, knew exactly what had been going on at Edwards Interiors and had the facts and figures to prove it. Which was all very well, but only if the person issuing the threats was aware of it. For all he knew, Alison had yet to go public and silencing her would make sense. But despite Wyness' efforts, and although we could hazard an educated guess, we had no hard evidence as to who that person might be. And there were a few people out there, the Vellacotts of this world, who would attack their target regardless out of rage or revenge.

A strategy occurred to me at that point, but one I didn't like. Alison had been at the receiving end of threatening emails. When I'd been on the force, our advice to people troubled in this way was on no account to engage. They might hit the ball over the net, but you should just let it bounce. What you should not do was hit it back. The moment you did that you were playing their game. But in this case? Perhaps a terse reply, polite but to the point, would do the trick. *As of today, they know.*

At neighbouring tables people came and went, lone business types in tired suits which had once been sharp, families with children and dogs, couples wrapped up in each other believing their love would last. Some of them would be right but many would not. My bleak view stemmed from experience, but statistics were on my side. Divorce rates were going up and would only begin to drop as fewer people got married in the first place. Increasingly, I was overtaken by the feeling that I, Douglas Hunter, was a little more than a ghost in the land of the living, observing other people living out their lives as if they mattered, people who still had hope. And it occurred to me for the first time that though I could live with it, by which I meant continue to function, there had to be more to life than that.

If I remembered correctly, the Good Book referred to bread cast on the waters. It didn't say whether it was wholemeal or not, but even if it wasn't you could expect to find it again after many days. What you were supposed to do with it then was open to question, but find it again you would. It wouldn't be lost and gone forever or eaten by ducks. Yet here I was, living as one who cast his bread upon the waters expecting it to sink, this negative attitude now a habit of mind.

If I sought advice, what would it be? *You show clear signs of depression, Mr Hunter. Why don't you try our user-friendly selective serotonin reuptake inhibitors? These should do the trick with minimal side-effects.* Or almost as scary, *what you lack is a sense of belonging, of being part of a wider community.* At which point I'd be advised to take up country dancing or join a choir.

Still and all, as a homespun philosopher might have it, to distract us from such things we have TV screens on walls. The set facing me was on a news channel, the sound turned down but the subtitles on. Scientists had announced the discovery of the oldest and most distant galaxy yet found, though what they were going to do with this information was by no means clear. An attractive girl who sang songs had just won eight Billboard awards, quite a haul. And closer to home, police were investigating the death of a woman in a chalet at the Craigendarroch resort. At present, they described it as suspicious but were withholding the woman's name till family had been informed.

When I finally made it home, I closed my door behind me with relief only to hear someone knocking a few minutes later. Mrs Clarke from the ground floor.

'Ah, glad I caught you, Mr Hunter.'

A packet had been delivered. Too large to fit through the letter box, the delivery person had rung her bell and asked if she wouldn't mind taking it in for me.

'As long as this doesn't become a habit.'

I thanked her and assured her it wouldn't. I hadn't anything on order and had no idea what was in it. But Mrs Clarke wasn't finished.

'While I have you here, could I just draw your attention to the rota for cleaning the communal stair?'

She assumed I'd seen it pinned to the back of the main door. She realised I hadn't been in residence long, but we all had to pull our weight. The lady could have given me a few years and I could have given her the brush off, but I knew she was right.

'If you don't have a bucket and mop you can borrow mine.'

45

OVER THE NEXT few days, I worked on my mind more than my body, though the process was similar, keeping as active as possible. I was determined to make progress on something. Anything. One morning, as I attacked my cereal and soya milk, I looked at the two unopened packets which had taken up residence on the kitchen table. What was in the larger one Mrs Clarke had handed in? I hadn't a clue, so I opened it. Inside were six gluten free pastas, each one a different flavour. I hadn't ordered them, MacNeil certainly hadn't, Wyness avoided anything promoted as healthy, so my benefactor had to be Alison. I picked up one of them, gingerly, as though I was handling an unexploded bomb. Zesty Garlic Spinach. That would go down well, but what would it do when it got there?

'You must admit,' she said when I phoned her, 'you've never been given to healthy eating have you, not left to yourself.' Translated from the diplomatic, this meant when not being nagged into it by Susan.

'You're speaking to a man who's just polished off a bowl of bran flakes!'

'Pleased to hear it, Douglas, keeps you regular no doubt, but they're not exactly nutritious, are they?'

I had no idea whether they were or not, so I conceded the point.

'You have to look after yourself, you know. Living on your own is no excuse for letting things slide.'

She meant well so I thanked her and steered the

conversation on to how we should best respond to the threatening emails. I was still tempted by the idea of replying, letting them know that the time for threats had passed.

'Now that the cat's out of the bag, you mean. Well I think the less we have to do with these people the better. They'll soon know anyway.'

As often happened when a company was taken over, one of its management team had joined the board of the merged group, the better to arrange integration. That was the theory, though according to Alison it seldom worked in practice. In accordance with this principle, a manager from Edwards Interiors was now on the Ergonomica board but had sent his apologies. Either he'd been genuinely unable to attend or feared being clapped in irons if he turned up. In any event, he would shortly receive minutes of the meeting from Eve Applebaum's fair hand, and the damaging information would be out there. And so we agreed to let the matter rest.

Two days later, MacNeil hadn't contacted me, as she wouldn't if she'd nothing to report. And then it came, late on a Thursday afternoon.

'It's me. I could drop by tonight.'

Coming close to asking in advance if she could come, this was unusual; she would normally have arrived unannounced, brushed me aside when I opened the door and taken over the flat.

'Good.'

'What's for tea?'

When I tried her with garlic spinach, she replied with an earful of abuse and a threat to arrive with buffalo burgers and chips. If I really had to have vegetables, I should cover that angle myself. Oh, and she wouldn't have rabbit food in the house, she said, forgetting the house was mine. But she made good, arriving with burgers half an hour later.

Although women often credit themselves with the ability to multi-task, MacNeil wasn't one of them, devoting all her attention to larding on the ketchup, biting, chewing, and swallowing. She could talk and drive at the same time, but when it came to eating, she was totally single-minded. After she cleared her plate, she spoke.

'You could do with a wee bowl.'

'What for?'

'Ketchup, salsa, guacamole, whatever. For dipping your chips.'

'Didn't you have one in Roseburn?'

'Two, but I didn't think of it then. Anyway, here's where I'm at.'

Learning of Torquil Abercrombie's criminal record, the local police had changed their minds and checked Jezebel for dabs. It was clear that an attempt had been made to wipe the place clean but some had been found, several partials and seven complete. Since Joyce Abercrombie owned the shop and had been called to it by the police when the break-in was discovered, her prints had to be among them. When asked to provide prints for elimination purposes she agreed, provided they wouldn't be retained when enquiries were complete. The upshot was that three individuals had been identified: Joyce Abercrombie herself, one person not on the database, and the errant brother Torquil.

This had proved difficult for the investigating officers, who had no idea if Joyce might still be protective of her brother or estranged from him due to his criminal activities. When they broached this delicate subject, Joyce led them to believe that she had as little to do with him as possible. It wouldn't do much for her reputation as the owner of a jewellery shop to be associated with a known thief. That's what she said, and it made perfect sense. But was it true? The officers couldn't prove it but believed that it was.

'You know what one of them said?' MacNeil asked,

going to the kitchen sink, washing residual grease from her mouth, and wiping it off with the dishtowel. 'He actually said *my antennae tell me she's telling the truth*! Antennae! You couldn't make it up.'

According to the sister, Torquil was barred from the shop and hadn't been anywhere near it for several years. The police verified this by questioning her assistant, Eilidh, who worked for her on a part-time basis, so they'd applied for a search warrant, which they would execute as soon as they got it.

'Where does he live?'

'Stirling.'

At this point, MacNeil reverted to the detective sergeant she once had been and produced a small notebook from her jacket pocket.

'A two-bedroom flat in Raploch Road. Oh, and some background on the sister. She used to live in an upmarket area, Orlochy Park. We're back in Dunblane now, by the way. But she sold it and downsized to a terraced house on Springfield Terrace. You know the sort of thing, two storey building, satellite dishes, cars on the pavement.'

'Right.'

'As far as I can see, when money was short she didn't turn to crime, she tightened her belt.'

'Interesting. Good to know.'

'So this should also be good to know. The likelihood is that Torquil's place will be raided late tomorrow morning. They've agreed to let us observe provided we don't muscle in. We'll find out pretty damn quick if the stolen items are there.'

'Excellent.'

'Couldn't have done it without that letter from Albion. Ex officer or not, they were ridiculously sniffy till I had it. We could go together.'

We would use my car, saving her paying for fuel, and

it would get me out of the house into the wide world, just where I needed to be to improve my state of mind. But she wasn't finished.

'I'm beginning to wonder about you, Douglas. You don't seem wholly present to me. You're not paying attention like you used to.'

I was stupid enough to take the bait.

'What makes you say that?'

'Shut your eyes.'

'Don't be daft.'

'Humour me. Shut them.' Which I did. 'Right, so I've been here a while now, we've eaten together. Tell me what I'm wearing.'

As far as I could remember, she was wearing a dark denim jacket, dark denim jeans and black trainers which had seen better days.

'They're walking shoes, Douglas, not trainers, and grey, not black. What about my top?'

Try as I might, I couldn't picture it at all.

'You've known me for years; what colour are my eyes?'

I knew they weren't brown, a colour I associated with the eyes of cows.

'Dark blue? Grey?' I opened my own. 'Look, Maureen, what's the point of all this?'

'The point,' she said, 'is that if you were involved, you'd remember more. But the fact is you're not taking an interest like you used to. You seem quite happy to let things slide. Take that packet on the table.'

'What about it?'

'It's been there for days. I know, I brought it in. But you don't seem to care what's in it.'

Without a by your leave, she tore it open and placed the contents on the table before me.

'Bluetooth headphones. Aren't you the one!'

If I was, this was the first I'd heard of it.

'For my phone.'

Knowing I hadn't a clue, she paired my devices for me, but wanting to know they worked checked for music on my phone.

'Latvian kokle music! What are you on?'

'You know it then.'

'Of course not. Neither does anyone else.'

'Cook does.'

'Apart from her, and she probably knits as well.'

'I like her.'

'You could do worse.'

'She's married.'

'You haven't heard? She's chucked him out. Kept on getting drunk and reading books.'

I'd never thought reading books was a bad thing, and neither had Cook until her husband preferred reading a book, any book, to spending time with her and it had become a habit.

'They say he's living in the shop now.'

In due course I checked this out with John Banks, and it was true. A marriage in name only, Cook had said, and Ruby's Ready Reads now boasted the added odour of stale alcohol, background no doubt, but detectable nevertheless.

Then the conversation took a turn I should have seen coming.

'There's not much point me going back home now, just to come back in the morning.'

I didn't see how this could work; I only had one bed and no sofa.

'Where are you going to sleep; in the bath?'

'With you.'

46

I DIDN'T HAVE a sword as there is in the story, so I couldn't put one between us as an earnest of good behaviour. I did have a kitchen knife, but that wouldn't cut it – not because it wasn't sharp but because it wasn't long enough. I heard her brushing her teeth in the bathroom. She was using my toothbrush, which suggested that sleeping with me had been an impulse not a plan. She hadn't brought one with her. And the same went for night attire. She borrowed a T-shirt and slept in her briefs. To my surprise, she kept her socks on. She saw me clocking this as she sat on the edge of the bed about to climb in.

'Good for the circulation.'

I slept fitfully that night, though the same couldn't be said of her. She went out like a light, snored a little, but not a lot and always quite lightly. The first couple of times she turned towards me I was ready to repel boarders, but I needn't have bothered. Nothing happened. After an hour or two, I realised she had no designs on me at all. As she told me later, a woman had standards and hers didn't sink so low. MacNeil was many things, but tactful she was not. She hoped I hadn't been disappointed. I was on the point of telling her that far from being disappointed I'd been relieved, but caution prevailed.

The following morning, she beat me to the bathroom, splashed water all over the place and left me with a damp towel. She refused my offer of bran flakes. Slamming the door behind her, she headed for the Breakfast Club and returned with two bacon rolls. Apparently, we had to have fuel in the tank and slices of dead pig met that requirement.

'You could do with a shower.'

I tried to sniff my armpit, no easy task for one so stiff.

'Doesn't seem too bad.'

'Not you, Douglas. Your bathroom!'

'Funny you should say that.'

She was amazed to learn that I'd already covered that angle; all I was waiting for now was an installation date. She'd thought such enterprise beyond me.

'By the way, that mattress.'

'What about it?'

'Bring it from Laurieston?'

'Yes.'

'Seen too much action. Needs replaced.'

Even in her sleep she'd detected irregularities, lumps. Anyone living with this woman would soon be worn out. We were clearing up when the call came through. The warrant had been granted; we should leave for Stirling at once.

We took the M90 all the way, a journey, she assured me, where even I couldn't get lost. This was a cheap shot. My map-reading was excellent, my sense of direction good. Except when it came to navigating my way through life, where it had clearly been deficient.

When we arrived, the police were already there, so we parked some twenty yards down the road, on the opposite side for a better view of proceedings. Even at that distance we could hear shouting, presumably the aggrieved Torquil in full throat. After things settled down, time passed slowly. What were they doing in there? Then an officer came out to the street talking into his two-way radio. Shortly after that, an additional police car and van arrived at the scene, quite a turn-out for a petty thief like Torquil. When officers from the van started taping off the house, we really began to wonder what was going on.

An officer spotted MacNeil in the passenger seat and walked over with a smile.

'Back again so soon? You just can't keep away.'

On the face of it he was referring to the area, but he was really referring to himself.

'It's your magnetic attraction, Colin.'

Did I detect a spark, a frisson of sexual excitement? He was good looking alright – fit, as they say these days – and so clean-shaven I assumed he lathered himself with shaving cream of a morning and smoothed it off with a blade. But apart from his looks, Colin had what we really needed. Information. They'd found a handgun in the cistern, unlicensed. This had come as a surprise since there was no evidence of violence in Torquil's record. They'd confiscate it anyway, but in this case a test firing might show that the weapon had been used in an earlier crime or crimes and that would be serious.

Meanwhile, they were taking no chances, conducting a minute search of the house for any other weapon and not discounting the possibility of explosives. As Colin was explaining this, we saw the family from the house next door being ushered out to the street for their own safety and taken away somewhere, a community centre or some such. They'd be barred from their house for four hours at least, probably longer. Their little girl, still in her pyjamas, was clutching a Teddy bear. And why not, we all take comfort where we can.

'How did he explain it?'

'The usual. The gun wasn't his. Looking after it for a friend.'

This was all very interesting, and more than we'd expected when we set off, but not what we really needed to know.

'So, Colin.'

'Ah, right. Ok. So we found several pieces of jewellery

in a suitcase under the bed. They were wrapped in a pile of old clothes but that would fool no one. He was right, it wouldn't, and certainly not an alert young man like Colin.

'Amber?'

'Some. They're taking them to the station. We'll soon know if they're from Jezebel; we have excellent photographs of nearly all the items.'

These had been taken by Joyce Abercrombie, who'd pictured them in their most advantageous light for display on her website. With matching descriptions, shots like these would be definitive when it came to identification. So good, in fact, that they wouldn't need Joyce to identify them, though as a matter of simple courtesy they surely would. And then the bad news. The seizure of the handgun would cause a delay, quite a long one. So much so that Colin advised coming back the next morning when more would be known. Surprisingly, this seemed to suit MacNeil, a woman who liked things done immediately, if not sooner.

'See you tomorrow morning then.'

She said this to Colin with one of her smiles, so rarely deployed that laughter lines were unlikely in her case, saving her the expense of anti-wrinkle treatments in later life.

'I think I'll overnight,' she said to me as Colin returned to the scene, 'how about you?'

Neither of us had brought anything for an overnight stay, bad enough for me but worse for MacNeil, who'd already spent a night with me she'd hadn't been prepared for. Was it possible she hoped to meet up with Colin in the evening, maybe even repeat her performance of the previous night but with added action? If so, the last thing she needed was a millstone like me.

'Count me out of this one, Maureen. I've had enough for one day. I'm going home.'

47

WE ALL HAVE duties to perform. That day mine included taking MacNeil to the Premier Inn where she, rather neatly I thought, conned me into providing my card details at reception. That way she could leave the next morning without checking out. Everything she owed would be billed to the card. Thinking I might as well see what I was paying for, I accompanied her to her room, which had a large double bed in better order than mine and, to her delight, a walk-in shower.

'Come and see this!'

I popped my head in and there it was, but I'd seen a shower before. Seen one, seen them all.

'You don't have one in the squat.'

'Not working.'

On arrival at a hotel room, the custom is to unpack your things, but MacNeil had none to unpack, a problem on hygiene grounds alone. She sat on the bed and consulted her phone.

'There's a B&M not far from here.'

'I don't need to know that.'

'Yes you do. I'll navigate.'

She emerged from the store brandishing a ten-pack of Gorgeous Girl disposable briefs. To me, this came as a cultural shock. Most things were disposable in these troubled times, from coffee cups to coloured plastic vapes, adding to an extensive range which already included such minor items as relationships and marriages. But briefs!

What next? Where did they all end up when the girls they adorned slipped them off?

According to the package they were small, according to MacNeil that was the only size they had in stock. A fresh delivery was expected later in the week.

'They'll do the job. I don't have a big bum.'

I didn't need to know that either, though I had to admit she inclined to the androgynous, so she was probably right.

'I got something for you.'

She presented me with a chocolate Easter egg which I assumed she'd bought at a reduced price, Easter being over. It was done up in a pink ribbon.

'Why, thank you Maureen.'

Getting a present from Maureen MacNeil was probably a first, and not just for me, for anyone.

She hadn't tracked down tops, so she intended to make do with the one she was wearing. She hadn't slept in it, after all.

'And,' she added, producing it from her plastic bag with a flourish, 'check this.'

She'd bought a toothbrush and plainly felt that she'd covered the last remaining angle for the girl about town set on an overnight stay.

'We should grab a bite to eat, it's been a long day and it's not over yet.'

I didn't take to the fast-food outlet we ended up in. It didn't seem to me that civilisation had advanced, providing food without the eating irons to consume it. Would the Victorians have tolerated this? I didn't think so. MacNeil didn't seem to mind, though. She tore into her cheeseburger as if she'd just finished fasting for Lent and didn't speak till she'd despatched both it and her fries.

'That was good. Haven't had one for ages.'

Wiping her fingers with a napkin, she took a swig from her milkshake, glared at my side salad and asked me a question.

'So, what do you make of the show so far?'

Footage had since emerged of Torquil being led from his house in cuffs, together with a woman thought to be his girlfriend. Most of it was shot on mobile phones by passing locals. On several of these clips a woman was heard shouting insults, the worst of which was "paedo", a term of abuse often used without regard to what it meant.

From what Colin had told her, it seemed likely that Torquil was our man. But that took us no further forward in figuring out whether his sister, the estimable Joyce, had any involvement at all. His past record suggested that the brother wasn't past stealing the milk from your coffee, but there wasn't the slightest reason to believe that his sister was that way inclined. Such evidence as MacNeil had turned up, suggested the opposite. Joyce Abercrombie appeared to be a woman who cut her cloth according to her means, and I had some fellow feeling there since the failure of my marriage had forced me to do the same.

'We don't have any evidence pointing to Joyce. None at all.'

'Not yet, but that low-life brother of hers might point the finger when questioned.'

This was possible, but Torquil was a man who had happily lied his head off in court, so without corroborating evidence anything he said would be worthless. If he had motto, it would be, *It wasn't me, it was him.* In Latin, of course. He'd blame anyone, including his sister, to take the heat off himself.

MacNeil heard me out and thought for a moment.

'The thing is, Douglas, you can't afford to be taken in by externals. That fact that the sister's a well-turned-out member of the county set doesn't prove a thing. You'd really have to meet her to suss her out.'

I hadn't thought of it myself. Maureen MacNeil came up with the idea for me, and when we went our separate ways, I drove the few miles from Stirling to Dunblane and ended up at Joyce Abercrombie's door much like a travelling salesman. I didn't even know if she was in. For all I knew she might be attending a gymkhana or the Perth bull sales. An alluring image came into my mind of the lady in jodhpurs, but when she opened the door she was wearing slacks and holding a duster.

'Yes?'

Quickly scanning my letter of accreditation from Albion Assurance, she led me into her living room and offered me a cup of tea. She was just about to have one herself, or so she said, though I suspected she was just being polite.

'Any excuse for a break from housework,' she said with a smile and disappeared into the kitchen.

Her living room, though small, hosted a remarkable number of objects: several prints on the walls and ornaments on every available surface, mostly porcelain with a couple of small metal sculptures thrown in. The sole exception was her coffee table, groaning under copies of Accessories, The Art of Jewellery and back-numbers of Lady, and Home and Gardens. I saw no sign of books, but Joyce Abercrombie had enough reading matter here to keep her going for months.

In the past, an investigator could sidle up to bookshelves and record racks, figuring out the sort of person he might be dealing with or, altogether more tricky, the impression an individual might want to give. *Ah yes, do check out my little collection on particle physics. Quite comprehensive, though I say so myself.* No thanks, mate, that can wait till another day which, if I'm lucky, won't dawn. But now, you could find yourself dealing with someone who streamed music you couldn't hear and read eBooks you couldn't see, and that told you nothing at all.

Joyce Abercrombie emerged from her kitchen holding a tray loaded with cups and saucers, a tea pot, a milk jug and

Demerara sugar in a cut crystal bowl. Supporting it with one hand, she rearranged her magazines into a reasonably flat surface and laid the tray on top.

'Red Bush. All I have right now, I'm afraid.'

She was so welcoming it crossed my mind that she considered me, an emissary of her insurance company, as the bearer of good news. We had looked into the circumstances of her claim and were pleased to report that everything was in order. That would be unfortunate. Also, in talking with her, I would have to be careful not to pre-empt the police, who would surely be darkening her doorstep very soon.

'I don't know if you've seen or heard a news bulletin this morning, Miss Abercrombie.'

I was on her sofa, and she sat opposite me in a bucket-style armchair with a fitted cream cover. Her hair was much as I'd seen it in photographs, up, and held in place at the back with a powerful spring-loaded grip a crocodile would have been proud of.

'Before we go any further, Mr Hunter, I refuse to be addressed as Miss Abercrombie in my own living room. Joyce will do me fine.'

Since she hadn't heard, I explained.

'The police have reason to believe your brother may have been involved in the theft of jewellery from your shop. They arrested him earlier this morning.'

Her reaction convinced me that this came as news to her. She put down her cup with a clatter and looked out the window.

'So that's it. Even to me.'

He'd sunk so low that even his own sister was fair game. Blood may have been thicker than water, but I had the impression that if his had congealed in his veins altogether and taken him out with a massive stroke or heart attack it wouldn't have been the end of her world. She wouldn't have wished it, of course, but wouldn't have been grief-stricken either.

The other thing I noticed was something she didn't do; she didn't enquire what impact this might have on her claim. My feeling was that Joyce Abercrombie had no involvement whatever in the break-in at her store.

48

JOHN BANKS SOMETIMES contacted me for a meet-up to celebrate the end of the working week. He had done this while I was still in the force, the place where he was still employed, albeit as a civilian. And he did so the following day, a Saturday. It occurred to me again that while he was a salaried man, and probably worth every penny, I no longer was. Unlike him, my working week never ended, I was always on the job. When I pointed this out, he paused for a moment and came up with a solution of sorts.

'All right then, why don't we call it a convivium?'

I could think of a reason or two but, after all, the man was doing his best. And we met, or foregathered as he would have it, at the Richmond Café not far from his place of work. I knew he liked it because of its excellent selection of goodies, and as long as the coffee was good that was fine by me. He ordered a baklava and tried to sucker me into doing the same, but I was happy with a scone.

'If you don't mind me saying, Douglas, when it comes to food you have a bit of a traditional tendency.'

I didn't mind at all; at least my stomach knew what was coming its way.

His briefcase was bulging, some files he was taking home to look over, but mostly his lunchtime sandwich box, now empty. One thing it always contained was raw carrot, very beneficial for the vision.

'So that's why donkeys like it,' I'd said to him once. But you couldn't crack a joke with John without him taking it seriously.

'I'm not convinced they realise that.'

I could see why he might be well adapted to the precise analysis of data, an exacting task of which he never seemed to tire.

'So it's true what they say about DS Cook.'

When he remembered, he was also discreet.

'And what might that be?'

'That's she's left Cook the Books.'

'Now that's interesting; I'd forgotten this information was in the public domain.'

A strange reaction from a man who'd put it there himself.

'It's true, I'm afraid. Though it would be more accurate to say that he left her when she showed him the door of the marital home.'

'And that would be after ejecting him from the marital bed.'

'I can neither confirm nor deny that Douglas, as I'm sure you must know.'

'I heard he was living in the bookshop now.'

'Who told you that?'

'You did.'

'Ah, right, so I did. Why the interest?'

I couldn't really tell him till I knew the answer myself, but if John suspected I'd taken a shine to her he was probably right.

'I'll tell you one thing Douglas, don't let her politeness fool you. She's as sharp as MacNeil was before her, just civilised with it. Which is worse in a way, you don't see it coming till it's too late.'

As he polished off his baklava, he glanced at the display cabinet but decided against a second slice. Look after the ounces, he said, and the pounds looked after themselves. Then he mentioned something I wasn't expecting.

'Do you know a Daniel Drysdale by any chance.'

'He starred in a viral video a while back.'

'I know. We reviewed it at the station.'

'I can't imagine why, it's not that good.'

Not by itself it wasn't, but they'd been alerted by the NCA that Drysdale had downloaded from the dark web a manual for the construction of incendiary devices in the kitchen. His credit card usage showed that he'd started to compile the necessary ingredients, not that he was doing it very well. Further to that, they'd been checking his email and phone records – not the content, just the meta data – and in so doing had discovered that a certain Douglas Hunter was one of his contacts.

'DS Cook thinks it's you.'

'It is.'

'She wants a quiet chat.'

This would only have worried me if my dealings with Drysdale hadn't been entirely legal, but as it was, I found myself looking forward to another tête-à-tête with DS Cook, or Anastasija, as she now asked me to call her. But Banks wasn't finished with Drysdale.

'He's been buying magnesium supplements online. In quantity. Much more than anyone would need to boost their health. He knows what he's trying to do but hasn't a clue how to do it.'

'I thought you said he had a manual.'

'He does. But you know how some people are, can't assemble flat pack furniture without calling in the joiners.'

I'd never tried, but that would probably be me.

'You won't believe this, but he's just ordered twenty-five containers of sixty capsules, a hundred milligrams each. Our best guess is he's planning to grind them down with a mortar and pestle thinking he'll end up with a useful quantity of flammable magnesium.'

'And he won't.'

'No way. For a start, there's more in these capsules than

magnesium: zinc, vitamins, not to mention the casings themselves. How does he hope to separate them out? In any case, what he's buying isn't pure magnesium, it's a compound.'

'Right.'

'Magnesium citrate, if you must know.' Which I most definitely did not, but data analysts don't know when to stop. 'Furthermore,' he added, and I believe this is what amazed him most, 'he's down on the deal a cool four hundred and seventy-five pounds!'

'You're aware he's crowdfunding.'

'That's for legal expenses, nothing to do with buying chemicals.'

'Check what he's spending it on, though. He's not picking up this bill out of his own pocket.'

I had John thinking now. Instead of police intervention, perhaps Drysdale could be stopped in his tracks by donors demanding their money back or threatening to sue him for fraud. Drysdale was an obsessive, a man with a bee in his bonnet. No matter how often he took off his hat it refused to fly away. But from everything John had told me, the only danger he posed was to himself.

We sat there for a moment or two in the warm glow of the knowledge that however inadequate the pair of us might be, we couldn't hold a candle to Dan Drysdale. But why would Cook want to talk to me about this young man; he was clearly no threat to society at large? Alright, he was a client, but there had to be more to it than that.

That same evening, MacNeil made contact again. I was back home by then, relaxing in one of her armchairs. The errant Torquil was being held at Randolphfield nick. He'd been interviewed twice, the first time represented by a lawyer from the list, the second time by himself. The lawyer had been a complete nonentity, a gormless pratt, a gutter-level oik. He would have done better with a chocolate tea pot. And so the insults had gone on. He may have been right in his assessment, but I doubted it. He'd expect to be released within five minutes on a legal technicality and when this didn't happen it was down to his brief.

'The gun. He claimed a friend had called late one night in a bit of a lather and asked him to keep it, just for a couple of weeks, no longer. That had been two years ago. The officers thought this was probably true, but since he refused to name the friend, they were nailing him for illegal possession.'

There was nothing surprising there, they'd have done that anyway.

'Did you get all that, are you still awake?'

'Yes, Maureen. Sorry. Go on.'

'Right, well at first he said he'd nothing to do with the robbery. And he stuck to that till they asked him to explain the fingerprint.'

'He wouldn't like that at all.'

'He didn't. Thought he'd wiped the place clean. So then he made a big play of fessing up. Alright, you got me there, now I'll tell you the truth. You know how it goes.'

I knew the song only too well and, in this case, had a good idea of the words.

'Right, so his story. Joyce put him up to it. Money was running out, he could rob the shop and sell the expensive pieces, she would clean up on the policy. That way they'd both win out. "Hit the jackpot" was what he actually said.'

'What a shit this guy is.'

'Just because you've got the hots for the sister.'

'I've only met the woman once.'

'She offered you tea and biscuits.'

I shouldn't have told her that. While it was true, it was hardly the equivalent of turning up on my doorstep with a winning smile and casserole, assuring me she could call back for the container in a day or two after I'd washed it.

'So how did they deal with that?'

'Very well, I thought. Just shows you can live in the sticks and still have a brain. They asked him if they'd discussed this cunning plan by phone or in person. He knew phone records would show he was making it up, it had to be in person. So then they asked him for a date.'

'He'd say he couldn't remember, wasn't sure.'

'He did, but they got him to narrow it down to one of three consecutive days. He couldn't remember which, but it had to be one of them. Took them over three hours, but they got there in the end.'

'Good for them.'

'And guess what? Joyce was in Dublin for a week at the time, meeting up with an old schoolfriend and taking in a craft fair while she was at it.'

'And the friend confirmed it.'

'Yes, and several people who'd talked with her at the fair.'

'Got him cold.'

'Exactly. I'm coming back tomorrow. No need to stay on here now. Colin will keep me posted.'

I was sure he would.

49

FOR ME, SUNDAY would only be a day of rest if I could turn my brain off. But since I couldn't do that, I took it for a stroll through the Meadows. And they were at it still, the women's exercise groups led by trainers with routines so well worked out that the calories the ladies burned off as they ran to the designated tree and back again for five minutes wouldn't be exceeded by the coffees and pastries they rewarded themselves with afterwards at Victor Hugo's. But if their weight didn't benefit, their muscles surely would. Sunday was a day for pious hopes.

Quite a few dog walkers were out too, only to be expected. In the past, the custom was to throw sticks for the animal to retrieve; now, though, coloured plastic ball launchers were all the rage, and I couldn't help wondering why people with hands and arms needed them at all. Alison had noticed this too, and asked me, with some asperity I thought, where all these plastic objects ended up when they died. *You've never asked yourself that, have you?* She put this to me in accusatory tone as if, because I had a dog, I was guilty of the habit too, though I never had been.

John's take on the subject was quite different. He knew how attached I'd been to my border collie, Ben, and how upset I'd been when the vet had to put him down. He'd also noticed – he was employed by the police after all – that my wife had left me for a bronzed outdoor type with more to offer than me. So now I had no one, I was all by myself. Alone. At this point I felt he was pushing me into Nobody's

263

Child territory and steered him away from the subject. But not before he suggested I should get another dog to keep me company, maybe a rescue dog from Seafield, who'd thank me for a good home, regular exercise, and meat on the bone.

But that was the whole point. I was living alone now and wouldn't be able to take a dog with me when I was working. And another thing he hadn't thought of. My previous house had a secure back garden where Ben had been able to amuse himself without fear of escape. True, there was a garden here at Gifford Park, but it was shared by several people, some of whom hung washing on the line and left the rear door open while they were at it. I didn't see how it would work. Being a reasonable man, he accepted these points before going on to suggest that if a dog was out of the question I could fall back on a goldfish.

My stroll took me through the Meadows and on to Tollcross. As I was passing the Heavenly Garden Chinese and Oriental Supermarket, I saw someone waving to me from the interior. Mr Chen. And I was struck by a thought. MacNeil couldn't squat indefinitely; her muscles would seize up. What she needed was a place of her own, and who owned five properties in the city? There he was, the man himself, Mr Chen, looking uncommonly dapper in his slacks and tartan waistcoat, one of those garments with a satin sheen at the back. I wondered which tartan it was. MacChen, perhaps, modelled for us today by MacChen of the Isles.

'Good day, Mr Hunter. On the trail of another miscreant?'

'Not today, no.'

'So what can we offer you?'

And I have to hand it to him, he tried.

'Our Meiji Hello Panda Biscuits are proving popular, as are our Sam Pan Char Siu Buns.'

I was sure they were flying from the shelves, but my interest lay elsewhere.

'Tell me, Mr Chen, do you have any vacant rooms right now?'

He looked surprised at the question.

'You are homeless?'

'Not for me, for a friend.'

'Ah.'

According to Mr Chen, the word "friend" was capable of several constructions, some of them dubious, so I explained that I was asking on behalf of a colleague who, like me, had also been a police officer. Reassured by this information, he told me that demand was high at the moment. So much so that he only had one vacant flat, and that because it was being redecorated.

'Would you like to see it now? It's just a short walk.'

In this case, putting two and two together couldn't have been easier. The flat Vellacott had trashed was just across the road in Lochrin Terrace and no one could have lived there till it had been cleaned up. We entered the blue main door from the street and went up the stairs to the flat.

'You will remember it as it was, of course. Not as it is now.'

The living room, recently a scene of splintered glass and gashed upholstery was now transformed, a new sofa and armchair on a new fitted carpet. The coffee table vandalised by Vellacott had been replaced by a circular rattan job with an oak-effect top. Since Chen knew from bitter experience that expensive furniture could prove to be money wasted, I assumed the table hadn't cost the earth and the top was veneer. He patted the sofa.

'This one makes down into a bed. No metal frame or springs, just foam. Saves a great deal of space. But I haven't got round to replacing the TV yet, I'm afraid.'

'I wouldn't worry about that, Mr Chen, the lady I have in mind never watches TV. She's into video games and has her own gear.'

'Video games?'

'I know. I've never seen the attraction either.'

'There must be better ways of employing the limited time available to us on this earth.'

I had to agree with him there.

'And so we kill time, till time kills us.'

He looked so thoughtful as he said this I wondered if he was quoting Master Kong or Lao-Tzu, but I wasn't well enough versed to know.

He led me to the bedroom and pointed to the area where Vellacott had spray-painted the words *UP YOURS BITCH* in red and black on the discreet floral wallpaper. Intended for his partner, Linda Hennessy, this message had been removed. As far as I could see, the old paper had been stripped off and replaced by new lining paper, then painted over with a bland vinyl emulsion.

'Waterproof,' Mr Chen said proudly, 'really intended for bathrooms, but as I know to my cost you can't be too careful these days.'

Mr Chen had done a good job on the flat and was ready to put it on the market again, but he agreed to hold off for a week till I could talk it through with MacNeil.

'This friend of yours can cover the deposit, I take it?'

Even if she couldn't, I could, and since MacNeil would cause no damage I'd get my money back if she left.

'You say she works for you.'

'She does.'

'Then you will act as guarantor?'

I hadn't a clear idea what this entailed, but I knew from my dealings with him that Chen was an honest man, so I agreed.

As we left the stair and made it to the street, Chen paused and handed me the keys.

'I have another set at home. Your friend will want to inspect the flat.'

You would think so, yes, but since we were talking about MacNeil that remained to be seen.

50

With the information available to me now, I had no doubt that the robbery at Jezebel was entirely down to Torquil, a conclusion reinforced by his bungled attempt to implicate his sister. It was possible he'd done this to get himself off the hook, but that was no excuse. Given some of the things he'd said during his interview, there was reason to believe he harboured a deep-seated resentment of his sister, a lady who would never qualify for businesswoman of the year but had always given it her best shot. Was she really a stuck-up cow? She hadn't come across that way. An arty farty ratbag? This was envy talking, and not making a good job of it.

Since there was no further progress to be made on the case, I summarised my findings in an email to Albion Assurance. Though Joyce Abercrombie's brother had been behind the robbery, Joyce herself had not been involved. The policy should be honoured. I had mixed feelings about this. Presumably, Albion had asked me to investigate with a view to saving money by not paying out. By this measure I had failed. But the company would have its good name to uphold. Refusing to honour the policy would be unreasonable and might end up with the financial ombudsman, or worse, make it to the complaints section of a national newspaper. They wouldn't want that either.

Attached to my findings, I submitted an invoice detailing the hours devoted to the case and the expenses incurred, notably MacNeil's overnight stay in Stirling. I had told Mr

Cameron that she would be leading on this one, and though I'd been with her for several hours I thought it best not to bill him for that. MacNeil could easily have handled it on her own. Reputations matter in every walk of life, or so I liked to think.

Though she'd been much in my mind, MacNeil had deliveries to make on Monday, so I dropped by to take her to Mr Chen's flat on Tuesday morning, only to find her in Linda Hennessey's room, leafing through a book of tattoo designs with worrying signs of interest. In our line of the work, the lower the profile the better; the last thing we want to do is draw attention to ourselves with piercings or tattoos.

Sneaking a closer look at the book, I found it rejoiced in the name *Expressive Skulls*, a come-and-get-me title if ever I'd seen one, but very much in keeping with Hennessey's Goth image.

'What do you think?' she asked, pointing to an illustration of a highly coloured skull, which called to mind a heat-map of a badly insulated house.

'Very striking.'

'That's what I thought.'

I wasn't sure if her interest was academic, or she was actually considering subjecting herself to Hennessey's dark arts. But if it was the latter, I had to avoid any attempt to put her off because, being MacNeil, that would reinforce her desire to go ahead.

'I like it,' she said, closing the book and laying it on the bed. 'So what's the story, doc?'

I told her it was a surprise, something I wanted her to check out, and by the skin of my teeth managed stop her forcing it out of me on the short journey to Lochrin Terrace. If we'd been going further afield, I wouldn't have stood a chance.

Unlike me, she hadn't seen the flat before and certainly

not in the state it had been left in. She went from room to room before joining me on the living room sofa.

'Not bad.'

I thought so too. It had everything the girl about town could want, including a full-length swivel mirror in the bedroom.

'Broadband?'

I had no idea. It hadn't occurred to me ask when Chen was showing me round.

'You know I'm into gaming, right?'

I did.

'And you know what's really handy for gaming?'

'Broadband. Alright, I'll ask Mr Chen about that.'

I could almost see her ears pricking up through her hair as she figured it out.

'This was Vellacott's flat!'

'Right.'

Then the conversation turned to money. She was fine with the deposit; since I'd get it back, she wouldn't owe me anything. But she'd never intended to swap her mortgage for a rent costing just as much. What would be the point?

'You're making money now, your deliveries and working with me. And you could always share with someone. Vellacott did.'

'Yes, but Douglas, come on, he shared with Linda, and not just the flat, the bed as well. Correct me if I'm wrong here, but this place only has one bedroom. What are you expecting me to do, round up a rent-paying man from the street and force him under the duvet?'

Unlike the broadband, this was a problem I'd seen coming. My solution was the sofa bed in the living room, thoughtfully provided by Mr Chen.

'Sharing would half the cost and you'd have a place you could call your own.'

'Cards on the table, Hunter, why are you so keen on this?'

Apart from the fact that I'd be happier if she had somewhere permanent, it would benefit the business. If she were called upon to testify in court, her residence would be the first thing to come up after her name. But as we both knew, that would do nothing for her credibility as an upstanding witness for the prosecution. I could just hear the defence lawyer now, in ham-actor's caustic tone. *And so, Ms MacNeil, you currently reside in a squat, which you and I both know to contravene section 68 of the Criminal Justice And Public Order Act 1994. And yet you expect this court to accept the evidence of a self-confessed lawbreaker when it comes to the accused?* At which point MacNeil would denounce this for the garbage it was, the Sheriff would intervene, and we'd be in deep trouble.

She could see the force of my argument, but who did I imagine she could share with?

'Linda? Seems a nice enough girl to me.'

'She is. I like her.'

'There you are then.'

But there we were not. Did I really think that after what she'd gone through in this very flat, Linda would want to come back?

'You hadn't considered that, had you?'

I had to admit I hadn't. Chen had restored is so well it was hard to believe it was the same place.

'And while we're at it.'

'Yes?'

'You've seen what Linda's like, a Goth to her silver toe rings. There's no way she'd settle for a sofa bed. She'd rather sleep in a coffin.'

I pretended to consider this.

'That could be arranged.'

51

I WAS SETTLING down to read the next instalment of James McLevy's casebook that afternoon when the buzzer rang.

'Hi, it's me. Anne.'

I opened the door to a young woman, mid-twenties or a little older, short, about five feet two inches, black hair parted in the middle. I'd never seen her before.

'Come in.'

'Thanks.'

I showed her into the living room.

'Ah, the famous chairs,' she said, sitting on one and dropping her carrier bag on the floor by her feet.

'You realise,' I said, 'that I have no idea who you are or what you're doing here.'

'Didn't she tell you? She said she would.'

'Who?'

'Your friend, Maureen. She said you wouldn't mind if I came round.'

'You were unconscious?'

As jokes went it wasn't the best, but her put-down took me aback.

'Don't be stupid.'

'I'm in my own house, I can be stupid if I like.'

'I shouldn't have said that. Sorry. But Maureen warned me you could be a bit weird.'

It was evident that MacNeil had not only told Anne about the flat but me as well, and while she was at it, the famous chairs. The person she hadn't alerted was yours truly, so

I'd have to find out for myself.

'I take it you're staying in the squat?'

'That's where we met.'

She worked as a manager in a supermarket. When she discovered her husband was cheating, he threw her out.

'This may seem an obvious point, Anne, but if he was the one who was cheating, you should have thrown *him* out.'

'Easy for you to say. His name was on the title deeds, mine wasn't.'

This was a story I'd heard before, there were too many Annes out there.

'When was this?'

'Three weeks ago.'

'Were you sharing the household expenses?'

'He paid the mortgage; I paid the council tax and the energy bills.'

Andrew was a specialist, dry walling and Ames taping, so he was bringing in money alright, but he'd been spending most of it on the fancy woman he was banging when Anne was at work. What he forgot was that Anne had friends and they had eyes. His cheating ways were bound to come out in the end.

'So you're thinking you might share with Maureen.'

'She used to be a police officer. If he comes hammering on the door she could sort him out.'

'Is he likely to do that?'

'He's done it already.'

'I don't get it. He cheated on *you*, he threw *you* out.'

But there was a remorseless logic to it. No longer living there, she stopped her direct debits both to the council and the power company. And who could blame her, but this hadn't been part of his plan.

'What happened?'

'Maureen saw him off.'

According to Anne's account, seeing him off involved kneeing him in the groin to the danger of his paternal prospects, putting him in a head lock and bouncing his head off the wall several times with special reference to his bald patch. It had Maureen written all over it.

'He wouldn't like that at all.'

'He didn't. Threatened to report her.'

'Did he?'

'No.'

That was a relief. Hunter Associates could ill afford another assault on our record. Knocking Gaines off his bike was enough to be going on with.

'He couldn't.'

'Why not?'

'Five of us were in the house when he arrived. We all said we'd tell the police he'd started it and Maureen was defending me.'

'She was.'

'Yes, but they didn't know that. They weren't in the room at the time.'

'I take it you want to see the flat.'

'If that's Ok with you.'

I drove her round to Lochrin Terrace, gave her the keys and waited in the car while she went up to look it over. I'd seen enough of it for one day. I turned the radio on. Choral Evensong from Chester, which didn't get me going at all, so I surfed my way to a drive time show. After an ordeal by jingles and wisecracks, there was a news summary on the hour. A group of lesbian abseilers had been arrested at the House of Commons, the story being so colourful that the point they'd been making got lost in the report. Volunteers cleaning up part of the Forth and Clyde canal had found three old prams and a sawn-off shotgun. And an update on the woman found dead at Craigendarroch; she had now been identified through dental records as a Mrs Jennifer Slorach. The police were appealing to the public for any information they might have regarding her recent movements.

'Slorach. An unusual name that.'

'Yes, Jim, I hadn't come across it either, so what did I do? I looked it up!'

'Good for you, Ellie, and what did you find?'

'Well Jim, it seems to have come from the word "sluagdach", which means "leader" in Gaelic. I hope I'm pronouncing that right.'

'So do I. Any native speaker out there who can set us straight on that, text us on 05868 and we'll call you straight back. You'll be on air before you know it.'

My pain was cut short by Anne opening the passenger door and getting in.

'It's not bad. It's really quite nice.'

'What did you make of the sofa bed?'

'It wouldn't do for a taller person, but it's fine for a shorty like me. And it's new, still has some bounce to it.'

'You checked that, did you?'

'Too right. Bounce really matters in a bed.'

I took her word for that and dropped her off at the squat on my way back home. I was just polishing off my lamb rogan josh when it occurred to me. Increasingly I found myself doing something while thinking about something else, then having to retrace my steps to make sure I'd actually done it at all. Had I locked the door when I left the house? Although I'd no memory of it, I usually had. In this case, though, I couldn't hope to reconstruct it; I hadn't been with Anne when she left the flat. She'd given me back the keys alright, but had she locked the door? The chance that she hadn't was a risk I couldn't afford to take, so I drove back to Lochrin to check. And sure enough, she had.

Just as I was leaving for the second time that day, MacNeil called.

'Something I meant to tell you, Douglas.'

But I'd met Anne already, knew where she was coming from and had a good idea where she was going.

52

THE FOLLOWING DAY was fallow except for two calls. The first was a video call from Alison, who had no deep reason for calling except that she wanted to make contact. Though come to think of it, that is probably the deepest reason of all. I was in the living room at the time, sitting on one of MacNeil's chairs surveying the walls, considering how to make them less bare. Alison was, as she put it, still on the horns of a dilemma; should she accept the post with Ergonomica or not? I had no idea, though for purely selfish reasons I hoped she would stay put. When I ran my bare walls dilemma past her, she perked up at once. This was just up her street and took her mind off the major decision she still had to make.

'Let me see them again?'

I gave her a slow panoramic sweep of the room, but other things were in the picture as well.

'Hold on a sec, what's that?'

'What's what?'

'That pile of junk in the corner.'

She had just seen MacNeil's gaming gear and knew it wasn't mine.

'Closer, please.'

I reluctantly obliged. The game was up and it wasn't Serrated Edge.

'A gaming console! That's not yours. You've never played a game in your life. You wouldn't know how.'

'They're MacNeil's.'

Even on my phone's small screen, her face was a study.

'You've impounded them.'

I told her that MacNeil, temporarily homeless, was living in a squat and had left her equipment with me for safe keeping.

'And how do you come to know all that?'

'I made use of her services recently.'

'Not in connection with the business, that wouldn't do at all. That,' she said, attempting to skewer me with a look, 'would be totally unacceptable.'

Though thinking quickly has never been a strength, I came up with a life-saving evasion.

'She delivered these chairs.'

'Out of the goodness of her heart, I suppose.'

'No.'

'There's a surprise.'

'She runs a delivery business now.'

I was spared further interrogation by an incoming call; she didn't want to, but she really had to take it.

'Sorry, Douglas, have to go. I'll deal with this later.'

I didn't like the sound of that. Was she planning to come through with an axe? The way out of this, if there was one, would depend on MacNeil. I walked to the squat, at high speed for me, and found her sitting cross-legged on her bed. She might have liked that position anyway, but she didn't have a chair. She was planning a delivery round for the days ahead.

'Well, well, if it's not the man himself.'

'What's left of him.'

She heard me out as I explained my problem.

'She still hates my guts, right?'

'You accused her of murdering her husband.'

'We all make mistakes.'

'Maureen!'

'Alright, that was a big one as these things go. Anyway,

276

how do you want to play it?'

'I don't know. It's a mess.'

'Want to know what I think?'

'That's why I'm here.'

The wisdom according to MacNeil was that I should level with Alison, but not all at once. Bit by bit, to lessen the shock. If I wanted her to keep quiet, she would, but she wasn't the only one who knew about our arrangement. Wyness knew a bit and Cook knew a lot. In any case, other jobs would come up. If we continued working together it would come out sooner or later. Probably sooner.

'And another thing.'

'What?'

'Keeping a secret like that, it's a strain, especially for a goody-two-shoes like you. Keeping up a front takes energy, and we both know you're a bit short in that department.'

She was starting to come across as my analyst, which was ridiculous, but she had a point.

'I mean, come on, Douglas. You're not here now because you're relaxed and at ease with yourself. Deception isn't your thing.'

I had just agreed to take her advice when Linda Hennessey walked in, like the Black Album remastered in the flesh.

'I'm off now. See you later.'

'Where's she off to?'

'The Scottish Tattoo Convention.'

The fact that there was one came as news to me. Life was passing me by.

'It's an annual event.'

She put her phone down on the bed and got serious.

'You've met Anne.'

'I have.'

'I think it'll work. We're planning to give it a go if you come up with the deposit like you said.'

At last, a bit of good news. They'd have the security of a place to stay, and in my mind's eye the setup was simple. MacNeil would play her video games in the bedroom, she used headphones anyway, the gaming type with mic, and Anne would watch TV in the living room when Chen had installed it. She liked game shows and reality TV programmes, which were just extensions of game shows anyway. Though MacNeil detested both of these things, she wouldn't have to watch them. Perfect! I agreed to visit Mr Chen and seal the deal.

'And there won't be my gear in your living room anymore.'

Noticing that I was growing restive with nowhere to sit, MacNeil led me out to the garden, where a wooden bench was available for those hoping to squat in the sun.

'You could do worse, you know. She's a nice girl.'

'She a Goth!'

'Not Linda. Anne.'

I couldn't believe it; MacNeil was trying to pair me off.

'She's only five foot two.'

'Give her a chance. She'll grow on you.'

53

BY THE GOSPEL according to MacNeil, the life of the solitary male was not the best. There was a regrettable absence of human warmth about it, and in any case, she added, I didn't want to die alone. Aside from the fact that this was a bit much coming from Maureen MacNeil, the very type of the unattached female, the thought that Anne would grow on me called to mind a tree weighed down by ivy. I didn't doubt she was a nice girl, and cuddlesome when the occasion arose, but this was a complication I could do without.

All such thoughts were banished by a call from DS Cook. We needed to talk, she didn't want to drag me down to the station, so it was her place, mine, or a neutral venue of my choosing. It couldn't be the bookshop, though; she was sure I'd know why.

'Where do you live?'

'Eyre Place. Can you be there at three?'

Cook lived on the third floor of a four-storey tenement and, amazingly, the main door to the street was blue. I was beginning to detect a theme here. Some people believe that there is no such thing as coincidence, but as my late father would have put it, I'm here to tell you there is. Because, really, my third blue door didn't mean a thing, and that put it in a very large category, since when you come right down to it, most things don't mean a thing.

On that happy note, I climbed the stairs to her front door and she waved me in.

'I'm not exactly hostess material,' she said, showing me

into the kitchen, but for you, Douglas Hunter, I have a choice of chocolate digestives or speķa pīrādziņi.'

Unlike my kitchen, there was no table, just a breakfast bar you could sit at on tall, chrome-legged bar stools. This arrangement was probably more up-to-date and therefore less satisfactory to a hum-drum individual like me who preferred not to perch. If I lacked a sweet tooth, I should plump for the pīrādziņi, savoury pastries with meat, cheese and onions. I was tempted; their crescent-shape reminded me of Cornish pasties.

'I hope you haven't gone to this trouble on my account.'

'Do you see anyone else here?'

Perched beside her with a coffee and one of her savoury pastries, she came to the point by way of a tangent.

'You have instincts.'

'I do.'

'Which you trust.'

'Yes.'

'My instinct tells me that you are basically alright but sometimes make bad decisions.'

'Like getting married.'

'I'm not best placed to talk about such things, as I'm sure you know.'

'The jungle drums have spoken.'

'As they do.'

She was referring to the way I was running my business. The fact that I had teamed up with Maureen MacNeil was a concern. I tried to excuse her.

'I'm sure you know this already, but Maureen is a force of nature.'

'So are earthquakes, hurricanes and tornados.'

Only time would tell if MacNeil would come good, she seemed to have done well in Dunblane, but Cook's immediate concerns lay elsewhere.

'You recently assisted a man called Daniel Drysdale

by providing him with an address where a film producer might be found. Chester H Burt.'

'That's true, I did.'

'Which Drysdale then used to harass the man on his own doorstep.'

'That's true too. But when he was asked to depart he did, and no violence was involved.'

'But Douglas, you have to think about this more deeply. Did you consider what he might go on to do with this information when he had it?'

'He told me he was going to challenge Burt on the question of image rights, pay him back in his own coin, so to speak, on film, and if that got him nowhere his intention was to seek redress through the courts. He needed an address for both of these purposes.'

'And you believed him.'

'What he was saying made sense.'

'Right, so tell me, when has court action ever involved firebombs?'

She had me there, of course, and her point was that I should think twice before agreeing to supply a client with information before I was sure how that information would be used. A client might tell me his wife was missing, he was very worried about her, when in fact he was an abusive husband using me to track down the house she'd taken refuge in.

Given my past history, this was a difficult one to deal with.

'I tried to track down my wife when she went missing.'

'I know, but you're not abusive.'

And then there was the recent case of Anne. If her errant husband asked me to track her down, I would certainly refuse.

'Anne?'

'Sorry. I forgot you wouldn't know.'

She listened with interest as I explained, nodded approvingly, but went on to make her point anyway.

'I think you need to exercise more discretion in the cases you take on. That's all I'm saying.'

'You're right, of course.'

'Good.'

At that point her phone rang and she left the room to take the call. I could hear her pacing up and down the hall as she spoke but couldn't make out what she was saying. From my vantage point on the bar stool, I looked round her kitchen. A frying pan rested on the hob and there were several magnets on her fridge and microwave. Some were notice board magnets in various colours, black, red and blue. But one on the fridge bore the words *The pies are finished*, and another beside it, *You eat it, you replace it!* One on the microwave also caught my eye; *Men to the left, women are always right.* It crossed my mind that Cook the Books had left the marital home following a less-than-subtle campaign by his wife.

When she ended the call and came back, her mood was sombre.

'What we were talking about before, these are minor matters. Something serious has come up. Have you heard of a Dr Iain Simpson?'

'No.'

This is really important, Douglas. Are you sure?'

'Yes.'

'Well, your friend David Wyness has, and this could drag you down.'

'I don't know what you're talking about.'

'I'm pleased to hear that. Ignorance may be your best defence.'

54

COOK DECIDED THAT before going any further I would need another coffee, if not something stronger.

'Sorry, I forgot, you don't drink.'

I did on occasion, I had nothing against it in principle, but this wasn't the time to indulge in petty distinctions. I wanted to know what she was talking about.

'So, Anastasija, about this Dr Simpson.'

She handed me a refill, and as she sat down beside me in one fluid motion, I realised she was more limber than I was, which wouldn't be difficult, very much better at easing herself onto a bar stool.

'I'll come to him in a minute. You follow the news, I take it.'

'Yes.'

'Ok, then you'll have heard of a case in Aberdeenshire, a woman found dead in a holiday chalet.'

I remembered my brief pit stop at Harthill and the TV on the wall. Closer to home, as the subtitles had it, police were investigating the death of a woman in a chalet at the Craigendarroch resort.

'Yes, I heard about that.'

'We didn't know who the woman was at first. She had no ID of any sort on her, either in her handbag or a coat or jacket pocket. Someone had taken the lot and she was in no condition to do it herself.'

'The local police suspected foul play.'

'Of course, but they had no leads. No one tried to drive

off with her car or use her cards.'

'So they published her picture in the papers.'

'Yes, but not before they'd checked for dental records. As you know, many dentists don't hang onto them after three years if a patient leaves the practice, but this time we were lucky. The lady had zygomatic implants.'

For the second time in our conversation, I had no idea what she was talking about.

'I hadn't heard of them either. With some patients the bone of the jaw isn't strong enough for normal implants, so they drill right through to the cheekbone and plant them in that instead.'

I heard her out in disbelief. I had cheekbones, but on the few occasions I looked in a mirror they seemed some distance from the jaw. Cook had cheekbones too, more prominent than mine and slightly improved by makeup. As far as I could see, implants to the cheekbone would have to be in the order of one to two inches long. This was a procedure which didn't bear thinking about.

'Sounds liked torture to me. You'd be better off with dentures.'

'You may think so, but in this case it made identification much easier. Not many dentists have the training to fit them, so we had relatively few to contact. We managed to identify the lady as a Mrs Jennifer Slorach from Arrochar.'

'Ah yes,' I said, in a vain attempt to slow her down. 'Slorach. Unusual name. Thought to be from the Gaelic word for leader.'

'How does knowing that help?'

It didn't, so I quickly moved on, suggesting that Mrs Slorach, being a married woman, suspicion would fall on the husband, a suggestion which fell on stony ground since the man had died five years before.

'The current take on it is that she was having an affair with a married man and was threatening to reveal all to the wife unless he agreed to leave her.'

Naturally, the police had tried to check her phone and email records. There was no phone in the chalet either, again suspicious, but interesting information was found on her laptop, which she'd left at home in Arrochar.

'And this is where Dr Simpson comes in.'

'It is. But such records as we found appeared to show that Dr Simpson had been in Mauritius at the time, so he couldn't have been involved, could he?'

'What do you mean, "appeared to show"?'

'Well, this is a bit beyond me, but our tech people were able to confirm that his residence at L'Oiseau de L'Ocean was faked. He wasn't there at all, but a lot of work had gone into giving the impression that he had been.'

'Right, so where was he really. Craigendarroch?'

'We believe so, yes. Let's just say a picture is beginning to emerge.'

'Mrs Simpson, is she aware of any of this?'

'Not yet. She still believes her husband was in Mauritius.'

Official reports had said the death was suspicious, nothing more, so Jennifer Slorach couldn't have been shot, stabbed, or strangled. But here the investigating officers had encountered a problem. Toxicology showed signs of recreational drug use, but nowhere near enough to cause death. The only thing they did discover was a puncture mark in a vein of the right arm.

'What did they make of that?'

'This is just a theory, nothing more, but our friend Dr Simpson is a consultant cardiologist, he knows his stuff. No one could be better placed to kill by injecting air.'

She slid off her stool, opened a kitchen drawer full of papers, took one out and handed it to me.

'Get a load of this.'

Her command of the local patois could be disconcerting. I found myself scanning an article entitled *The*

Progression of the Air Embolus in 115 Middle-Aged Patients.
Every one of them had died, but the article also made it clear that there was some divergence in professional circles regarding how much air would prove fatal in impeding the function of the heart. However, a cardiologist would be on top of all this, he would know the score.

'We're currently talking to locals in Craigendarroch, Ballater, Braemar, Aboyne and so on in the hope that someone saw him. We're also checking filling stations in case he had to fill up and used a card.'

'Who booked the chalet?'

'She did.'

'Too bad.'

'But Douglas Hunter, here's my question. How do you think Dr Simpson managed to give the impression that he was in Mauritius? His wife phoned his hotel twice and got through. That's what she thinks, anyway. How was it done?'

It was obvious that this was what she'd been leading up to, and since she'd already mentioned Wyness, I could only suppose that Dr Simpson had paid him through his side-line, Parallel Lives, and probably at his much-vaunted Service Level Three. This was an enterprise about which I was supposed to know nothing. And that was true as far as Wyness was concerned. But though I wasn't involved in any way, there was my heart-to-heart with a certain Sylvia Gathercole at the Elephant House who, if asked, could confirm that she'd told me all about it.

'There's something you should know.'

55

I TOLD COOK everything about my meeting with Mrs Gathercole. I also admitted that before that, I'd had my suspicions that Wyness was up to something, though he wouldn't tell me what it was.

'So, to be clear, you have never, at any time, discussed Parallel Lives with David Wyness.'

'At no point, not a word. He doesn't even realise I know.'

'Therefore, it couldn't be said that you have endorsed his scheme.'

'I couldn't, could I? As far as he was concerned, I knew nothing about it.'

'Yet when this Gathercole woman asked your opinion of him, you gave his character your seal of approval.'

'Yes, but Anastasija, only to the extent that he wouldn't abuse any information she gave him about herself.'

'He wouldn't use it to blackmail her.'

'Exactly. I didn't paint him as a compendium of the moral virtues.'

She thought for a moment, my fate in the balance.

'Well, Douglas, I don't consider you criminal in any way, or even guilty of sharp practice, but it seems to me you have been negligent in this matter. You should have intervened to nip it in the bud.'

'Yes, I see that now.'

Though I wasn't in court I was being judged and risked a thought in my own defence.

'What he was doing wasn't actually illegal.'

'Which made it all right? I don't think so. I'll tell you how all this strikes me.'

Taking the Drysdale and Simpson cases together, Hunter Associates showed a regrettable tendency to provide services to clients without due consideration as to how those services might be used. Incendiary devices and homicides didn't inspire confidence.

'We had nothing to do with Dr Simpson.'

'But one of your named associates had. People won't see past that.'

Having felled me with one well-aimed blow she followed up with another, reminding me that in the course of her work she met members of the public the force couldn't help but a private investigator could. She had considered referring such cases to me but now, under the circumstances, she no longer felt able to do so.

'I'm sorry, Douglas, but there it is.'

I had the feeling that she was putting me on probation. But as it was right now, ethics might come up against income. I had no new cases on my books. One might come my way which didn't meet her ethical criteria. What then? Risk it and take it on, or decline it and starve in the warm glow of her approval? Just as well I still had money in the bank.

'So what's the way forward with Wyness?'

'We've tried to contact him several times both by text and email, but he hasn't replied. 'Our number won't be in his contact list, of course, so he'll feel free to ignore us.'

'He might think they're just nuisance calls.'

'Very likely.'

A woman adept at covering the angles, Cook then revealed another reason for wanting to see me.

'But you *are* in his contact list. If you phone him, he'll pick up.'

In fact, he frequently didn't, but I agreed to give it a try. If he answered, I'd hand my phone to Cook. But he didn't answer me either.

'You've rung his bell, I take it.'

'And knocked on the door. If he doesn't respond in the course of the day, we'll be round tomorrow morning. Neighbours tell us he's a night owl, seldom to be seen before noon, so that will be our best chance of finding him in. We're going mob-handed, as you would say, with an enforcer. We have to clear this up.'

'You intend to smash in his door?'

'He's leaving us no choice.'

'You should see his bolts, really heavy, top and bottom, never mind the locks.'

'I intend to. From the inside. After we're in. And by the way, I could see the man far enough; I've had to cancel a hair appointment to deal with this.'

'I assume you've booked another.'

'Easier said than done. Estelle needs a four-hour slot for this procedure. How many of these do you think she has? I can't get another one for three weeks.'

When I suggested she was having me on, Anastasija set me straight.

'My hair is naturally dark. As you've probably noticed the blonde is growing out, especially obvious along the parting.'

'Gentlemen prefer blondes.'

'I really don't care what gentlemen prefer. You prefer receding at the temple and thinning on top. I, Anastasija Bērziņš, prefer blonde. But,' she added, striking a technical note, 'Estelle advises me that on this occasion she should bleach my hair twice before applying the dye using multiple layers of foil. Involves a spot of balayage, don't you know.'

She said this playfully, well aware that I'd no idea what she was talking about.

'It all takes time.'

'And money.'

'That too.'

56

THAT EVENING, I brought Alison up to date by email. I considered calling her, but she would surely have asked me as many questions as Cook had done; one grilling a day was enough to be going on with. Repeated attempts to call Wyness got me nowhere.

The following morning, I had breakfast at six in case the call came early, but the text when it arrived read *Ten o'clock, be there*. So I walked down to Leith Street to be met by Cook, Hector Robertson, and two uniformed officers with an enforcer, red in colour, hard to miss. To avoid blocking the road, they'd left their vehicles round the corner on Waterloo Place. Not wanting to miss the action, a curious crowd had gathered, including some homeless souls from the Access Point, no doubt grateful for the first time and only time that they didn't have doors to break down.

'Ok?'

We filed through the main door and climbed the four flights of stairs to Wyness' flat. In a last-ditch attempt to gain entry by less dramatic means, Cook called Wyness again and Robertson hammered on his door. All of which caught the attention of the gentleman on the opposite side of the landing, who asked us who the hell we were and what we thought we were doing. Cook gave him a sanitised version and told him there was nothing to worry about, while Robertson warned him that there would be some noise, but it would be of short duration.

'So I'd stay inside for the moment, sir,' he advised.

To ensure that he did, Robertson ushered him back into his own home and closed his door. He looked indignant to me. If the police hadn't been there already, he'd have called them to complain.

'Right.'

I knew very well how articulate Cook could be but, on this occasion, she was restricting herself to single syllables. Detective Sergeant Cook, woman of action. Because of the heavy-duty bolts on the inside, it took the uniformed officers three attempts with the enforcer, but they finally succeeded, leaving the door hanging from one of its hinges.

'Mr Wyness!'

There was no reply and I assumed that, very unusually, he wasn't at home. But I was wrong. They found him in his Command HQ, slumped over one of his keyboards, his screens still displaying changing currency movements in their customary reds and greens. Robertson quickly looked them over.

'At least it's not porn.'

Cook thanked the uniformed officers, and as they left checked Wyness for signs of life. Even at the best of times these could be hard to detect, as she was finding now. He was still breathing, though very lightly. Prodding him in the ribs got no response, nor did shouting in his ear.

'Call an ambulance, Hector. This is a blue light job. Tell them there's a pulse but he's out for the count, totally unresponsive.'

Robertson had it figured; Wyness had overdosed. But Cook wasn't so sure.

'Is he a user? I assume you would know.'

'Alcohol and tobacco, yes. Drugs no. Never.'

As Robertson put in the call, she looked round the room, taking in its moth-eaten curtains, closed as always and stiff with the stench of stale tobacco. There were three beers cans on his desk, two of them empty, and the remains of a burger in a polystyrene container.

'This leaves a lot to be desired.'

'It does. It always has.'

She looked at the Wyness waist, flesh overflowing his belt. For Cook, who had her fastidious side, it was the last straw.

'This is an associate you can do without.'

'It looks like I might have to.'

'Right, Hector, the gear.'

Robertson surveyed the screens on the desk, the computers under it and what looked like a printer, a scanner, and several external hard drives.

'I know. There's a lot. Take it down in stages, we'll be here for a while.'

As Robertson began to disconnect the hardware, Cook strode to the windows and drew the curtains. One came apart in her hands. Apart from letting light in, she hoped fresh air from the street outside would clear the room, but unless it could strip the paper from the walls as well there was small chance of that. The first window had been painted in so well it wouldn't budge, but the combined efforts of Cook and myself managed to raise the other a few inches, an exercise which brought us close together; though whether she smelled as good as she looked I'd no way of knowing, so toxic was the atmosphere in the room.

'Well, Douglas, shall we see what else this place has to offer?'

Not a lot, as it turned out. The bedroom was a mess. By the look of it, the sheets hadn't been changed for months and the pile of dirty clothes in the corner suggested his washing machine was broken, though this proved not to be the case. By that stage, nothing in the kitchen would have surprised us, including the pile of dirty dishes in the sink and two mouldy scones in a cupboard.

'He doesn't even have a dishcloth!'

If he'd been a lazy person like me, he'd have let his draining rack take the strain, but he didn't have one of those either. And so we progressed to the bathroom, where Cook checked the contents of the cabinet for any clue to his present condition. Apart from aspirin and paracetamol, it contained four different indigestion remedies, Senokot, Imodium, Buscopan and peppermint Rennies.

'I think it's fair to say your friend Wyness has digestive issues.'

And that was what the paramedics said when they arrived, though quick to point out that none of these over-the-counter remedies could have led to his present condition. One of them had struggled up the four flights of stairs with oxygen, just in case, while the other conducted basic checks, including blood oxygen, blood pressure, pulse, and pupil dilation.

'It's not looking good.'

The lead paramedic spoke to us while taking bloods.

'I can't be sure till we get the results, but it looks to me like hyperglycaemic coma. We'll have to take him to A&E at once.'

This was clearly a good idea, but the person preventing it was Wyness himself.

'How heavy would you say this guy is, Màiri?'

'A good sixteen stone. He's grossly overweight.'

'We'll have to call in another team.' She turned to us to explain. 'We don't need the ambulance but we do need the muscles.'

In the fifteen minutes or so which elapsed before the second team arrived, Robertson completed the transfer of the computers, drives and hardware to the police car. But even with four paramedics, two men and two women, heaving Wyness off his chair and onto a stretcher, then manoeuvring his bulk down four flights of stairs proved a major challenge.

After they'd gone, Cook phoned for a carpenter to board up the front door.

'It won't look great, but it'll do the job. Hector, turn the water off. I'll check the electrics and gas.'

On way back down to the street, Cook turned to us.

'These people are amazing.'

She was referring to the paramedics. This had been my experience too; whatever their job threw at them they handled.

'Shouldn't we wait till the joiner's secured the door?'

'So, technically yes, Hector, but thanks to your efforts there's little left in there worth taking.'

57

LATER THAT DAY, I brought my colleagues up to date with developments at Wyness' flat. MacNeil, who didn't know him very well, assured me that either he'd make it or he wouldn't, something I'd already figured out for myself. Alison knew him only too well but would have preferred not to. *Well, what can you expect from someone with a lifestyle like that, though in his case, use of the word "style" is hardly appropriate. Really, Douglas, I wouldn't waste much sympathy on the man, he's brought it on himself.* I had to hand it to them, in their different ways they were both correct. For a split second I toyed with the idea that they might get on with each other but dismissed it as the fantasy it was. Even if they could, neither of them would want to.

Then the plumber called. Callum. I'd forgotten about him, but due to a cancellation he could bring my job forward. He could start today if that was alright with me. He arrived just after lunch complete with tools and the new shower unit still in its box.

'There are no isolators in your bathroom, so I'll have to turn the water off at the main. If you want to fill a kettle or anything, now would be the time.'

I filled a kettle and pan, which was just as well because Alison turned up on the doorstep at two o'clock without a word of warning. She brought a lemon drizzle cake, a gift or a peace offering, I'd no idea which.

'Thought I might catch you in.'

'You have.'

Sitting in my front room on one of MacNeil's chairs, which she wouldn't have done if she'd known, she told me she'd been thinking. Nothing new there, so I asked her what she'd been thinking about.

'I've decided to take the job.'

For me, this wasn't good news, but it wasn't surprising either.

'Well,' I said, 'offers like that don't come your way every day of week.'

'Exactly. Just what I thought. Gather ye rosebuds while ye may, and all that.'

If I remembered rightly, that line concerned human relationships, sex even, not dry-as-dust accountancy work, but that was best left unsaid.

'When do you start?'

'Next week.'

Her eyes strayed to the corner of the room in search of gaming gear, but to my relief MacNeil had already taken it to her new residence in Lochrin Street. At that point, the sound of Radio Forth came wafting through from the bathroom.

'Good grief, what on earth's that?'

Without waiting for answer, she went through to find out and sized the situation up at a glance.

'A shower unit.'

'That's right, Mrs Hunter, a big improvement on the taps.'

A stickler for detail, she could have corrected him but on this occasion showed unusual restraint.

'Mrs Hunter indeed,' she said with a smile when she came back; an offer she hadn't received and would never have accepted anyway. My mobile rang. It was Cook.

'You're in? Good. I'm in the area.'

She arrived shortly afterwards, and I could hear Alison's cogs in motion. What was my connection with this woman, exactly?'

'I have news.'

She sat down on the other chair to deliver it, obliging me to take a director's chair from the hall cupboard for myself.

'His bloodwork confirms what the paramedics thought. A hyperglycaemic coma. Wyness has type 2 diabetes.'

'Well there's a surprise! Booze, burgers, tobacco. Hardly to be wondered at.'

Cook gave Alison an appraising look, a woman who didn't mince her words. In fact, she didn't mince anything. Mince was below her, never to be found on the menu.

'When I phoned the hospital, they were ridiculously cagey.'

'You're not family, Douglas.'

'True,' Alison agreed, 'but he could have claimed to be his brother. Over the phone they'd have no way of knowing. A bit more enterprise would do him no harm. He doesn't need to play it straight down the line every time.'

Starting to feel I was under fire in stereo I left the room, had a quick word with Callum then went to the kitchen to put the kettle on, hoping they might start on each other and leave me out of it. But when I returned with coffees and slices of cake, that was not what had happened.

'DS Cook has just brought me up to speed with this Parallel Lives business. Outrageous! I can hardly believe it.'

'I had nothing to do with that, Alison.'

'So I hear.'

As the conversation progressed it became clear that Cook hadn't told her I'd known about Parallel Lives for some time and done nothing about it.

'How is he now?'

'He's out of the coma but they're keeping him in for a while, stabilising his blood sugars and checking for possible brain damage. No visitors till tomorrow.'

'It ill behoves me to speak ill of the dead,' Alison said, not meaning a word of it, 'but if they'd looked for brain damage *before* the coma, they'd have found it.'

'He isn't dead yet, Alison.'

'I was speaking metaphorically, Douglas. In any case, as I'm sure you know, he's always been dead to me.'

'Karma.'

Alison glanced at me in case I knew what Cook was talking about.

'I beg your pardon?'

'A clear case of karma, wouldn't you say?'

This was a word which would never pass Alison's lips, so she definitely wouldn't.

'I'm not sure I know what you mean.'

'Simple, really. If we hadn't been investigating Parallel Lives we wouldn't have broken into his flat. Parallel Lives saved *his* life.'

'I hadn't realised,' Alison said, 'that the force was employing New Age officers now.'

Not caring for the way the conversation was going, I changed the subject.

'Alison's taking up a new job, did she tell you?'

She hadn't, so Alison told her about her investigation into Edwards Interiors, the impending legal action against Ergonomica's accountants and how, as a result of her efforts, she had been offered the post of chief financial officer at the new, enlarged group.

'My goodness,' Cook said, looking at me, 'I don't know about you, but this puts my level of crime in the shade. When do you start?'

'Next week. Well,' she said, suddenly getting up, 'angles to cover, things to do. Good to meet you, DS Cook.'

She promised to contact me later that evening, after she'd dusted her surfaces and checked her plants. When she left, Cook came out with a Major Statement.

'Well, Douglas!'

After a suitable interval, she offered me her thoughts.

'Mind if I come straight out with it?'

'Of course not. Why would I?'

The gist of it was that I was in trouble. My IT expert was out of the picture for the time being, maybe for good, and my partner, Alison, was leaving town. As far as she could see, the business wasn't bringing in much work as it was, so this was white knuckle time at Hunter Associates. Decisions had to be made. Delaying them wasn't an option.

I couldn't find fault with anything she was saying, but at the same time had no idea what these decisions might be.

'What do you mean, Anastasija? Decisions?'

'You should wind up the business. You've given it your best shot. The bird won't fly.'

'Right, and what do I live on then?'

Cook gave me a long, hard look.

'What are you living on now?'

Callum knocked on the door and came in, his work complete, he was ready to leave.

'Finished. Want to see it?'

Cook and I joined him in the bathroom, which didn't leave a great deal of space. Callum, clearly pleased with the result, gave us a quick demo.

'It's really simple. With the lever down, your water comes out the taps; pull it up and it comes out the shower.'

'So it does. Excellent.'

'Some of these units don't work if the water pressure's too low. This one will though.'

Reminding me that the invoice had to be settled within thirty days, he left us to it.

Back in the living room, Cook went to the window and looked out into the street, her eye caught by the True Jesus Church.

'Religion, water, you have it all on tap now.'

She turned back into the room and said she should be going too, but before she did, she had a suggestion to make, something she'd been thinking about for some time.

58

AND SO THE evening came and with it evening thoughts. I popped a meal for one into the microwave and hardly noticed I was eating it. Cook had faced me with unwelcome facts concerning Hunter Associates, and everything she said was true. I was scarcely scraping a living as it was, but with Wyness and Alison gone the outlook was bleak. Each of them covered angles I was incapable of dealing with myself and MacNeil, useful as she was on the ground, couldn't cover them either.

The idea of winding up the business troubled me most when it came to MacNeil. Despite a few hiccups along the way, she was starting to come good. She'd thrown her cocaine habit, no mean feat, and had just moved into Chen's flat with Anne. But her delivery business, while bringing in money, wasn't bringing in enough. How would she make ends meet without the money coming in from me? The thought that her fresh start might fail if I wound up the business troubled me greatly. When I put this to Cook her response was a deft combination of the uncompromising and the practical.

'When it comes right down to it, Douglas, we must all take responsibility for our own lives. You have tried to do this after your wife left, I have tried to do it my when I showed my husband the door. As for Maureen MacNeil,' she added as an afterthought, 'by all accounts she's an excellent driver. I say that because there are several delivery companies out there who'd be only too happy to sign her up.'

As suggestions went, this one was eminently logical, though I doubted whether MacNeil would take kindly to having her rounds organised for her and her progress constantly monitored by the company app. But it might come to that in the end. Which left me. Before leaving, Cook sat down for five minutes and ran her proposal past me. I listened in amazement.

'Re-join the force!'

'We're short staffed.'

'But Anastasija, I left under a cloud.'

In fact, I'd been left with no choice when our IT people had detected irregular use of police databases when trying to locate my wife.

'I've been looking into that.'

'Then you must see the problem.'

But according to Cook, there wasn't one. I hadn't been dismissed from the service, I'd resigned. The fact that I'd done it under pressure didn't alter that fact. And most importantly, because I'd chosen to leave, no charges had been brought. So as far as my record was concerned, it was spotless. Some people knew the background of course, John Banks and Hector Robertson, but neither of them would bring it up. As for DI Maitland, the officer in charge at the time, he had retired.

'In any case,' she pointed out, 'who's he to talk? He gave you a bottle of Highland Park.'

I looked at her in astonishment. Alright, she'd done her homework, but how on earth had she dug that one up?

'John Banks told me. Selkirk bannock too, according to him. Anyway, if you choose to apply, I'll do what I can to support your application.'

Her phone rang and she took the call in the kitchen. And as I listened to her talking through the wall, I tried to think through her suggestion.

'The Craigendarroch case,' she said when she came

301

back in.

'How's it going?'

'We can't prove that he injected the Slorach woman with air, nor that he used a topical analgesic before inserting a syringe into her vein. Neither are detectable by autopsy. But the Aberdeen police are confident that's what he did.'

'So it has to be circumstantial.'

'Yes. They're currently setting out to prove that Dr Simpson wasn't where he said he was, but was where he said he wasn't. If you see what I mean.'

'He wasn't in Mauritius but he was in Craigendarroch.'

'Exactly.'

'So it will come down to witnesses.'

'That and Wyness' records.'

'Wyness kept records!'

Knowing him, I found this hard to believe.

'He had no choice, he had to keep track of his moves. Liars have trouble keeping their stories straight; not a problem for people like us, we don't have any, but not so easy for him. We found them on an external drive. Full details. Chapter and verse.'

Cook believed they'd get Dr Simpson before the week was out. His story would unravel, his lies would catch him out. He'd already been sighted lunching with Mrs Slorach at the Learney Arms two days before her death. He may have felt Torphins was sufficiently distant from Craigendarroch to be safe, but he was wrong. Yet hopeful as Cook was, I had the feeling that nothing short of a confession would do in the end. Morphine if he'd used it, yes, that might have nailed him, but Simpson had been smart. One thing he'd never needed to do was steal air from the hospital dispensary.

'You're more confident than I am,' I told her.

She had a reply to that.

'Most people are.'

I went to bed that night my head too full of ideas for

restful sleep. For any sleep at all. If there was an OFF button somewhere, I couldn't find it. My wayward thoughts resembled clothes in the washing machine I'd cleaned my duvet cover in. The laundry had a catchy line; *Tumble in and give them a spin*. Great, but what if you didn't want to. My thoughts were tangled together like so many shirts and socks. Wyness. The Simpson case. Alison appearing as star witness in a negligence suit. MacNeil setting up her gaming gear in her new home. And Cook's suggestion about re-joining the force. Back to square one, an occasion for wry thoughts if ever there was one, but a tempting opportunity best avoided.

There was no repose to be found. Till I looked over to my bedside table, actually a chair, noticed my mobile phone and Bluetooth cans, and finally found repose in the soothing sounds of kokle music. Who'd have thought it? Not me, a few short weeks before.

Wasn't there some mention of harps in connection with heaven? I was sure there was. And surely the kokle was a stringed instrument much like the harp though in the horizontal plane. Who knew what harps were like back then anyway?

And these cascading notes, a balm to the soul, were accompanied by fleeting though agreeable images of Anastasija Cook, a woman who, it seemed to me, was opening a door and asking me in.

If you enjoyed reading *A Habit of Mind*, the author would be grateful if you would leave a review on Amazon.

Printed in Great Britain
by Amazon